LOST ROMANTICS

– stories –

Jim O'Donoghue

First published in 2023
By LateVixenBooks

Printed in England by Clays Ltd, Elcograf S.p.A.

ISBN: 978-1-7398080-1-3

For Mum,
who taught me to read
and write.

Carson's Trail was published in *Let's Be Alone Together*, a Stinging Fly anthology, September 2008; **My Breakfast with Gumbo** in Short FICTION, University of Plymouth, 2008; **Sweetheart, I'm Telling You** in the Dublin Review, Summer 2010; **My Animal Passion** in the Dublin Review, Winter 2011; and **The Sixth of November** in the Dublin Review, Autumn 2015. **Unmarried brunette on the London train** was longlisted for the 2006 Arvon International Poetry Prize and appeared in the anthology.

Far be it from me to stand in the way of any reader
who just wants to read and run,
but to enjoy this book to the max I suggest
reading these stories in the order given,
in the same way as you would sit down and listen to
Dark Side of the Moon or *Hejira* or
From the Choirgirl Hotel
or *New Gold Dream*.

No se puede vivir sin amar.

My Animal Passion

Until late summer last year, I worked in IT for a securities firm on Upper Hatch Street, but when my contract came to an end it was not renewed. Strange to say, my dismissal came as something of a relief; something would have to shift, and I would have to shift it. At the approach of middle age, it is all too easy to coast until the time comes to pack your bags and make your final move to one last place of rest. When I was laid off, I saw that this notion had troubled me for a while without my even knowing it, much less seeking a solution.

Still, I had to pay the rent. The house I rented lay out in the suburbs beyond Castleknock village, on one of the estates built around a decade ago. Some might say that it lacked soul, but I had always admired its quiet modernity, clean lines and the little garden at the back. It had all the advantages of a rented place and few of the disadvantages: when something broke, a plumber or electrician would turn up promptly to fix it, but the landlord lived in England, only dropping in on us every six months or so to make sure we had everything we needed.

If there was a disadvantage to this arrangement, it lay outside the house and somewhere inside me. The estates themselves were the essence of labyrinthine:

there was a roundabout at one end of the road and another at the other end, a pattern that recurred again and again over many square miles. When I first moved in and still went for walks, I was always losing my way coming home; whenever I took a turning, it was always the wrong one – I was forever mistakenly convinced that *this* must be *my* roundabout, almost to the point of marching up to the wrong front door. After a few weeks of these misdirections, I curtailed my walks to within a certain radius, taking in the nearest pub or shop, or I headed straight for the station and caught the train into town. The odd thing was that I was on my own in my confusion; when someone came to visit, they never had the slightest issue with finding the house, never even mentioned it as a problem. Maybe this anomaly was what made me think up a scenario whereby I rarely had to go out and, instead, people came to me.

At the start of September, my housemate announced that he would be moving out at the end of the month to live with his girlfriend closer to town. He may have felt that he was leaving me in the lurch, but in truth his decision was serendipitous. An enterprise had come to mind in the weeks since I lost my job, a notion that could only have been put there by the financial crisis. It seemed obvious that I should use the resources to hand – my own raw materials, you might say – and on the day he left I sat down to design my website. Compared with those already out there offering similar services, it was somewhat rudimentary. I had no testimonials, and the only recent photos of myself were taken by, or with, my second wife. After cropping her out, I was left with a series of sunny images of me on a beach, on the deck of a holiday cabin, in the shade of a redwood in Big Sur, wearing trunks and T-shirts and, in one case, a sarong.

I finessed the website and researched the fee, which I set low on the grounds that I was inexperienced and my place was a long way out. Then I placed a rather primly worded ad in an online publication devoted to personal services and, surprisingly quickly, the women began to turn up. At first they arrived in dribs and drabs – but word spread, and by mid-November I had several bookings a week.

The mechanics of my new profession were not quite as I had imagined. My ideal scenario had me beginning the day with a woman who wanted a vigorous fuck. I fancied that those who wanted nothing more than a gentle tumble might arrive around lunchtime, when a bowl of olives, bruschetta and a glass of Pinot Grigio might be thrown in, or toast and marmite for the more down to earth. I had thought to spend the afternoons on a less labour-intensive activity, such as oral sex or a foot massage. But I soon learned that it would not be possible to arrange matters this way: women would turn up after work, fresh from the rush hour, in business suits and with the office smell still on them, wanting whatever they wanted. Some of them knew what they wanted, while others were painfully reticent and undemanding, would arrive in a rush and often, despite my best efforts, leave in a rush as well, clutching their orgasms to their chests.

I was no longer a young man, and the rigours of the trade were testing, to say the least. After a week, I went to see my doctor, who prescribed me a couple of boxes of little blue pills, with a warning that they might be bad for my heart. I did not tell him, and he could not have guessed, the purpose behind my request – that my use was industrial rather than personal. No one could have guessed, since even with a new haircut and a better pair of shoes, I still looked more like an out-of-work IT consultant than anyone's idea of a gigolo.

As in any form of self-employment, there were little periods in the day when there was nothing much to do. Now and then, I might have a lady whose husband was either dead or inattentive, who needed little more than a hug. One of these was Marietta, a stately brunette slightly older than myself, in her mid-forties, who would pay for an extra hour just to sit with me in the conservatory. Even in winter, the conservatory was snug; with the light from the lamp down low on the mahogany table and the Mexican rug on the floor, it was a cosy enough place to mull over our various escapades.

'When you were twenty-one,' she asked me, 'what did you see yourself doing in twenty years' time?' She sat in the wicker chair, tucking her naked heels beneath her buttocks. 'I mean, where did you hope to end up?'

'Well, right here with you, of course.'

Marietta laughed. 'Don't be gallant, Jerry. I want a real conversation.'

'I was happy to be wherever I was in those days. It would never have occurred to me to think of being anywhere else.' I thought for the first time in a while of London in the 1990s, how to begin with I had slept under bridges and between parked cars and how little any of it had bothered me – how I would have worked for sunlight. I looked into her warm, broad face, a face in which there was still the occasional hint of the girl she had been. 'In those days, though, I was desperately shy.'

'Well,' she smiled, tugging at her sleeve, 'it's lucky you've shaken that off.'

Marietta, under the loyalty card system I had devised, would come to me three times a week at about nine o'clock, ostensibly in search of sex. But once we lay down on the kingsize bed, which the landlord might almost have bought for the purpose, she would gently withdraw; I was left looking longingly at the slightly puckered skin of her breasts on which, as a younger woman, her hopes must have hung. She did not have to squeeze every penny of value out of her hours with me, and not just because of the discount. She was one of those fortunate people – there were some, of course – who had done well out of the credit crunch. She was more than flush; she would arrive in a vintage Corvette, which she parked discreetly, at some distance from the front door, since it was so incongruous among the almost identical German and Japanese models that dotted the estate – family cars whose alarms went off all the time, under no provocation. We even talked of her setting up a standing order to pay for my services, although all she was paying for was eye contact and a certain amount of honesty.

In the end, she became a source of frustration to me, since she put me in the position of desiring what I most disapproved of, which was in any case not on offer – and perhaps that is why, one evening in the first week of December, we fell out badly over politics.

'You know who else has thrived on the collapse of the banks and the craving for some kind of kindness, however cheap and shop-worn? You, Jerry, *you*.'

It was Marietta's parting shot as she stormed out of the dimly lit conservatory – I never saw her again.

Of course, my thoughts were often drawn to what she had said, a truth that was hard to deny – that I was just another pirate, a profiteer. But part of the magic of complicity is the way it makes itself disappear, a magic that springs partly from the seductive nature of supply and demand. There were always new people to please: more clients joined up than left, until my diary was crammed with names. I maintained the sabbath, kept Sunday for myself, but the rest of the time was so busy that I barely had time to consider the ethics of my profession – or for that matter the failures, of which inevitably there were a few. It was also in the nature of the business that some clients left unsatisfied. There were women with whom it simply failed to happen – we were a bad fit, we rubbed along badly – and those occasions were painful, not so much professionally as personally. I felt rejected, of course. I had tried my best to be loving and lovable, but my best had somehow repelled her; she had disliked my smell or my taste or my style more generally, perhaps just the shape or size of my penis. But I was professional enough to keep my hurt at these rebuffs to myself.

After Christmas I put up my prices and still suffered no shortage of clients. I was making two-thirds of my gross monthly wage in my former job, but since there was no way of paying tax on my new salary it came to more or less the same amount. I began to buy things for myself: new shirts, a fountain pen, Gene Clark's solo LPs on the original vinyl. But I also put money back into the business: I splashed out on a new mattress and a Turkish rug for the bedroom and had an electrician come in and install a dimmer switch. I bought a better coffee machine and some coffee-table books for the conservatory where, now and then on a busy day, clients would wait for me to become free.

Naturally, I was surprised by this popularity and wondered at its source, but I came to the conclusion that the reasons for my successes were just as mysterious as the reasons for my failures. In short, there was no particular reason. I was reasonably well preserved, but then I had never been more than averagely good-looking, even as a younger and more elastic man. The answer when it came to me was both alarming and reassuring: I sold well because people knew where to find me, because I was *there*, just as chocolate digestives are always on the same shelf in the supermarket or, to take a more apt analogy from our part of the world, puppies can be bought from puppy farms all the year round. The puppy you bought was loved because you had paid for it – that was all it came down to. This insight was enough to make me forget myself in the transaction, and for quite a while I went on that way, regarding myself purely as a commodity.

This only made my encounters with clients more surreal, of course – the fact that, while my interest declined in my own reactions to our sex, I still had an interest in theirs. I became lost in this asymmetry. Of course, I knew that it must be a bit weird for them to confront their mirror image in my hallway. I disguised my curiosity as well as I could, but now and then I could not help catching the glance that a departing customer gave to a new arrival, when an ageing vamp made way for an anorexic career woman, say, or a curious bohemian, covered in tattoos and with a purple streak in her hair, passed on the doorstep a lonely émigrée who had scraped together enough spare euros for an hour of human contact. One cloudy afternoon, a Trinity student from a rich family brushed shoulders with a handsome church-going type, dressed in tweed, who had walked across Phoenix Park with her lapdog. The student followed the woman down the road with her eyes before turning to ask,

'How can you touch us both in the same hour? How can you ride her and then ride me? I don't understand.'

No doubt she had a point – that what I was doing required quite a mental or physical leap – but what I did

13

seemed banal when set against who they were. During that autumn and moving into winter, women as a species moved a step closer to me, until I saw past their types – beyond the middle-aged divas, the little red riding hoods and ladies who lunched. I saw past the facades of all those plaster saints and stone foxes, saw through the expressions on the faces of troubled souls and mischievous young witches. When she came into my room, dropped out of her clothes and wore that look of agony, I saw in a way I had never known a woman whose animal passions took their own peculiar form. It was tiring sometimes to be the object of all those beastly urges – but when she revealed herself that way to me, I took the revelation in both hands and, if I still had the strength, held it up to the light to study it.

By January the house, with its ceaseless flow of visitors, had become cosier than it had ever felt when I lived there with a housemate – but the air around it was a constant blurred and grainy grey. The trees, pavements and recycling bins of our estate were shrouded in mist, through which grey figures moved without appearing to make progress. The air had that spectral stillness that has always made those first two months of the year, for me, the hardest to live through. To perform the act I was paid to perform, I had to up my dosage of boner pills, cut down on the wine, meditate a little longer in the mornings. I could not afford to succumb to depression. Something about my situation began to pall on me; whether it was the routine and repetitious nature of what I did for a living or something else, I was unsure.

As if to encourage spring to arrive and dawn to come earlier, I took to walking the streets again, as I had when I first moved in – at the end of my shift stumbling out into the stark suburban lamplight, getting lost in the mist in the early hours of morning. On such a walk, a fortnight after Epiphany, I passed through the estates and went along Porterstown Road until I reached the church of St Mochta's, where I crouched with my back to a buttress and smoked a joint. As well as being one of the few true landmarks, the church was the only edifice in the area that looked presentable in all weathers. These days they put up a building with little regard to how it will look under low cloud or harsh sunlight; walls that shine like burnished gold in summer will glower by late autumn like the walls of a jail. Not so the church of St Mochta's, whose blonde stonework seemed to shimmer in the moonlight, more evident now that I was off the estate. Of course, I had never been inside; on Sundays, while others poured through its doors, I sat in my conservatory and read reviews in the papers of films I would never see, since my evenings were too busy.

I crouched on the church steps and thought about a visit I had received that morning from a neighbour, a thin man with a narrow moustache and a birthmark on his left temple. He was a lawyer by trade, which was no doubt why he had been delegated the task of carrying a petition, signed by 87 other neighbours, to the effect that I should cease carrying on a business from my home. People were aware of all the comings and goings, he said – as how could they not be, when everyone's house faced everyone else's. It was, as he told me with the glimmer of a smile, bringing our quarter of the estate into disrepute.

He had obviously accepted the task with reluctance, and stepped around the subject by means of various distractions, asking for sugar in his tea and then, when he found I had them – inevitably, since I had everything to cater for all tastes – accepting sweeteners instead.

Sitting at the kitchen table, he patted the several sheets of A4 that comprised the petition.

'The trouble is, to be honest, we're not even sure who we should present it to. After all,' he went on, glancing about the kitchen, searching presumably for giveaway signs that he was in a house of ill repute, 'this is not really the sort of thing that Fingal is used to dealing with.'

'You can present it to me if you like,' I told him – and he looked at me rather sharply, but again suppressing a grin. He was a naturally jaunty type who was, at that moment, trying to restrain his natural jauntiness.

'You're not supposed to run a business out of these houses,' he went on, scratching his upper lip. 'At first we thought you were just very popular with the ladies. Then some of our housewives – and indeed some of our house husbands – began to pick up on certain details. The duration of the visits, for example, the footfall, the churn...' He faded out, looking away and turning his attention to the innocent-looking clock with its birdsong chimes, a survivor from an era when I was merely an IT consultant and no one had even known I lived among them. He was thinking, perhaps, what I was thinking – that it was ten minutes to the hour and that in a minute or so a client would arrive. He showed me again the long list of names, as if to bring us back to the point, then drank up his tea and left.

He could not have suspected it, but his visit changed everything. Until his intervention, it had never seriously occurred to me that I was being watched or that, if anyone had noticed what was going on, they would attempt to intervene. Sitting on my heels on the church steps, inspired by the marijuana, I saw into my own double thinking: I had assumed that I was safe from criticism – that the unspeakable nature of what I was doing would cause people not to speak of it and that, at the same time, they would silently admire my entrepreneurial get-up-and-go, even desire to emulate it. And now I knew that none of this was true, how could I go on?

Gazing out from my alcove into the black night, adorned by its silvery strands of drizzle, each strand lit individually by the one lone streetlamp, I was surprised by how painful I found the notion of being separated from a profession I had taken up almost thoughtlessly. Perhaps it was the memory of my last client that made it so hard – a girl in her late twenties, not beautiful exactly but evidently an original, a rare bird. It was true that, while she was in bed with me, I had savoured her secretly, licking my lips behind her back, knowing that in real life no one like her would ever have picked me out from the crowd, out in the free world beyond my suburban bordello. But no, I thought, that was not it.

The spliff was extinguished by a drop of rain and with some trouble I relit it, sucking hard, while at my back the buttress grew colder. I had gone out into the pale afternoon and bought marijuana from a man in Coolmine. I did not like to think of myself as the kind of old hippy who got wasted at the first sign of a crisis, or an ageing idealist who wandered the streets at night and got stoned alone on the steps of public buildings – but who was I if not an old hippy, a faded idealist, a disillusioned gigolo? Once I had not had to ask myself that question, because once I had been a married man, with a married man's point of view. In fact, I had been married twice, the second time not even dignified by the hard period of a decree nisi; my second wife was still out there somewhere, legally bound to me but far from my ken. In all that time when I was somebody's

17

husband, I had no need to wonder who I was, but in all those conjugal years what had I learned? That marriage was not a fine romance decreed by medieval poets, admen or the movies, nor was it a loveless convention sanctioned by church and state. Marriage was just a litany of not enough – the starter home on the outskirts not enough, not enough all those days when we sang and danced and smiled into one another's eyes, not enough all those holidays in the sun. All the couples counselling was not enough, not enough all our knotty conversations so long into the night. Sleeping around was not enough, staying faithful not enough – and then all that yelling in a rage, all that begging for forgiveness, was still not enough. Always, as if it were part of the formula, there was never enough of anything: never enough sex, never enough love and the love, when it happened, never enough.

The joint was way too strong, ridiculously front-loaded – but then I had rolled it with my eyes closed in the dark. But for a moment I saw through the darkness, and I saw that in all the little deals I had done over the months with my clientele, deals where I held up my end and they kept theirs, it was never possible to feel short-changed. If a client felt ripped off she would rarely say so, she would simply never come back, but for me to feel cheated was unthinkable. Even so, I thought it now – that throughout all those little love affairs with total strangers it was not enough – and I saw that it had felt that way from day one. Why in that case did I want so much to keep on doing it? Did I believe that, through sheer repetition, something unsatisfying might become a source of fulfilment? Was that how I had lived my life, forever on repeat, forever hoping that it would be different the next time?

It was easy to dismiss such twisted visions, brought on as they were by a few drags on a joint, not least because by their nature they were instantly forgettable. Other perfect insights into my process had no doubt occurred to me in times past and been forgotten the very next second. But these questions stayed with me all the way home, upstairs and to bed – they followed me even into my dreams, and more than once I woke up laughing at the fact that after all these years I was looking at something that had always evaded me, or which I had always avoided. I woke and slept and woke through an endless night of interrogation, travelling on until I was exhausted through worlds of confusion and revelation.

Needless to say, little was left of this world of extremes when I woke the next morning – a gloomy morning with a lowering sky, steely grey, promising further downpours. No petition or sudden enlightenment could stop its harsh descent or halt the flow of women who arrived in their dribs and drabs. It was a typical Tuesday at the start of a new year, in other words – exactly the kind of day when you wish you could take a break, when you regret you have a business to run.

Then into all this drabness walked Cait.

She rang as I was boiling myself an egg – over the phone she was breathless, as if fitting me in between tasks. 'I can't promise you I'll be any good,' she said, as we set a time. 'Men are often disappointed in me.'

I laughed, taken aback by her unusual take on the customer-client relationship. 'Well you don't have to worry about that with me, at any rate. I'm not paid to be disappointed.'

She sounded reassured and rang off after making an appointment for six. By lucky chance – and again, no doubt, there was serendipity involved – she was my last appointment for the day, and somehow I knew not to tack on anyone after her. I replied regretfully to a couple of emails and a text, saying I was fully booked up. After that, the day went by in its usual way except that, contrary to my long-established rule, I caught myself watching the clock. Midway through coitus with a surly girl from Sligo, it struck me how odd it was for me to be waiting in such nervous anticipation for a woman I had never met and had spoken to only once, on the phone. But there it was – that was the fact of the matter: I was waiting for Cait.

My strange state of foreshadowing sounds a little trippy, even to me, when I think of it now – and it is true that the night's excesses still ran in my veins. I had one of those dope hangovers that makes every mental object seem weird and remote, while it promotes a kind of maximum sensitivity in the nerve endings. The young woman from Sligo, who did not seem like someone accustomed to paying for sex, who mumbled her requests for pleasure and declined to remove her top, doubtless sensed nothing unusual in our long hour of restless position changes. I spent the whole session in a state of abstraction but trying not to explode whenever, as it were accidentally, one of her hands brushed some part of me. She appeared unaware of the lopsidedness of our encounter; she grunted in dull satisfaction at the last minute, just when our time was up, and left looking as grouchy as when she arrived. In the old days, just 24 hours before, I would have marked her down as a bit of a wrinkle and watched the website with an eye out for her review. But those were very much the old days – because now, it seemed, all I did was wait for Cait.

By a quarter past six, when she had still not arrived, I went downstairs and flicked through all the terrestrial channels and some of the satellites; then I turned off the TV and pored over my accounts, which were absurdly healthy – really I had never been so flush. For a while, I looked at the wares on eBay, vintage baseball caps and the like, very much the sort of tat I would have splashed out on in the beginning, without putting in a single bid. The wait was not just frustrating but filled me with an inexplicable anxiety, as if my destiny were in some way being thwarted. It had seemed that morning when she had called that she was anxious to see me, almost as if it was a matter of urgency – or was this just another illusion, a byproduct of my night of madness, a flight of desperate fancy?

Finally at loss for any further ways to fritter away the evening, I went upstairs. Every five minutes or so, I went over to the window to peer between the blinds at the pavement below, hoping that any steps I heard would end at my door. Half past six came and went, and at a quarter to seven it began to rain, pelting down in that heedless manner beloved of Tuesday nights in northern Europe. I had made a rule against it – I was, in my own small way, quite good at rules – since it could not be said to enhance my performance, but in a fit of pique I rolled a joint and smoked it on the kingsize bed, occupied these past three months or so by a succession of Maeves and Sinéads, Maires and Claires, Fionas and Deirdres and Eimears. Those at least were the names they had given for the purpose of our encounters – but who knew, perhaps even Marietta had been an alias. On reflection, it did seem an improbable Christian name for someone from this country, like something out of a book; but I had met her on my first day on the job, more or less, before I became at all sceptical, and the name had suited her. It was odd, come to think of it, but I had never bedded a Cait – and perhaps that was it, all I wanted was a Cait to add to my collection. Perhaps that was all I was doing out here in the suburbs, where other men collect football scarves, toy cars and first editions – collecting them to me, name by name.

This fixation on someone I had never met and knew only by name, only over the phone and for no longer than a minute, felt irrational at the time, even slightly deranged. But now I understand it: there are moments in life when a particular hunger produces something, or someone, out of the blue – or, in this case, out of the mist. Desire itself creates the incarnation of the desired. The problem here was that my desire had summoned her up and then, just as she was on the point of manifesting, she had disappeared again. Why was I waiting, wherever had she got to, and who was she anyway? As I asked myself these hopeless questions, I imagined a girl in a goth top with a band name on it, black and billowing to match her figure, pause at the turnstile at Connolly Station and count out her cents, then shake her head and turn back again – deciding instead to buy a new winter coat, momentarily embarrassed at her own foolishness.

She could have no inkling of my impatience to see her, which in the stoned haze of my boudoir increased by the minute. I knew this yearning could not be right, but now I could only let it grow. Something had shifted, it was true: for months without a thought I had hired myself out, sold my body to anyone who could match my price – but now all at once it was as if I had forgotten that such a transaction was even involved. All at once, my body was not just this thing I had flogged for a dime – it was *me* again, the same me who had won a bronze for the 100 metre dash on school sports day, swum in the icy waters off Portstewart, threshed about to *Teenage Kicks* in adolescent cider ecstasy. It was the same body that I had dragged halfway around the world more than once and which all this time I had fed and clothed, sometimes with joy and sometimes begrudgingly – the same body which, on a drunken evening at Hanlon's Corner, had almost died when a juggernaut cut across me as I turned left into Prussia Street.

The night flowed on, humid and vast, full of this frustrated promise. I rolled out of bed and stubbed out the joint, then standing up straight I grabbed the ends of my dressing gown cord and pulled it tight. I felt sadly abandoned, as you do when a date fails to show – I went over to the window that looked down into the rainy night garden, flung it open and breathed deep of the sodden air. Over the fence in the murk, my neighbour's blind and decrepit dog barked at an invisible moon, as he had been allowed to bark every night, at least since I moved in, despite the furious entreaties of all the other neighbours to please keep the thing indoors. But I was glad of his barking now, since it contained its own message. It told me what I wanted to hear: that I could get back to my old routine, all was not lost, I could wangle it somehow with the powers that be and ignore their petition, things could go on as they had before. I could forget this pointless wait for Cait – I needed no denouement after all, no twist to the tale: all I needed to do was to go on regardless, barking like a dog, and no one could stop me.

At that moment, of course, the doorbell rang, and I ran downstairs in all my dishevelment. 'I'm sorry,' she said as she came in, shaking out her umbrella. 'I know I'm horribly late.'

Kicking off a pair of soggy sling-backs, she took off her headscarf and shook out a mane of damp blonde hair. She was dressed quite haphazardly, not so much for the dead of winter as for autumn or early spring.

This fact distracted me for a moment from other aspects of her appearance – her long, pale face and green eyes under drooping eyelids, which made her look as if she was just waking up or just about to fall to sleep. In her hand was a large black leather briefcase, which proved very light when I took it from her and put it down beside the coat stand. Later she told me that she carried it about with her as a matter of course, to appear more like a commuter. When she took off her coat, baggy and beige, in a material that had begun as something fluffy and become shaggy with age, I saw that she was as plump as I had imagined her, but for a different reason: she was pregnant.

Bewildered by all my mental shifts and in something of a trance, I led her upstairs and stood watching as she peeled off her jogging pants and a once classic but now tatty Benetton sweater, underneath it a T-shirt with the print of a cartoon owl – and below the owl the legend, *Whoooo*. She dropped heavily onto the bed with its rumpled coverlet and closed her eyes.

'Did you come from far?' I asked, hovering in the doorway. It felt as if she were the first person to visit me in an age, as if I was actually unused to callers, although the room seemed to reek of dope and sex.

'Lucan,' she said. 'The buses were atrocious.' This was not news to me: the buses, such as they were, were always atrocious. Then she opened her eyes and smiled at me somewhat groggily. 'Aren't you going to get into bed?'

I came round behind her and undid the clasp of her enormous bra. 'I must admit that I've never made love to a pregnant woman,' I said, hanging the bra by its strap on the bedpost. 'Or not to my knowledge.'

'Ah well, I'm not quite as far gone as I look. The baby's not due until May.' She grinned up at me from the bed as I went over to close the window, powerfully aware of the layers I was wearing and of what was underneath. 'You're looking a little nonplussed,' she said, still grinning. 'Are you one of those people who like to turn out all the lights? Have you never seen a naked body before?'

Slowly I loosened the belt of my dressing gown and dropped it on the chair, on top of her bits, and stepped towards her in all my glory.

'I have, but have you?' This fatuous reply was made partly out of panic, but partly also out of a conviction, coming from who knows where, that I must elicit from her some important fact.

'Oh yes, I have, many times.' Cait sat up on an elbow and watched me calmly, eyeing me down the length of her fine nose. 'We have the same CV, as it goes. We work in the same industry,' she said, as if we were copy editors on rival fashion magazines. I must have looked fairly flummoxed, because she laughed; then she laid a hand on the massive pale bulge of her belly. 'He's tickling me,' she told me – like a natural conclusion to these revelations.

She lay back on the pillow and put her arms above her head. She could not see past the hump of her unborn child to where I pulled her knickers down over her ankles, balled them and tossed them onto the chair, to where I ran my tongue between the tight curls of her yellow hair and the lips of her sex, parted as if caught mid-sentence. With my hands on her waist, I could feel the baby tumble beneath my thumbs. 'Oh Jeez, oh Jeez,' said Cait – and down in the street a horn sounded one long blast, a car alarm stopped bleeping and the neighbour's dog, satisfied at last that the moon was still up there, however unseen, abruptly ceased to bark.

Afterwards she lay still, neither opening her eyes nor stirring, and I tugged the sheets from under her and draped her in a blanket. It had been quite a while since I spent the night with anyone. Sometimes a client would fall into a doze after she came, finally able to relax in a place where she had no errands, no need to converse, no responsibilities. Depending on how busy my diary was, I might give her ten minutes before blowing gently in her ear to wake her or, if there was a large enough gap in my schedule, leave her on the bed for a bit while I made myself coffee and read the paper. That night I went downstairs and turned off all the phones, closed down the laptop and dimmed the lights. Then I went up to the bedroom again, got into bed beside her, switched off the bedside lamp and allowed myself to fall like a stone into the darkness.

When we woke in the morning, I half-expected to find the baby lying between us, wriggling and gurgling, the fruit of an earlier lovemaking fallen early from the tree. But no, it was just me and Cait for a little while longer; the baby could wait a while. And there is still a little time before he appears, a month or so at this point – time that we have both used rather well. Since that auspicious night, she has moved in with me, bringing precious little in the way of belongings besides a lava lamp, an alabaster egg from a long-ago Roman holiday and a couple of Annie Lennox CDs. As she says, all the baggage she has she now carries inside her, everything she earned she has saved for the baby. Similarly, I have hung on to the capital accrued in my months as a sex worker, a precious packet that will be useful to us in the summer.

Cait has retired from the trade and set herself up as an online agony aunt, just as I have given up my work as a professional pleaser of women and taken a job at the delicatessen in Superquinn. Some weekends I do a shift in The Carpenter in Carpenterstown, where I pull the pints and look with fresh curiosity into punters' faces. There was a time when I saw only the surface of people – but now, in the blink of an eye, I can picture them getting dressed, see the care and deliberation with which they choose their clothes, see the room in which their clothes are kept.

In a bid to hold on to what I have learned, on Tuesday nights these days I go to a men's group, presided over by a lugubrious old German named Uwe, in the ugly modern hall attached to the church. We sit on hard chairs in a semicircle, listening to each other until it is our turn to speak. And then we talk about the decisive moments in our lives, times we have imitated our parents and times we have been ourselves. We reveal to one another our surplus of strange qualities, curious quirks and surprising virtues, our attempts at honesty. We talk in turn about our experience of love and madness, our moments of freedom, our animal passions.

Sweetheart, I'm Telling You

The girl was sitting in the buffet car when Jack came in for a beer. He was surprised to see her again; they had been sitting across from each other when the train left Gdańsk, at the start of the journey, and she had caught his eye once and smiled. She was dressed in the typical style of a Polish student, elegant but inexpensive, in a thin green blouse and pale blue jeans. When the train reached Tczew she had left their carriage with her overnight bag, and he thought he had seen the last of her – but there she was, sitting in the buffet car and looking out at the March sunlight bouncing from the snow-covered plain.

He stood in line while an old man wearing the grey and claret outfit of the state railways served bigos and rolls to the customers ahead of him. It was still only eleven in the morning, early for a drink, but he wanted something to dull the day's extreme brightness. While he waited, he watched the back of the girl's head. She was not a girl – she was a woman, of course – but he saw in her an unfinished quality, a girlishness that was sad and appealing. In two years of living in Poland, he had got into the habit of gazing at the women around him, as if through his gaze he could possess them, feeling a shameful power all the time he did so at this secret invasion. Her neck was slender and her skin a greyish white; a lick of light brown hair reached the collar of her blouse. After the man at the counter had given him his beer and change, Jack went over to sit at the table behind her, facing the direction of travel.

There were few other passengers in the buffet car, only a middle-aged woman and two young cadets, who sat side by side but drank as if alone. Overheated air poured from vents at their feet, making the carriage unpleasantly stuffy; outside the sun shone remotely, hinting at the possibility of a new season but without bringing a thaw – its light fell in stripes across the tables marked with the state monopoly's drab insignia. In the turn of her head towards the window, he saw the girl look for a change in this environment, in this struggle between cold light and airless heat. Then she stood to rescue her bag when it slid into the aisle, and he saw how neatly she fitted into her jeans. Her grey eyes caught him in their orbit for a moment as she glanced about her; she must be ten years younger than him, he thought – she was pale, but her pallor was somehow radiant.

Tilting the bottle of beer to his lips, he thought about the previous night, so typical but also so bizarre, the kind of night that would stay with him. He had walked home as usual from his lessons at the British Council studium, where he taught on Thursday evenings; when he approached their block and saw his wife waving to him from their kitchen on the second floor, as she often did when she expected him at a certain time, he had waved back – and his wedding ring, always slightly too large for his finger, had flown off into the bushes at the foot of the building. Kasia had come down with a torch, and they had spent half an hour searching the undergrowth while the neighbours watched silently from their windows, until his wife had stood suddenly, brandishing the ring. It was a miracle, really, that she had found it in the dark, among all the dead leaves, under the pressure of all those watching eyes. It was a shame that they had not stayed in and had a glass of wine together to honour this miracle.

Today he was on his way to London, with the ring in his pocket for safe keeping. After the train to Warsaw he would fly to Heathrow, then take the underground to Chiswick where his mother lay ill, possibly dying, looked after by his sister. Kasia had not wanted to come and he had not tried to persuade her – she and his mother had never got on, and he was glad of some time alone, not for any reason in particular but just to be free of her. After a year and a bit of marriage, he was still not used to her constant presence; it was as if they were always together, without a break, even during the day when he was at his work and she was at hers. Now as the train rocked along its tracks she became more distant with each telegraph pole and snowy field, and he felt bereft and exposed but at the same time released.

He held on to the plastic table with one hand and lifted the bottle to his lips with the other. The halting, juddering movement of the train on its tracks filled him with dread. As a child, he had loved to travel, loved nothing more than to watch from the window of a train as it hurtled onwards, swaying on the rails – but now he saw in its every hitch and skip the potential for disaster, some high-speed derailment. He had been this way for about a year without saying anything about it to anyone, not even Kasia. At Christmas, when friends suggested taking a ferry across the Baltic to Karlskrona for a few days, he had made some lame excuse not to go. There was no way he could come out with his real reason – that the Baltic in his mind was an angry sea with tall black waves that were only waiting to swallow him up. But his fear did not stop there – it attached to all forms of transport. At tram stops he hung back and stuck to the wall of the shelter, convinced that otherwise he would somehow tumble onto the tracks at the very moment when the tram pulled in. Car journeys down the narrow backroads through Kashubia for their weekend breaks were just as nerve-racking.

He knew that his fears were groundless, that he was only suffering from some expatriate neurosis that came of being so far from what he had known before – but the train began to jolt across the river bridge into Malbork, and he could not reason them away. He held on tight to his bottle of beer and made himself look across the river and into the trees on the bank beyond, trying to recall whether the bridge was made of wood or metal, seeing in his mind's eye all the carriages slide rapidly into the water and sink beneath the surface. It was absurd and impractical to give in to these feelings – he had the flight to come after this, and the plane's endless circling as it queued in the air for a runway, and then the ride into town on the underground, fire-prone and crash-prone.

As it passed the central point of the bridge, the train slowed almost to a halt, and he closed his eyes and let the bittersweet harshness of the beer catch him in the back of his throat; when he opened them again, he saw the woman ahead of him staring down at the frozen river. He followed her gaze to where, close to the bank, a swan was stuck in the ice, with only its white back and the curve of its neck showing above the waterline. It must have been caught there somehow – it was as if the temperature had dropped so quickly that it had no time to fly away. The train picked up speed then, just as the sun emerged from a cloud above the walls of Malbork

Castle, a cloud shaped like a radial wing – and it came to him all at once, not like a thought, like a sensation, that impossible leap from the icy runway at take-off and the give in the wings as the plane hit turbulence, its high-pitched mechanical whine that measured out the long minutes in the sky. He swallowed and shut his eyes once more against the glinting sun, but in the dull and repetitive thud of wheels across the cross-ties he heard a premonition of the awful thump as they hit the ground at landing, engines screaming in back-thrust, the terrible panic of braking.

He felt something brush his sleeve, and came back with a start to find the girl's hand on his arm, a look of concern on her pale, plain face.

'Are you okay?' she asked him in Polish.

'Oh, sure,' he said, answering in English – his Polish was still too stilted for anything more complex than an order at the bar. 'I'm fine,' he told her, smiling. 'I just had a big night last night, that's all.'

Her name was Julita, she told him, as she took a seat on the stool next to his. He was right in thinking her a student: she was in her final year of economics at the University of Gdańsk, on her way to a job interview in Warsaw. In a moment of easy agreement, he fetched her a beer, and they sat side by side as the train headed south.

'I shouldn't drink this,' she grinned, 'but I need the courage.' Her eyes, now that he saw them up close, were green more than grey, the colour of her blouse, with little golden spurs. He took her in: her top button was undone, and he saw the dip at the base of her throat and the start of her small breasts. She seemed very aware of her hands, thrusting them now and then between her thighs as if to warm them. Her self-consciousness was touching – but after a few pulls on her beer she quickly lost her shyness.

'So you want to work in Warsaw?'

'No,' she said, 'not really. I'd rather go to London, like you. Warszawa is a terrible place, *strasznie brzydka*. Terribly ugly.'

'London is ugly too,' he said, 'in parts.'

She allowed her hands to escape and dance in front of her eyes for a moment; then she folded them between her thighs again and leaned towards him, smiling. 'I would like to see the parts that are not.' She smiled all the time, but he could not be sure what it meant, her smile; now and then it flickered off, only to brighten again in an instant. 'So why was last night so big for you?' she asked him.

The night before had not been big so much as foolish, on the usual petty scale of things. After Kasia had found the ring, he persuaded her to go out with him to meet their friend Joe at an Irish pub called Scruffy Murphy's. Joe was one of a handful of Irishmen in a city that had several Irish-themed pubs, where they even celebrated St Patrick's Day in an ersatz kind of way. Joe was already drunk when they arrived, and Jack had worked hard to catch up with him while Kasia chatted to a French guy and his Polish wife, a couple they often bumped into in these expat hangouts. After an hour or so, an American friend of Jack's had swung in, a goateed Californian called Bill, along with his wife Beata. Their arrival was a signal for the night to turn awkward, when Joe sidled up to Beata and proposed, in his teasing way, that they should sleep together. Bill took umbrage in the ultra-pacific West Coast manner that Joe despised, and Joe tried to punch him in the face. His drunken right hook missed by an inch or more, but the bouncer had made them leave all the same.

Julita watched him impassively, smiling at his story with its little catastrophes; while he told it, he avoided the word *żona* – avoided the word *wife*.

'You guys sure know how to have a good time,' she laughed, in a phrase she must have picked up from a movie.

'Let's drink to that,' he said, draining his bottle and offering her a second.

'It is really not a good idea,' she laughed – but when he pressed her again she accepted, as if nothing she did could be that important, no consequences could be too damaging.

'You can always brush your teeth,' he joked when he came back with the bottles – but something in what he said passed her by, either the words or his tone; she failed to understand, and shrugged and frowned at the table between them. With the sun falling into the buffet car and the artificial heat all around them, he felt a fragrance rise from her, musky and sweetly alien, the scent of her *charme slave*. If he wanted to remain as long as possible within her aura, he must take care to speak slowly and in sentences with transparent content, or she would shrink from him as something simply foreign, necessarily separate.

But while they worked on their second beer she loosened up and became more animated. In explaining the hardships of student existence – all those tales of retaken exams and compulsory physical education that he had heard many times from other students – she let her hands go, waving them around before her face as she talked. Not listening closely to her predictable tales, he watched the spell her fingers wove before his eyes, as if she were making a little cage for his attention. In a sudden gesture at one point she reached up and untied the turquoise scarf that held back her light brown hair, and her hair fell forward over her forehead as she tied the scarf around her thigh, above her knee. Everything she did was so natural, he thought, so unforced and pretty; he wondered how long he could keep her with him, and hoped it would be as far as Warsaw.

They entered a long culvert, where the train ground almost to a stop; at the end of the buffet car, a door swung open and closed, squeaking on its hinges. In the buzz of alcohol and sweetness of the early spring light, the train's gentle rocking as it crawled on between the banks with their tall silver birches was strangely provocative. Although she remained perched on her stool, Julita seemed to come closer and pass into his space. For an instant, he shut his eyes against the light that dashed through the silver birch branches; when he looked about him again, for a minute or so he saw nothing but the points of light that fell between her fingers. He watched her mouth, not hearing what she said – he had heard all her stories before, in the same broken English. It only made him feel lonelier to hear his language spoken that way; but the language itself was lonely, tired of being mumbled in classrooms full of chalk dust by young people who had never travelled anywhere it was spoken. He could not bear to meet her round eyes – their innocence rumbled him, made him feel old and at a disadvantage.

The train began to move off again, still rocking while it gathered speed. Julita finished her beer and slid from her stool. 'I have to go and change into my suit,' she said. 'We're getting close.'

She was right, he saw from his watch – they were only half an hour from Warsaw. When she picked up her bag, he followed her past the compartment they had shared at the start of the journey until they reached the end of the corridor, where they stood in the chilly gap between carriages, teetering together with each reckless sideways movement of the train as it hurtled along. He looked over her shoulder at the perishing rubber that bridged the gap between the cars. How unsafe it all seemed to his western eye – all those carriages held together by strips of fatigued metal and running helter-skelter on rusted wheels – and instead he looked down at the top of her head, as she hesitated by the door to the WC. Then she put her hand on his arm and drew him in with her, closing the door behind them.

She leaned back against the door and kissed him for a while, her tongue flicking inside his mouth, one hand fluttering about his face with what he took for uncertainty. But then with the other hand she loosened the belt on her jeans and stepped out of them in the cramped little space, then bent down and folded them and put them on the lid of the toilet. He unbuttoned her blouse and pulled it carefully from her arms, their greyish flesh covered in goosebumps from the cold – he was taken aback by the newness of her body, its pretty density. They kissed again and she pressed against his leg, then took his hand and put it inside her knickers and tilted herself towards him, standing on her toes. Jack lifted her and put her down on the edge of the sink and ran his hands along the inside of her thighs to her almost colourless lips, where he put his mouth, which parted under his tongue. The thought flashed across his mind while his tongue played inside her, *Kasia will never find me here*.

Then he undid his own belt and, holding her away from the filthy floor, entered her slowly while her breathing quickened and slowed, stopped and started in sharp little pants. He made love to her standing up, trying not to look down at the muddy blue plastic of the floor beneath them, gluing his mouth to her neck where

36

it sank down to her breasts, so swanlike and perfect. Little was left in his mind between entering her and coming inside her – he was aware of her weight in his hands and her tightness around him, the lilywater sweat that started out of her as they moved together and the smell of her hair in his eyes, but that was all. She came all of a sudden, with a yelp, biting his tongue – and he put her down.

They sat in their former compartment and watched the approach to Warsaw. As long as the capital remained in the distance he could stay with her, hold onto her – but soon the outskirts were followed by the suburbs, the towering anonymity of massive housing projects. They stopped at several outlying stations; at one, a little Romany boy came into the carriage playing an accordion so large that he could hardly get his hands around it to press the keys – but he played, and Jack gave him a couple of złoty. When the boy had gone, Julita smiled at him and shrugged. '*Co można zrobić*?' she said. 'What can you do?'

Long, straight boulevards passed below the raised tracks, fringed with dirty snow, sunlight glinting from stationary cars – then they crossed the river again and were in Warsaw proper, looking down on shanty stalls where traders from the old routes, timeless old women from somewhere in the east and their ravaged men, sold plastic toys, batteries and cut flowers. Jack remembered how much he had wanted to write about all this when he first arrived in Poland – and then, when his lack of talent became too painfully obvious, how instead he went from street to street taking pictures of the few walls that remained from previous versions of the city, still bullet-scarred. Gdańsk had seemed magnificent to him in those days, when its fragments were still held together by his vision, the hope of his wedding day, the energy of that union. For a while, the act of taking a photograph was enough to hold the fragments together – by making a stab at art, he could contain the chaos inside him, up to a point. But beyond that point nothing held together, and his life began to spill from the frame in bits and pieces.

Julita sat next to him, her legs crossed, barely speaking until the train entered the lightless cavern of the central station. They walked down a concrete tunnel and climbed to the level of the bewildering concourse, where lines for tickets stretched half its length. The other half was taken up with gypsy beggars with missing eyes or arms, ageing bureaucrats in once fashionable brown coats who might have been somebody under the old regime, junkies who wandered backwards with their eyes tight shut, oblivious to their open wounds and muttering to themselves, gangs of younger men in uniform, presumably on furlough from national service – and dotted here and there among them a few members of Poland's newly moneyed middle classes, who watched over their bags with cold impatience.

He said goodbye to her outside the station, in the shadow of the Palace of Culture. Julita took a piece of paper from her bag, wrote something on it, folded it in half and handed it over to him. 'Phone me when you get back to Gdańsk,' she told him. He told her he would and watched her cross the wide and dangerous road and disappear down Emilii Plater, her hair tied back once more in its bandanna, until her brown head was lost among the milling ciphers. On the bus to the airport, he felt for her number in his pocket; he should take it out and memorize it, or Kasia would stumble upon it – and what would he tell her, if she did? He could say that it was the number of an admirer; she had told him once that his problem was he lacked admirers. He could tell her it was someone with a job offer, although he already had enough work. Or he could tell her that it was the number of someone he had met on a train – he could tell her what happened. And what then? This phase of their lives would be over; they would go their own ways and never speak to one another again.

The airport's cool white walls and orderly groups of solitary travellers came as solace after the melee at the station. It was a sealed environment, shutting out what he did not want to see, exclusive enough that it felt like a space created for him and his kind. He recognised the irony of the fact that, as much as he hated flying, even so he loved the logic and privacy of airports, where everything was always under control and pointed to one moment – the moment of departure, however long the delays.

In this case, his flight was on time; for an hour, while he waited for his gate to be called, he stood by the high windows in the duty-free zone and watched robots wash the ice from wings of local light aircraft and men with giant scrapers clear snow from taxi lanes. It was only when he went to join his queue that the day's two elements came together in his mind: what he had just done and what was about to happen. As he stood in line with passport in hand, he let his eye fall on a small plane that seemed to taxi forever without gathering speed, until finally it rose and climbed for a minute with desperate haste into the middle air. For a long instant, the ground looked as if it might change its mind and pull it back down to earth. But then it broke free – shook off gravity and went on climbing to a point below the clouds where its wings became a golden blur, until a cloud shadow fell across it and turned it black. Then it levelled out and flew west in a straight line, until it was too much of a speck to show.

While his gaze hovered at the place where the plane had vanished, he wondered where she had got to, Julita, what she had done when her interview was over, whether she had gone to a bar and sat there thinking about him, asking herself whether he would call. For a minute he was lost in this dream of her – but then in a flash that was like a memory, a sudden recollection of something real, he saw that they were nothing to each other, not even strangers. What they had done together was as unrelated to either of them as he was unrelated to the land he stood on now, an accidental collision in a soiled room. He had seized the moment when it came – grabbed hold of it as if he were alone in the world and flying through mid-air and she could stop him from falling. Her face appeared before him again, her look of lust and round-eyed innocence, and he hoped that she had forgotten already what had taken place between them. He hoped that in the toilet afterwards when she changed into her suit, she had washed him out of her, that his seed had not grown cold inside her and spread the chill of his fear.

He took the crumpled ball of paper with her number from his pocket and held it briefly in his palm before dropping it into a bin before the final screen. Radiation saw though him and security made no comment, and he walked out across the frosted tarmac to the plane that would take him to London. He watched his step on the slippery ground until he reached the stairs – then he raised his eyes beyond the frozen wing to a dazzling field of light, the setting sun that fell on a crust of snow.

Constant in the Darkness

One late afternoon in early spring, Mark Drake sat on the riverbank and watched the sun go down. The dirty city water turned gold at a certain point, when the sun hung over the roofs of the suburban houses; then it fell below the skyline and the water turned black. This was his cue to go home and make dinner – but when he stood he found that the world had gone dark before his eyes. He climbed the embankment steps, expecting his sight to return at any moment, but when he reached the road he still could not see. Setting off slowly towards the bridge and the muted thrum of rush-hour traffic, he walked for a minute before colliding with a passer-by. It was a woman, he could tell from a certain atmosphere around her – her scent, and something else.

'Why don't you look where you're going?' the woman asked him. 'Have you forgotten your stick?'

'I'm not blind,' he said, 'I just can't see right now.' He was aware of how odd this sounded, but the woman said nothing – he only heard her rapid intakes of breath; she must have been running when they bumped into each other. 'Could you take me to the bus-stop on the bridge? I can find my way from there.'

'Well, I don't know,' she said. 'I'm in a hurry, I have to pick my daughter up from school.' A car swept along the embankment behind her. 'What happened? Can't you see anything at all?'

'I was watching the sunset,' he said, 'for longer than I should have, I suppose.' This time she laughed; the sound of her laughter was close at hand, while below them, at the bottom of the steps he had just climbed, a duck landed on the water with a flurry of wings – he could almost see its webbed feet plough the surface. It was surprising how much he could still see from memory.

He felt her sudden motion as she looked at her watch. 'You'd better come with me to school,' she said. 'I don't have time to take you to the bridge. I'm late for Janet as it is.'

She took his arm – but even so he stumbled to begin with, unsure where his feet would land, until he began to relax and let her guide him. Her scent hung in the air about them like unlabelled stock, citrous and something else, almost covering the smells of soil and grass that came from the embankment gardens. Then the school sprang up before them in a welter of voices, and they came to a halt. 'Where *is* she now? I can't see her,' the woman said – but she was looking at the side of his face, her breath on his cheek, until he felt compelled to speak.

'I'm Mark,' he said, 'Mark Drake.' He paused to let her answer, but she said nothing in return. 'I'm sorry if I've slowed you down.'

She turned away and lit a cigarette – he heard the rasp of a lighter, a sigh as she exhaled. 'Janet will be out in a minute,' she said. 'She's always late on Fridays – the teacher keeps them behind to say prayers.'

They waited side by side in the playground, a grey expanse he remembered from his own schooldays. Moisture rose in the air as the sun fell towards the horizon. All around them parents chattered, the fathers' dull monotones mixed in with the mothers' soothing trills. The two of them stood without saying anything for what seemed a long time. 'If you pointed me in the right direction,' he said at last, 'I'm sure I could find my way. I grew up around here.'

'Oh, but I can hardly let you wander blindly around, can I? Anything could happen,' she said in her mocking way, 'you might fall under a car.' A child's quick footsteps approached them then and stopped, and she guided her daughter's small hand into his. He held the damp palm in his own for an instant, the little row of fingers. 'This is Mr Drake,' the woman said. 'I found him by the river. What do you think? Shall we take him home with us?'

The girl still held on to his hand – he felt her looking up into his face. 'He's *Captain* Drake, not *Mister* Drake,' she said.

The woman took his arm again, laughing in that way she had, as if they were surrounded by an empty space that had a few amusing things in it here and there. 'That's right,' she said, 'it looks like he sailed around the world just to be with us tonight.'

The chorus of voices grew quiet as they left the school behind, smothered by the river's watery run and their footsteps echoing as they entered the backstreets. The three of them walked on into the Meadows, a mile-deep stretch of Victorian terraces that lay between river and town; he sensed that was where she was taking him. The woman's invitation, if that was what it was, had come as a surprise – and now he was swept along through the chill evening air, turning one corner after another, while he tried to retrace their steps in his mind, the path they had taken from the riverbank. But the way they had taken had too many twists. Twenty years ago, as a boy, he had been at home in this labyrinth, but since then he had rarely been back, and now he had no idea where he might be going.

When they stopped at her door and she let go of his arm to find her key, he wondered whether it would be better to walk away, try to follow the walls back to the river and the river to the bridge. But then the door was open and she ushered him through, and he went upstairs after the little girl.

The woman sat him at the kitchen table and opened a window, letting in a cool tang of dust and ash. Unable to see the changing light, he had lost any ordinary sense of how much time was passing. There must have been lapses when he was unaware of minutes going by, of the hour – because all at once late afternoon turned into evening. He felt it in the change in the air that came in through the window, damper and cooler now. Behind him a cupboard door closed and a cork popped, and he heard the light gasp of wine as it fell from the bottle into a glass.

'Cheers,' she said, putting a cold glass in his hand, tapping his glass with her own. He heard her sit down facing him across the table. 'It's nice to have a visitor. My last was a disappointment. I regretted my decision, shall we say.' In the next room, the little girl was talking to herself, water in a pan was coming to the boil, a pipe ticked in a wall nearby – otherwise the house was remarkably silent. 'He tried to leave his mark on me, to tell you the truth, and not in a good way. You don't look like someone who would want to leave a mark.'

'So how *do* I look?' The first sip of wine tasted harsh, even acidic, made his eyes water; he put down his glass and laid his hands out flat, palm down on the table.

'Have you forgotten already?' she laughed.

Hearing her swallow, he picked up his glass and took another mouthful. This time the wine tasted sweet and fresh – it took him back to a valley filled with olive

44

trees, cypresses and cicadas. Her chair scraped the floor as she stood, the oven door slammed, a pan clanked on the stove, and the child appeared at his side; he felt her small hand on his shoulder, heard her voice close to his ear. 'You know Captain Drake is a pirate, mummy, like Bluebeard.'

'Ah, yes, that makes sense,' her mother said. 'After all, I found him wandering around by the river. My guess is that he fell asleep and ran aground and his ship sank. He was washed ashore, but his shipmates are all down with the mermaids on the riverbed. Isn't that right, Captain Drake?'

'Some of them,' he said, smiling at the room, unseen but felt. 'The rest are in The Aviary, playing pool and drinking lager.'

'Rum,' the daughter insisted, 'pirates drink rum.'

The girl asked to sit on his knee, and he lifted her up. Her talk and warm presence were reassuring, but he wished he could speak plainly with the mother, who seemed to hide behind this childish banter, take refuge in her child's imagination. Janet played with his ears and hair while their dinner cooked – sauce spat in the pan, throwing out strong aromas of garlic and basil. It was remarkable how sharpened his senses were, how with every mouthful of wine the flavour became more intense.

The woman brushed past them to the next room, he heard a needle drop onto vinyl – and a song played on the stereo, one he had heard many times before but changed now by where he was and who he was with, being able to hear it without the distractions of sight. The voice flew from the speakers into the room, through the window and out into the world, where it soared into the sky and painted streaks of feeling in the air – in the next instant flying from those same feelings on its wings of sound.

After dinner, Janet went off to bed and her mother sat with him at the table over a second bottle of wine. The room was very still. Out in the street a single bird sang the same note, over and over; in the end even the bird fell silent, and the night was altogether quiet except for a faint whistling of wind, a calling of ducks and gulls from the river and the distant whoosh of traffic from the bridge.

'The food was very good,' he said, after a minute or two of this wordless hush.

'You're welcome.' She paused, and he imagined her lifting her glass to drink, her lips on the rim of the glass. 'Don't you like the silence? You seem to want to break it.'

Her question came from the far side of the kitchen, and through clenched teeth; another cork popped from another bottle. Was this their third bottle, then? He remembered her saying, 'One for you and one for me,' but perhaps he had counted wrong.

'I was just making sure you were still there,' he said. 'For a moment it seemed like I was alone.'

'Is that a feeling you often have?' she asked him, closer again, swallowing – he heard her swallow.

'Yes,' he said, 'it is. I don't know why – there are always people around.'

She refilled his glass then took her seat again, facing him across the table. He felt her eyes on him; he wished they could stay this way for a long time. 'Do you feel as if I'd kidnapped you?'

'Kidnappers tend to lock you in the cellar with a piece of bread, or so they say.'

'Well, I feel like a kidnapper,' she told him. 'It's a pleasant feeling, really.'

He lowered his head and stared at the table – seeing nothing, knowing nothing. 'Really? What is it like?'

'A delicious feeling of power,' she laughed. 'What *shall* I do with him next?'

He reached slowly for the stem of his glass, carefully so as not to knock it over. 'What are your options?' he asked, or thought he asked. Somewhere in the house he heard the girl stirring in her bedroom, the creak of her bed and a sigh. Neither of them spoke for a minute or two; there was silence again, almost perfect this time; even the cars had stopped their flow across the bridge. 'Even human speech is just music,' he said, in the end. 'We make all these sounds, but none of it means what we want it to mean.'

'Are you sure?'

'Yes, it's impossible to say anything really – all we can do is sing.'

'Maybe,' she said, after a pause. 'But there's nothing wrong with that, is there? There's nothing wrong with just singing.' She leaned in closer, bent towards him across the table – he sensed her nearness. 'So what do *I* look like,' she asked him. 'Do you know?'

Her voice was rich and warm; as she breathed, he could almost see her chest rise and fall – he felt her gaze on his sightless eyes. 'You have brown hair,' he said at last, 'dark brown. Your eyes are light blue, you have a lot of freckles. You're pale, but the wine has put colour in your cheeks.'

The room emptied for a beat or two – for a few seconds her breathing seemed to stop. 'Well,' she said, 'you're right, in fact, I'm a brunette with blue eyes, with a lot of freckles and rosy cheeks. You have described me exactly.'

47

Her even tone made him aware of his own stillness – yet there was an inner rising in him, which he knew she would be able to see. She stood abruptly, her chair scraping the floor, her glass landing on the table with a clink.

'Let me show you another room,' she said.

She led him through two doorways to a room smelling of linen and lotions and began to undress. Static crackled as she pulled her top over her head – from the corner of his eye he saw sparks, or so he thought. When she went to open a window, in spite of his blindness he seemed to catch a glimmer from the streetlights on her pale breasts. A slight commotion, a mix of voices came through the open window, then dwindled away. The pubs had just closed – last orders were done.

'Take off your clothes,' she said, 'and I'll hang them up for you.'

It was quiet again as they lay down, apart from the ticks and groans of the house. The feeling of her skin against his own sent points of light into a space behind his eyes – and when she touched him with her hands, her touch turned into sweeps of colour. Her breath on his face shot purple lines through his mind's eye, the pressure of her thighs brought a shower of red and gold. Then all at once he was inside her and all colours merged into black, and he made his way in the dark towards the promise of an opening until he arrived on her shores – she was an island, he realised, and he had just walked across her, and now he was walking her sands. But the land all at once was awash, a wave swept over both of them and he was buried, lost to himself.

Afterwards they lay on the coverlet in a breeze from the open window that chilled his skin, until she got up to close it. Again he thought he saw her pale figure

48

gleam in the light thrown by the streetlamp, but he was mistaken. He held his hand up in front of his face – he could see nothing. She lay down beside him again, and their sides touched, but the touch seemed incidental. She was more remote now than when they had first collided on the riverbank or walked together through the Meadows or talked in her kitchen. He would have liked to say something to break up this rhythm, the rhythm of them coming together and falling away, to ask her if this was what she wanted; but when he opened his mouth to speak, he understood before a sound left his lips that she could not hear him. She was already asleep; her breathing quickly settled into a pattern, and he turned on his side, closed his eyes and fell into a strange measureless darkness.

He dreamed that a meteorite fell from the night sky and landed in the market square, in the centre of town, soaking all the buildings in its orange light for an instant before melting them all in its heat. It was no longer possible to find his way around the city now that it had no buildings, no streets, now that the street signs made no sense. Waking from this dream, he floundered for a minute in layers of shadow, nauseated by this depthless black swell, either because of his blindness or because the night was at its darkest. It was only when he felt the woman stir beside him that he realised he was really awake. Putting his hand on her side, he found the curve of her belly, flowing down to a hollow. Her body trembled slightly as it filled with the dark night air.

Then something woke him up, and this time he was wide awake. He opened his eyes, expecting them to be filled with the sight of a strange room, a woman's face – but there was nothing, not even the palest motion. He felt her stir and tug back the duvet, sensed her looking down at him, her breath in a warm trickle, reminding him of the wine. 'You were laughing in your sleep,' she said.

'Yes, it was strange, I was dreaming,' he began – and automatically he started to tell her about the meteor; but an alarm clock started to bleat, and she leaned over him to shut it up. 'How late is it?' he asked.

'It's not even light yet.' She sat up suddenly and got out of bed. There was a splash from a sink somewhere and then hangers clicked, cloth brushed against itself; when she came back, she bent over him and touched his shoulder – she was dressed. 'Time to go,' she told him, and helped him into his clothes. She did not want her daughter to see him in the morning, it was easier if he just disappeared – no doubt this was what she was thinking. He did not question her logic, or the logic of taking him out into the street when he was still blind. After all, what could he say? He could tell her that he wanted to stay, but he doubted that anything he said would change her mind.

She led him downstairs and unlatched the door. As they paused on the threshold, he took a deep breath and drank in the cold spring air, listening out for the sounds of distant traffic, cars and trucks that poured across the bridge half a mile away. Then she took his arm and they walked together as they had the previous afternoon, their heels rapping the flagstones in the cool morning. The city was slow to shake off the oddly ornamental quality it had acquired overnight in his dream; it was as if the streets and houses were fabrications, figments of somebody else's imagination, unreal places lived in by real people. Until that morning, he had always thought of it the other way around – that the city and its streets were real and concrete and it was the people who were made up, fictional.

Doors opened and closed around them and other footsteps joined theirs, before moving away again and leaving them alone. A spoken word, a woodpigeon's call startled him by its nearness. Other sounds began to emerge from all sides, at all angles, as if from small speakers placed along their route: water gurgled through the drains below his feet, while above him a jet engine drew an arc of noise across the sky's unseen parabola. They turned any number of corners, and for the first time since they met he felt that he was at her mercy – as if he was a stranger here, and she was the only person he knew.

'How will I find my way back?' he asked her. 'To you, I mean.'

She stopped then, let go of his arm and put her hand on his cheek, taking him in for a moment, studying him in the daylight. 'Well,' she laughed, 'you'll know next time. Never leave home without your ball of string.'

In a minute they turned the final corner; a blast of wind swept up a handful of dirt and threw it in his face, spattering his eyelids. He could taste the city on his lips, bitter and gritty – they crossed the road, and for a few seconds the traffic was all around them, a loud and almost angry noise. But then it was behind him, and he became aware of the river below, slopping against the arches with its lapping echo.

'We're on the bridge,' she said, 'at the bus-stop. You know the one I mean?'

'Of course,' he said.

She slipped her arm out of his, took his hands and placed them on the parapet, where he stood and was blown about, buffeted by the breeze. He felt exposed, high above the water, exposed to the dawn light and rush of traffic at his back. He gazed down to where the rising sun coaxed the water's surface into life so that it shone in fragments, changed constantly by the currents and gusts of wind. These shards of light appeared like hundreds of eyes peering up at him from the river, until a cloud blew over the sun and the eyes turned away, or they sank to the riverbed.

He turned from the water and looked quickly about, but there were only the usual sights of morning – white vans driving out of town with their loads, a woman in an apron opening the shutters of a café. There was no one with him on the bridge.

My Breakfast with Gumbo

It is Monday morning and I am having breakfast with Gumbo on the pavement outside a small café, in the early spring sunlight, in the brisk wind that courses down the street. It is the main street of our southern coastal town, the kind of street on which dramas such as this are played out daily, with no witnesses beyond a waitress, a schoolgirl playing truant and the old man who empties the bins.

Gumbo sits across from me, his face red and his hair a wild tangle, like dirty candyfloss, sucking his missing finger – the last joint on the middle finger of his right hand. He lost it when we were five years old, playing tag with my sister. Since then, I have heard him tell how a monkey bit it off at London Zoo, or how he snapped off a digit in a fist fight over the Albion or in a game of Russian roulette, played for fingers not for brains. Only I remember Jeannie slamming the parlour door, the crunch of wood on bone, the screams and blood and wah-wah of the ambulance that took him to the General.

Gumbo prefers his fairytale versions of events, because he is very childish. But then so am I. We have been childish together for over thirty years.

'Let's not beat around the bush,' says Gumbo. 'We're here for a reason, Morgan' – the last word a sigh of disgust with my name in it.

Gumbo wants to know whether I have ended my long-going affair with his wife, Lorna, who at this moment is almost certainly asleep, but whose absence makes itself felt. Lorna, too, has something missing – not from her hands or feet but from her chest. Without the missing breast she would be too perfect; as it is, she twirls invisibly between us, a tiny figurine of a woman with her one wrinkled dug.

But I do not want to discuss Lorna's Amazonian tit or her face with its thrusting jawline, her buttocks clinging to each other in tension or ecstasy, her out-turning navel, her pulsing throat, the hairy nape of her neck. We had three good years together, three years of each other's reckless wit and personal hygiene, three years of licking and nibbling, tugging and fiddling, three years of biting and scratching and stroking. They were the three happiest years I have known, but how can I say so to her husband?

'Yes, let's not beat around the bush,' I say – and I smile through the glass at the plain Jane who serves here on Mondays, hoping for a distraction. But I cannot catch her eye; she is too busy lending an ear to her colleague, a regular chatty Cathy who is no doubt going through her old repertoire, her usual litany of bus fare, funfair and unfair. Cars swish past, God bless them, never thinking that the end will ever come. A teenage hustler in noxious pink jogging trousers goes by, nudging my shoulder with her hip. We would be better off indoors, but Gumbo and I have chosen to sit outside; our business is a little too intimate for all those old ladies with balding pates, headscarves and *Daily Mails*.

But it is cold out here, the sour chill of April a week after the clocks change.

'Barbara came by to pick up her stuff,' he tells me.

'So I heard,' I tell him back. It was all over town in a minute – how Barb arrived with a Transit van and how Gumbo tried to kill her. Barbara is Lorna's mother, a lady of pensionable age who rules her daughter with a fine-toothed comb, picks out her lingerie for her from the discount racks, fields her phone calls. She is the kind of mother-in-law who plays footsie with you over Christmas dinner then stabs you in the back when you are washing up.

But I would rather not think about all that now, when my breakfast is congealing; the egg has stiffened as it is, the yellow gone turgid. On the other side of the street, the shadier side, is the sex shop – and above it, in a rented room, Lorna and I made love. As I twist my fork in the unyielding yolk, I recall the insides of her elbows, the silky crook of her arm, where I took her more than once – but then I took her everywhere more than once – while we put out of our minds the boiler's steady pounding, the driving away of cars and thrum of buses, the ratatatat of cash registers and moans of customers downstairs...

Gumbo is waving his knife in front of my face, to attract my attention. 'So I said to her, *Barbara, what have you done with my wife?* Naturally the woman denies any responsibility, says Lorna is free to choose whether to stay or go, all her usual fork-tongued shite. I admit, Morgan, that I would have liked to grab her by the throat and pin her against the sideboard, that thought was for a minute at the forefront of my mind, but whatever she says I did not, I did not raise a hand against the old boot. Anyway, it doesn't matter anymore – Lorna's gone, and her goods and chattels too.'

Gumbo is my oldest friend and was, until he discovered my affair with his wife, my best.

'Well,' I said. 'Well.'

'Yes, Morgan. *Well, well.* But what I want to know is, now it's all over, now the showboat's sunk and the circus animals are drowning, what kind of compensation do I get?' Gumbo clears his throat. His voice is a great, gruff, rattling thing at the best of times; today it is reminiscent of Billie Holiday towards the end of her career. If Billie Holiday had been a distributor of greetings cards working out of Shoreham industrial estate, she would have sounded a lot like Gumbo this morning.

'Compensation?'

'Yes, Morgan. Of course, I can't *force* you to recompense me, I realise that. Nor can I appeal to you on emotional grounds since, evidently, you don't have much regard for my feelings. All I can do is state my case – that you ruined my life, and so on – and see what kind of package you come up with.' Gumbo sticks the stump of his finger into the froth at the bottom of his mug and sucks it. He looks like an ageing baby in a wig, I think – but the thought only brings me pain.

'I could drive that load of condolences to Hastings for you next week,' I suggest. Gumbo raises his head slowly from where it has almost sunk, nose first, into the leavings of his sausage sandwich; he grins a grin that is savage and forlorn then in one rapid swing of his arm sends me tumbling from my chair. The evil-smelling teenager, coming back our way on her beat, steps over me with a laugh.

'Have a heart, Gumbo.' I stand and brush the dust from my chinos. He reaches over and takes the croissant from my plate, works it east-west into his enormous mouth. I right my chair and sit back down, motioning through the glass to the waitress inside.

What adventures we have gone through, Gumbo and I. As lads in the 1980s we clubbed together, hipped and hopped through the night, took in a little casual thievery, downed a handful of pills. At a church fete we crashed in Haywards Heath, one afternoon in '82 when we were both nineteen, we met the woman who now twirls between us – touting tickets for the tombola, her churchy mother in close attendance. She looked so wonderfully out of place, a hussy with orange hair, fool's gold hoop earrings, Duran Duran patches on her denim jacket. We called her Horny Lorna, teased her till she cracked; and then we liberated her from her stall and took her into town, where for a year of Saturday nights she cavorted with us, laughing with Gumbo but winking at me... And then two years later, in a fit of mad optimism after a night of Thunderbird and Diamond White, she married him.

A decade passed, almost a decade and a half of mutual regard. Older and both hitched, we hinted slyly at our wives' bizarre proclivities over buckets of cider from Middle Farm, over cans we split at the bottoms of our gardens. When my own dear wife, Mrs Morgan Hackett, fled to the wilds of Dorset with a vet, Gumbo was solicitous and hilarious by turns. I never tracked down her captor to demand compensation – but then I knew what a mistake he had made in taking off with that repressed and repressive woman, whose trash-talking ways and skin-tight outfits, complete with camel toe and elephant's knuckle, had turned me into a laughing stock in our small corner of Hove.

'We have known each other too long, Morgan.' He has finished chewing my croissant. I think that this cannot be the end of his sentence, I await the next clause. But I wait for a clause that never comes – just as in our youth we waited for buses that failed to arrive and hitched home from Peacehaven and Saltdean, from Seaford and Hassocks and Burgess Hill, laughing all the way. Oh, Gumbo.

'You still have the business,' I point out. 'Besides' – I feel bound to register this particular fact with him – 'you and Lorna have been drifting apart for years. And I was hardly the first guy to take advantage.'

'But you are the only one of them I know by name.' And so, I suppose, the only one he can ask for something in return. Gumbo is right in principle and yet in practice not so right. He cannot mean financial compensation, I see that. But what else I might have given him – a lasting tribute from his former wife as to his sweetness and light, his agility in between the sheets, his prodigality as a breadwinner – is all made impossible by one thing. Lorna could not stand his bearish paws on her, she could not even bear to be seen with him, or not for the last five or six years of their marriage. It was frankly a miracle they lasted as long as they did.

I hear a soft voice at my shoulder and am handed a plate by the waitress, and on the plate is a fresh croissant. The lookless waitress is taking my side; she bends over me, tending to the gash in my left temple with a napkin. When she leaves us, I say to him with the right amount of hurt and wonder in my tone,

'Gumbo, I am amazed,' meaning, amazed that he would actually draw blood over this issue between us.

Yet there is no need for amazement. This is the same Gumbo who used to squire so many girls to midnight dinner dances, girls who already had boyfriends; after a while I became accustomed to seeing some affronted male rear up out of the shadows and Gumbo take him down with his trusty right hook. There was always a kind of violence in him, I see that now. And now, as we enter our troubled mid-forties, it is my turn to bleed. Gumbo eyes my hand full of French pastry as it approaches my mouth, watches so closely that I rush the job and choke.

'The thing is, Morgan. Well,' he ponders, 'what *is* the thing?' His eyes leave my face; he gazes down the road, past my shoulder, towards the junction where every few minutes a double-decker threatens to smear some mad jogger across its fender. Suddenly Gumbo's expression softens; I know he must be thinking of someone dear to him, but when I turn I see only the grubby nymphet in her jogging pants, coming back our way for her own no doubt nefarious reasons. Then it strikes me that she resembles Gumbo's daughter, Glenda, albeit a less cossetted Glenda in less clean clothes.

What a family they were, in their time – Gumbo, Lorna and Glenda, in their rambling two-up, two-down in Fishersgate. Arthur 'Gumbo' Gaston and his triangular family would string their street with bunting on royal weddings, cup finals and funerals and all those other occasions of national celebration. On Sunday afternoons they would set out for the Hove seafront and Marrocco's, for an icecream smothered in strawberry syrup, coated in hundreds and thousands. Gumbo and Lorna flung cocktail parties all summer in their small square of back garden, into which their nutso neighbour flipped empty cans of special brew, pot noodle cartons, pigeon fanciers' guides and table legs, to be seized and run off with by the dog, Marley.

Lorna christened the dog but it was Gumbo and Glenda who called the cat Perky Jean.

'So do you get to keep the kid?' I ask.

Gumbo's wet gaze follows the brutish teen, who crosses onto the shady side of the street and leans up against the sex shop, one knee jutting.

'Glenda wants to stay with her mother,' he replies. He screws up his napkin and dabs at his left nostril. 'No doubt so she can learn something more about seduction and betrayal. I mean, Morgan, more than she learned from having you around the place. Ah, well.'

He has gone from violent recrimination to maudlin resignation in a moment, I see – and I relax. But I see something else as well, something that would cause a stronger man than me to wince. I see that Gumbo is about to write me off, write me out of his story.

'They do a great cinnamon pie here,' I tell him.

'She hasn't even come back for her toys,' he goes on.

'But Glenda is not a child, Arthur.' I find myself unconsciously mimicking Lorna, the object of all our affections. Lorna, who had an unhealthy fascination with her daughter's emotions, would sometimes expound on how fond poor Glenda was of me. Leaning up on an elbow, lighting a Benson with half an eye on the time, Lorna would feed my vanity and stoke my pride.

'She sees authority in you, Morgan,' she would say.

'Authority? Really? In an old jug of wine like me?'

'She admires you, Morgan – she has more respect for you than she does for her own father.'

'That's not good,' I would always say, out of sympathy for my cuckolded friend. Then Lorna would plant my hand between her thighs and my lips on her breast, and we would start all over again in that little room above the shop.

I do not think that Glenda respected me, as such. I was for a while the object of her suspicion, as she picked up on countless sly glances that passed between Lorna and me – and at the same time, for an unhappy period, her adolescent crush. Perhaps she wanted to work out what it was her mother saw in me; at any rate, as a troubled cherub just over the border of puberty, she went through a phase of pursing her lips and rolling her eyes, putting a hand in my hair, sitting in my lap and calling me Morgie. Now that I was a dead man to the Gastons one and all, the thought that I had let the kid down was piquant. But there is no way to spell this out, of course, to her dad.

Gumbo concerns himself with his pets, now that all the humans have fled. The dog, out of necessity, stays with him. Barbara is afraid of Marley, who sees her for what she is – a bitch.

'She took the cat, of course. It will probably kill the bloody thing, moving house at her age. But what the heck.' The cat, Perky Jean, is about thirteen years old and very frail. 'And Glenda hardly even calls. God knows what tale they've told her, the witches. I see her everywhere now, whenever I go out, wherever I go.' Gumbo puts his head on the table for a minute; when he raises it again it is redder than ever, with grains of sugar stuck in his eyebrows and a smidgen of cappuccino foam across his hairline. 'Ah, well. Those women sure know how to strip you of all you have.'

'But your general health,' I say. 'Your gallstones and stuff. How do you feel in yourself?'

'Pardon?'

'Seriously, Gumbo. I worry about you, I really do.'

'Morgan, you're such a bag of shit.'

I know that I am doing him a favour, sitting here and letting him talk to me like this. It is as much compensation as I can afford to give him. But what if I were to tell him that Lorna and I have gone our separate

61

ways, we no longer have the room over the sex shop and, although Barbara keeps a handsome caravan in her backyard that would do the job nicely, I have never visited it? What if I admit that Lorna has not stopped making love to me from some guilty impulse, is not repenting too late or punishing herself for her adultery by denying herself now she's single? What if I were to confess that, sadly, simply, our genitals have grown tired of each other?

But I remember a time when it was not that way at all, when I would stretch her out and lick salt from the walls of her red river valley while we lay, a couple of English desperadoes under the ivy – when even her toes ached with desire for me, or so she said.

For three years our affair survived undetected, masked by that suburban jollity by which a man may laughingly make some outrageous comment about the body of a woman who does not belong to him, even make a grab for her arse, and be regarded as just another bon homme in a world of bonhomie. It began, as these things must, in an act of treachery. My wife had just left and Gumbo and Lorna were taking care of me; I came to see them so often I was like an extra member of the household, fitting somewhere between Marley and Perky Jean. We were Marley the dog, Perky Jean the cat, Morgan the… what? In those days of humiliation and well-milked grief after the departure of Mrs Hackett, my status was unclear; I knew only that I had a friend in Gumbo, an ear, a loyal companion for those long nights of extravagant solace.

Then one afternoon I came round and he was out – Lorna alone was in. It was a Sunday afternoon at the start of our new century; in those days, as I recall, she had two breasts. I shall never forget the way they swung before my eyes, braless beneath the hem of her floral dress, already slightly wrinkled but still swell. They swung as she danced about the kitchen, pissed on leftover punch from last night's cocktail bash, measuring her steps to the plastic floor tiles, taking in a medley of Sister Sledge numbers before she fell sweatily into my arms.

Part of me would like to tell Gumbo of this grand beginning, because part of me still loves the notion of full disclosure, getting it all out in the open, part of me believes that being honest with him at this late date might make all the difference – but most of me knows it is a very bad idea. And if I cannot tell him the start, I certainly cannot tell him the finish.

Gumbo is stuffing a piece of cinnamon pie in his mouth, clotted in cream. He wears a short-sleeved shirt that reveals his once powerful arms, strong from lifting crates of cards. Over the years the crates have become lighter, his biceps less pronounced. We are all more or less falling away, I think – my gums are melting, my feet are all bunions, my ears do not pick up the crickets any more. And then I think of poor Lorna and a story she told me soon after her op, while we lay in bed one afternoon. Glenda came into the bathroom; she was twelve and carrying some puppy fat, but still flat-chested. She pointed to her mother's remaining breast and said,

'Mummy, when will *I* get one of those?'

'I wonder,' says Gumbo, his mouth full of pie – and I look up into the dazzling sunlight that floods the street this morning. 'I wonder.' He clears his throat. He sucks the stump of the middle finger of his right hand.

'Yes?'

'You know what this is like, Morgan? It's like it's *us* who are getting divorced.'

'Do you think we'll ever go fishing again?'

'That's what I was wondering.'

Gumbo and I catch each other's eye and look away. It is true, I think, that he and I have loved each other as men rarely do, with a pure love made up of shared notions of rightness, an ability to grin through pain, a desire for things to remain essentially light. Neither of us likes the dilemma facing us today, forcing us to get heavy. We would both rather pretend that this is one of our silly fallings-out, just a naive spat, and not the weighty matter it is. I understand that he hit me only out of frustration, because we cannot laugh it off the way we used to, and I forgive him for that. But my forgiveness cannot alter the issue I have spawned between us, or I would hold out my hand to him across this breakfast table.

What have I loved most about Gumbo, now I have lost him? Mainly it was his silliness – how he made the kind of joke that a funny *girl* would make, late on at a party where everyone else was too drunk to speak, when he would go down on all fours and pretend to be his pets or imitate, with exquisite tact and each in turn, all the other party guests. How he threw himself into his projects, big or small. How once he printed a job lot of obscene wedding cards, only to discover that someone else along the coast had already sold a bundle to all the shops with the same tasteless gag. How once he built a kennel for Marley that collapsed into a pile of planks as soon as the dog reached the end of his rope. How once, on the anniversary of the Queen Mother's death, he stayed up all night, spray-painting his Mazda in the colours of the Union Jack.

'I hope we will,' I tell him.

'But you know we won't.'

Gumbo stands and goes into the café and pays the bill. It is his last generous gesture towards me – I realise that – and my eyes are so bleary with tears that I hardly notice the girl pass our table again, her pink jogging trousers stained at the knees, her hands flashing about her crotch as if she were doing the hand-jive. When Gumbo comes out and asks me where his mobile phone has gone, I point to the rapidly vanishing point of her grey hooded top, her dirty pants, her stolen footwear in which, no doubt, she keeps her money. He swears under his breath, searches his pockets, looks around in vain for the long arm of the law.

But that is just like this street for you. You let down your guard for one moment and some rampageous minx just out of kindergarten slips your mobile down her knickers, with no witnesses beyond the blind man tapping his cane, the balding old girl who looks up briefly from her rag, the waitress who comes out onto the pavement and watches Gumbo hobble in the wake of the little felon.

Travelling South

Coming out of her bedroom on the Saturday morning of their departure, Sally heard a crash from the kitchen. She walked slowly down the cool lino of the dusty corridor in her bare feet, a towel wrapped around her waist. Lenny stood at the end of the corridor, raising his whiskery face as she approached; he skittered away as she bent down to stroke him, and the towel came undone and fell to the floor where the cat had been. She stood like that for a moment, naked and feeling the summer breeze come in through the cat-flap, tickling her ankles.

From the kitchen she could hear Emma's steady stream of curses, though not what she was ranting about – the individual words were swallowed up by her anger. She knew that whatever had made Emma angry would be something far off and hard for either of them to change, not something in the here and now. Was Emma tidying up whatever mess she had made while making breakfast? It seemed unlikely – and no doubt they were about to avoid having a conversation on that very subject. She picked up the towel, tucked it under her armpits and crossed the sunny lounge to the kitchen.

Emma sat at the kitchen table with her chin resting in her hands, the *Guardian* on the yellow formica surface between her elbows. It was not even today's newspaper – but yesterday's news could leave Emma in a rage for weeks.

'Can you believe these fucking Americans,' she said, 'fucking it up for everyone else.'

Her bare shoulders jerked forward every time she used the F-word; she sat tensely in her chair as if braced against the information she was taking in, with her fingernails digging into her cheeks, not looking up. Her eyes were fixed on a photo on one of the inside pages – the page spread across the table, one corner soaking up a puddle of coffee. And this, thought Sally, was the person she was about to spend two weeks with in Spain. She made her way between the cat litter tray and all the other debris that covered the kitchen floor – a cycling helmet, a bag spilling out-of-favour skirts and t-shirts for the chazzas, a bunch of rarely used cookery books that had somehow come down off the shelf – and poured the last lukewarm drops from the cafetiere into a half-clean mug. Then she stood beside Emma, putting her hand on one of her quivering, beautiful shoulders. Emma flinched.

'Hi,' said Sally. Emma did not respond – and Sally had time to recall the 'joke' that Aaron had told her in the pub the night before. 'You know the only thing worse than one week in Spain, Sal? Two weeks in Spain, haha!'

'Hey, what happened with all the cookery books, flatmate?'

Sally sat down and tried to look into Emma's eyes, but Emma's eyes were too involved with a picture of a US Marine in his uniform in Helmand, crouching in his uniform and talking to a boy. The soldier and the boy were smiling at each other – the boy was reaching out, touching the soldier's gun with one small finger.

'They fell,' said Emma.

'You scared the cat,' Sally laughed. Her laughter sounded forced – and if it sounded forced to her, she knew it must sound doubly forced to Emma.

'It wasn't me, it was them, the fuckers jumped,' Emma said in her careless theatrical way, pointing accusingly at the books that lay scattered at her feet. This was one of her things, making light of her little moments of irresponsibility, dramatizing them until they became weirdly attractive. '*They* did it, *they* scared the cat.'

At Gatwick they were told that the travel company had booked them into a non-existent hotel and on a non-existent flight. It was not a deliberate con, apparently, just one of those things, a cock-up and not a conspiracy. They were offered Crete instead.

'Same difference,' said Emma, as she dropped her bag in the waiting area. 'We can sing Viva España in Greece just as well. We can sing Una Paloma Blanca and dance about in our plastic sombreros.' She laughed her husky laugh and opened her book, resting it against her thigh with one foot up on the seat so that anyone who passed could see her knickers. She was in her element – Emma always loved it when things failed to go to plan.

They had two hours to wait for their rearranged flight, during which Sally wandered around, looked through the ties at Tie Rack and chose one for Aaron. She wandered on, deciding against a Starbucks mocha; soon she would be in Greece, where she could drink Greek coffee. As she made a tour of W.H. Smiths and picked out her airport novel, it struck her that Aaron never wore shirts with collars, and she took the tie back and exchanged it for a pair of comedy socks. She felt a bit tragic, buying socks decorated with Dali clocks for a man nearly twice her age, but it was the kind of gift he would be grateful for. Socks with clocks would not impose any great burden of debt on him – he need not reciprocate. He would wear them once, then put them away in a drawer and be funny about it.

In her wanderings, she often passed the place where Emma was guarding their bags, with her foot up on the seat as before and her nose crinkled in concentration. Sally thought that other passers-by must have noticed her, too; she looked so intense and natural and almost flawless, from her heart-shaped face framed by the glasses she used for reading to her unvarnished toenails, falling out of her tatty espadrilles. Emma glanced up from her novel – something long and deep by someone dead and French – and smiled her freckled smile. Sally knew that her friend was far from flawless, but at such moments even she could be taken in.

By the time they had done the coach ride from Heraklion to the resort and found their hotel, it was around dinnertime. The hotel was small, hidden up an alleyway, its front draped in bougainvillea, but when they changed into their evening wear they found no running water came from the taps – and in the shower there was a cockroach, still alive.

'Fuck it,' said Emma, 'we can wash in the sea.'

She tripped lightly around the pretty whitewashed room, dropping items of clothing in every corner, putting on her bikini. They had shared a flat for a year but they had never had to share a room, and Sally resented how shapeless Emma made her feel in such proximity. She stood in front of the mirror in the floral-patterned dress she had bought for hot evenings in Spain and pulled her hair back from her face. It was a hot evening in Greece, and her cheeks looked flushed and her eyes tired from the early start.

'My hair,' she said, 'my one beauty.'

Emma laughed; it was looser and happier than her English laugh, as if a simple move southwards had relaxed something in her throat. 'You're so vain,' she said, as if Sally had been serious. 'I never knew you were so vain.'

But when they had followed the promptings of locals down to the beach and been in and out of the sea, they both relaxed. The water was not exactly clean – a kind of fluff lay on its surface amid unhealthy rainbow swirls – but it was warm and buoyed them up. Afterwards, Sally lay back on her towel and listened to tourist voices near and far, a restaurant singer just up the beach who ran through *Baker Street*, *Wild World* and *Take It Easy*, the discreet hush of the Mediterranean. Half a mile away, in a part of the bay with more restaurants and bars, they heard squaddies yelling and chanting.

'Ugh,' murmured Emma, 'hark at the little Anglo-Saxons discovering alcohol.'

Emma sat up and rubbed at the salt on her thighs and tugged at her bikini strap, fidgeting, looking about her, while dusk made inroads into the blue sea, turning everything on the beach a little bluer. Out at the mouth of the bay, white lights on a pleasure boat came on all at once and the air appeared to darken around it, as if it was the stage for something, a piece to be played out on deck.

Sally saw how Emma's pulse beat in her throat as she turned and looked down at her, and recalled a night in mid-winter when Emma had come in drunk at two in the morning with a love bite in the same place. She knew it was two because Emma had woken her up and

70

talked to her for an hour about sex and war – some theory she had come up with about the psychology of invasion. In the end, she had fallen asleep on Sally's bed, and Sally had taken the spare duvet to the couch in the living room. She had never asked where the love bite came from, and anyway it faded pretty quickly; what she had really wanted to ask was whether they were not a bit too old for hickeys.

'D'you reckon Aaron will remember to feed the cat?' Emma said.

'He'd better.' Sally felt her own tummy grumble and put a hand on it to still it.

'What is it with you and Aaron, anyway?' Emma wrapped her arms around her knees and gazed seawards to where a lone figure stood on the upper deck of the pleasure boat, looking back at them on the shore through binoculars. 'Do you have some sort of Platonic relationship? I never hear anything from your room.'

'Maybe we're just very quiet.'

Emma laughed. 'He doesn't look the quiet type, to me.'

'How do you mean?' Sally sat up, so their heads were close together, momentarily in line with the setting sun.

'Men that ancient usually want to make a big performance out of it, in my experience. They like the rest of the world to know they're still up to it.' Emma looked around quickly, her eyes glinting briefly from the sun's last ray. 'Don't you find?'

'Aaron's just a friend,' Sally said – and she would have said more, that Aaron was virtually impotent from all the cigarettes and beer and that he made his impotence an excuse to treat her as his sexless ally against the world of females that had defeated him throughout his life. She felt like saying all of it, but it seemed like too much for the first night of a two-week holiday. Emma's face was so close to her own that she felt her breath on her lips; it was really getting dark. Then the English voices from the bars exploded in a sudden chorus, filling the hot Greek air with ugly sounds from home.

'Fucking squaddies,' Emma said, but still laughing her new southern laugh. She stood and threw Sally her dress. 'Put it on and let's go and get us some paella, mi querida,' she said. 'I'm hearing that you're hungry.'

After a heavy, oily meal of squid and olives and Retsina, they went back to the hotel and changed again for the clubs. This time the water was up and running; they showered and went out quickly into the 'Attic night', as Emma called it. The clubs were packed full of English girls, along with some Italians and Germans, and they were pressed in tight as they danced to loopy eurotrash. Emma pulled off her tie-die t-shirt and spun it about her head; underneath she wore a Disney bra, Mickey over one nipple and Minnie over the other. The Italian men drew closer to her on the floor and followed her to the glass-topped, zinc-framed bar that took up a whole wall of the club. They laughed when she ordered a glass of water and threw it over herself – but the next one she threw over them, splashing the nearest one full in the face, hitting him in the eye with an ice cube. Security descended on them, and in the melee Emma was allowed to put her shirt back on and they were made to leave.

Out across the sea, the moon had risen and made its enormous way skywards, licking the waves with bright white light. They sat on the sea wall, listened to the waves and watched its progress. Coming from the water swilling below against the wall, Sally could smell engine oil, rotting seaweed and the salt of the sea itself. Emma sat close so that their shoulders touched, still panting from her exertions in the club, sat with her back straight and her eyes fixed on the horizon, a subtle demarcation between two darknesses.

'Aaron and I don't do anything in bed.' Sally leaned back on the palms of her hands. 'He can't. He may be the first name in the dictionary but he's useless with his dick.'

Emma remained as she was and did not laugh. 'That's very funny,' she said after a pause, 'and very sad.'

A yell came from somewhere not too far away, and then a roar, and two men emerged from the awning of a darkened restaurant a little way along. They swore at each other in English, but incomprehensibly. The louder man picked the quieter one up and threw him over the sea wall into the rank water, then everything was almost silent apart from the shouts of the man in the sea.

'It's not really that sad,' Sally said. 'It would have been wrong, anyway.'

They started back for the hotel; as they passed the place where the man trod water, shouting up at his mate who had long since departed, Emma laughed throatily. She flung her arm around Sally's shoulders and pulled her close for an instant. 'How English can you get,' she said. 'A midnight dip in a sea full of shit.'

Emma took off her t-shirt and skirt as soon as they stepped in the door; she flipped them across the room, towards the one chair, but they fell short, landing in the middle of the floor. She lay down on top of her bed without pulling back the coverlet. Sally got slowly undressed and chucked her clothes haphazardly at the chair, not wanting to seem to be making a point. There was a place for tidiness and untidiness, after all. Greece was an untidy place. But her concerns were lost on Emma, who looked dead to the world, though she stirred when Sally sat down on the edge of her bed. The pants went with the bra, Sally saw: Mickey embraced Minnie on the rise of her mound.

In the mottled darkness of the room – they had left the blinds open, carelessly, letting in the bugs and moonlight – Emma opened her eyes and watched Sally watching her. 'I like your knickers,' Sally said. 'They're not what I expected.'

'You underestimated my underwear.' Emma sat up and undid the bra and dropped it on the floor between their two beds. 'Should never do that. Everyone wants to get inside, no one ever knows what's underneath.'

She lay back down and wriggled out of her knickers – and Sally did what she had wanted to do all day, or all year, and leaned in to kiss her on the tuft of hair below the bone, more or less where the cartoon mice had been kissing.

The next two weeks followed the same pattern: Sally woke in the morning to find Emma gone and ate her breakfast of yoghurt and honey on the garden terrace at the back of the hotel; she swam in the sea, read her airport novel and had a slice of pizza for lunch. Emma was never in the room at siesta time and often failed to show up for dinner, but some nights they would meet in a club. If they met, Emma would seduce her, kiss her on the mouth in front of the squaddies and tourists; when they trailed through the English stag parties and gangs of international students on the seafront on their way back to the hotel, she would swing her round and kiss her again, very publicly. Back in the privacy of their

74

room she would go on kissing her – but it was all one kiss – and make love to her drunkenly on one of the beds.

But if they missed each other in the clubs, Emma might not come back to the hotel at all, and Sally could end up not seeing her for 24 hours. On one of the nights when she failed to find Emma, Sally let an Italian man pick her up, but she disliked the intense way he held onto her on the quay; she ran away at the first opportunity, when he loosened his grip on her to look at some other girl.

One afternoon, while Sally was taking her siesta, Emma snuck in and tried to get some things from her bag without waking her up. But it was impossible for Emma to do anything without making a noise – she knocked the alarm clock off the bedside table, and Sally sprang suddenly awake, dazed and with a headache and a vague memory of some hot nightmare. She sat bolt upright and shouted, in a kind of reflex,

'Emma, what the fuck are you doing here?'

Emma's reaction was muted and insincere; she sat down on the other bed and yawned theatrically; then she reached behind her for her French novel and held it out to Sally, with a beseeching look from which Sally had to turn away, it was so fake.

'Can we swap books? I've finished this one.'

Sally had not finished hers, but she handed it over even so, although Emma would not enjoy it, and she would not be able to read the one she got in exchange.

Emma left, and she got up and wrote Aaron a postcard, trying to make a joke about spending two weeks in Greece like the one he had made about Spain in the pub that night; but to make it funny, she would have to fill him in on at least one real detail, and it was unimaginable that she would tell him about herself and

Emma. So the joke did not look like a joke at all, more like an odd complaint – and that night, after she hooked up with the same clumsy Italian and let him do more or less what he wanted on the path up to the ruins, lying on the hot stones with a storm of cicadas in her ears, she realised that the secret was not to do those things that you would only complain about later. It was a lesson learned, but a lesson learned too late in this case. She was stuck in Greece, lying awake, alert and alone most nights, dirtying the sheets with the beach tar on her feet, listening to the stag parties beat each other up to the tune of *Viva España*.

But the day came when it had to end – the day of the flight, a Saturday. Sally woke up with bright glitter in her eyes, the sun reflected off the sea through the blinds she had forgotten to close. It was early and Emma was nowhere to be seen. Sally rose and began to move about the room, putting her things into her suitcase, ignoring the other things scattered around on the floor – Emma's things. But the sunlight was so insistent that she did what she had wanted to do from the first morning: she went out on to the balcony naked and stood there, letting the warmth of the sun and the sea breezes play on her thighs, shoulders and breasts. She watched the light of the just risen sun bounce from the water and cover her with dapples, let it flicker over her, tracing the lines of her body.

Inside there was a loud bang and a curse, and the sound of things scattering across the floor. Sally stayed where she was, not turning around at once; after a minute or two, she went back into the room and sat down on her bed. From where she sat, she could see some of herself in the mirror: her hair had gone blonder, bleached by the sun, and she was brown everywhere she looked. Emma sat on the other bed, wearing only the Disney lingerie. Through the open bathroom doorway over her shoulder, toilet articles were strewn across the floor. She seemed already to have returned, in spirit, to England – her brown hair was tied so tightly into plaits that her scalp showed through, in a way that was painful to look at. When she looked up and met Sally's eye, the look in her eyes was absent, withdrawn. When Sally moved to sit next to her on the bed, she shrank away, as if suddenly averse to intimacy.

Sally tried to imagine what it would be like, the two of them together again in England, sharing a flat, knowing what they knew about each other now. In her mind, she placed all the ordinary household objects where they would normally be – the cookery books on the shelf, the cat in the corridor, yesterday's newspaper on the kitchen table, her impotent boyfriend in her bed. Could it ever be like that again?

'Well,' she said, without moving from the bed, 'let's not miss the plane.'

Emma cleared her throat. 'I'm sorry, I fucked up.'

'We both did,' Sally suggested.

'No, we both did not. It was me,' Emma told her. 'It was me who fucked up. We could have had a nice time.'

'We did have a nice time.'

'Don't be stupid, you know what I mean.'

Emma stood up abruptly and undid her bra; she stepped out of her knickers.

'I know you think I'm kind of lame,' Sally said. 'You think I'm an idiot.'

'I don't think you're an idiot,' said Emma, pushing her down on the bed. 'You opened up to me. You know no one ever does that, right? You know it's not the done thing.' Emma knelt on the bed, straddling Sally with her knees, placing her hands gently on the dips of her waist.

77

'Everyone does something else instead, no one ever just opens up. I think you're brilliant, actually.' She leaned in then and put her hands on Sally's breasts, bringing her face down close so their noses touched. 'I'm just a fucked-up scaredy-cat.'

Then Emma got up again and closed the blinds and shutters against the heat – but while they made love on their last morning in Greece, the light crept in through the gaps. It crept in through the slats of the balcony shutters and the gaps that the builders had left between the wall and window frames, came off the sea outside and found its way into the room.

Unmarried brunette on the London train

The little town was baked in pretty heat
and you in a dress with frogs on it, so
edible, and not just from the legs up,
from the mouth down – and seaweed too, seacows,

seahorses and a kind of zebra thing
or a unicorn, and no ring on you
anywhere, miraculous, sublime – to
see a girl like you without a ring and

what wonderful grey skin, how English can
you get, and a haircut from another
decade, another century even,
and all this lowkey beauty going north

with frogs on it and seaweed, to the big
town baked in ugly heat, wearing no ring.

September Funeral

A whitish late summer haze hung over the English Channel that morning. The sea itself was unmarked by anything other than a few buoys, a swimmer or two and a yacht that cut across in front of them with sea-soured sails. Scott and Aidan sat out on the hotel terrace under a parasol, watching the water from a distance. Their father had been a fisherman – he had died ten years earlier off the coast of Scotland, his trawler swept away in a freak storm. This was when they were introduced; they had been born only nine months apart but to different mothers, Scott the older of the two. Coming late, when they were twenty, the bond might not have meant much to them; their lives were dissimilar in many respects – they did not even look much like each other. But for Scott the meeting had been so significant that it was hard to remember what his life had been like before that funeral in Glasgow, where they had shared a moment over the fate of their unlucky dad, laughed and gelled.

Afterwards they had stuck together, for a while sharing a flat and friends, although Aidan's friendships tended to be short and violent while Scott's were longer term and sentimental. One of those friendships had just come to an unnatural end, which was how they came to be down on the coast that morning, although Aidan had no intention of going to the service – he had just come along for the ride, he said. As he sat with his brother, taking in the sea's fierce reflections, Scott thought again about the small darkness of that end – the garage, its running car and toxic fumes, the gradual asphyxiation. This thought was what had kept him at the hotel the night before, after check-in, while Aidan went out on the town; he had wanted to sit for a few hours and try to make sense of it.

He saw that Aidan's gaze was drawn the same way as his, towards the splinters of light reflected from the water's surface, sharp despite the haze. It was one of those things they had in common, a fascination with the sea – an aversion, almost. Neither of them wanted to get any closer to it than they were now, separated from the water as they were by the seafront and road. Scott had noticed this before on foreign holidays, when everyone else had raced down the beach into the waves and they were left together on the sand. Perhaps it was because they were both brought up inland and it was alien to them, perhaps it was because of how their father died – it was hard to say; but they were both mesmerised by the sea's surface that morning, its constant action. Even this early, at nine, people were out water-skiing, while children played on the stones along the shore.

'Are you going to change into something more appropriate?' Aidan asked, putting down his coffee cup and looking around for the waitress. 'I'd love to see you go to Zak's last fling in your Hawaiian shirt. The poor bastard would have appreciated the anarchic gesture.'

Scott had not changed for the funeral yet – there was another hour before he had to set off. Even Aidan was more suitably dressed, in that he was still in the blue pinstripe suit he had been wearing when he came down straight from work the night before. With his eyes red from his all-nighter, black stubble and ludicrous beard – two lines that ran from the ends of his moustache to join the circle of hair on his chin – he looked like a cartoon Mexican bandit, comical and go-getting. They had taken a double room, but Aidan was a compulsive clubber and devotee of singles bars, and Scott had seen nothing of him until he barged in at five that morning.

'Zak, anarchic? He really wasn't.' Scott drank the last of the watery latte the hotel had served him after breakfast. 'His anarchism was pretty skin-deep, at any rate – underneath he was as conventional as they come. He'd want us all to take his last rites seriously, dress up in the right gear and cry at all the right moments.'

'You're pretty sore about this suicide, aren't you?'

Scott shrugged. 'Like everything else he did, I guess it wasn't his fault.' But it was true – he did feel sore. His broken sleep and the brittle feel of the occasion had left him fractious and impatient to get it over with.

Aidan replied with his eyes fixed on the skyline. 'Whose fault was it then? Did God tell him to do it?'

'That wouldn't make it God's fault exactly, would it? Anyway, Zak would never have listened to a God who didn't wear some shit he found in a skip or eat out of a veggie box.'

Aidan grunted, flicking a cigarette from the packet that lay between them on the table. Watching him light up with shaking hands, Scott took in his brother's wired look and bloodshot eyes, and how otherwise he seemed unaffected by his bender. He envied Aidan the way his experiences seemed to wash through him and leave no residue.

'So no Jesus for Zakky.' Aidan exhaled into the air. 'So why is he being buried in a church and not having his ashes sprinkled along a ley line?'

'He asked for the church in his note, I guess. You know he left a note? He must have wanted a procession, a reading or two – you need a church for that, at the end of the day.'

Aidan snorted. 'That fits. I never really did get why we hung out with him, even back in the day when he was still a gas, relatively speaking. He was your typical New Age charlatan, old Zakky, the way he took himself so seriously and could only talk the walk. You could see it in his furrowed brow – all that righteous monomania.'

'Yeah, it was like he wanted some kind of prize for enlightenment.'

As ever, Scott was swept along by the reckless fluency of his brother's negativity about people; but he shifted in his seat, aware that Aidan's need to be caustic often ended up fixing on him – as it did now. Aidan went on with a half-glance in his direction, stroking his beard. 'But then that's what you want, isn't it Scotty? Some kind of recognition, a medal, something to take home to your mother. Not that she'd notice anything you brought her, of course.' Aidan leaned forward in his chair, his brown eyes blinded by conviction. 'You're so pathetic around that woman, Scott. You're like a cat bringing a chewed-up rat into the house and waiting for a round of applause.'

There was no defence against this observation: over the years, Aidan had turned its partial truth into an absolute. It was just one line of attack in a long battle between them, a war over something never spoken out loud. This battle could not have gone on for so long if both of them had not wanted it – Scott understood this, but he was powerless to stop it, unclear about what he got out of it himself. He saw that Aidan was at his happiest when locked into their struggle, and whatever it was possessed him and carried him away, whether it was jealousy or spite or inverted love. Each time one of these arguments happened he longed to escape – and he wished, a lot of the time, they had never met. But he felt a wrench now even so, when Aidan suddenly got up from his seat and said he was off to get a beer in town.

'You're right,' he said, looking up into his brother's face, darkened by shadow as he stood with his back to the sun. 'It's true, I do want recognition from the world – but then you get all the recognition you need from yourself. Remember the song? *Aidan will never be left on the shelf because Aidan he's in love with himself.*'

Aidan hovered for a moment with his lip curled and a look in his eye as if he was deciding whether to laugh. 'Always someone else's words,' he said finally – then he turned and leapt the few steps from terrace to pavement and walked off towards the Steine, his suit flapping in the breeze, leaving Scott alone with those feelings that recurred in strict sequence, almost a rhythm, every time they met up: a hatred of that stocky muscularity, that bullish certainty he found so repulsive yet grudgingly admired, a contempt for himself for admiring it at all.

Since they had first met, Aidan had found himself a job in the City, earning a sum that Scott could only guess at – but the Square Mile had not given his brother these habits. Aidan the floor trader was the same person who had partied away the early nineties, living on ecstasy and crashing on people's sofas – the same macho tearaway who affected to know everyone's secret, who had an instinct for spotting people's flaws, who took a slash at whoever crossed his path. This power to monster the situation was channelled now into making money, but he was the same player who had been penniless before – Scott had watched it unfold before his eyes.

He leaned back in his seat and closed his eyes to the sea for a while, trying to relax and enjoy what remained of the morning before he had to set off for the church. It was one of those September mornings full of promise, with an uplift in the air – precisely the sort of morning, in fact, he had come to associate with disappointment. Such days often seemed to drift to a murky conclusion from a highpoint of brightness and clarity. It had begun to happen a couple of years ago, when he turned thirty, this odd tendency for a bright promise to go dull. But now there had been a death – one of his friends had died, even if it was one he had rarely seen in the last few years – and surely that sacrifice would be enough to insure the day against the usual downward trend? This was an old superstition: when he was younger, around the time when he first met Aidan, he had seen all his small humiliations and catastrophes as downpayments on fate, little deposits on his luck. For a while he had really believed that, if one thing went badly, something else was bound to go well. These days it seemed the deal no longer held: nemesis still followed hubris, but an upturn did not always follow a downturn.

He opened his eyes again on the sea – its constant motion breaking up the light, breaking in on his own reflections. As another dinghy zipped towards the piers from the marina, a teenage girl came up onto the terrace from the street and glanced at him for an instant before walking over to the open doorway. She wore turquoise lycra leggings and a new pink t-shirt with the legend in silver lettering, *Millennium Bug*. He turned in his seat as she went in and watched as she stood at reception, dancing impatiently after ringing the bell, kicking the boards of the desk with her trainers. The receptionist came, and she launched into a breathless inquiry after a guest of the hotel. Of course, it felt shameful even as he wished for it, but he was sorry that the man she asked about was not in some way himself – a version of him with more presence, more distinct but also more typical, closer to the type who looked like success.

The receptionist fobbed her off and coldly waved her away, and the girl came back out onto the terrace where she stood, filling his field of vision for an instant as if wanting to ask him for something, parting her lips to speak but saying nothing. Up close she looked about eighteen, but something sour about her mouth, a kind of bitterness made her look as if her youth had been lost somewhere. Her body had a sort of poisoned fullness – a child's body still, but flooded with toxins. Another waif and stray, he thought, and he felt a rush of lust towards her lostness, her sad availability – but he could hardly sit her down and offer her a drink. The bartender came out then to shoo her off, and he watched her limp away along the seafront into the still rising sun, the dazzling east.

There must have been fifty mourners at the ceremony in the country church, in a village full of Edwardian mansions, set in a fold between the sea and south downs. Stepping off the bus from town, Scott was in the churchyard before he could prepare himself. Funerals were a way bearing a misty-eyed witness to the final disembodiment, so it was shocking to see so many over-dressed people in the little field of stones. The stiff card telling the order of service and the usher who handed it over felt like figments of a dream; his upright bearing and tan seemed to upbraid him as he walked the asphalt path to the door of the flint-faced church. The gloom as he went in was hyperactive – bright spots danced before his eyes while he took his seat. He had assumed that his own vitality would carry him through the hour and a half of readings and singing, but it did not altogether. At the end of it all he felt overwhelmed by something – not death itself but the spin put on death by the vague and euphemistic Anglican service.

When the church spat him out into the graveyard along with the pallbearers and coffin, he looked around at his fellow mourners, some his age but more of their parents' generation. The older mourners knew how to act, expressing their grief with glib formality, all handshakes and headshakes, in a routine of dignified acknowledgment. He had to turn away from this performance – he hung back from the lip of the grave, keeping his eyes on the sky while the dead man's mother threw in her handful of soil. But then it became apparent that they were all expected to do the same, walk in procession and chuck earth into the grave; so reluctantly he followed the crowd, choosing his handful with care, as if it mattered which portion he dropped on Zak.

He was aware of people ahead and behind him in the line who were doing the same thing. Some of them he knew from parties from that time five or six years ago when he and Zak saw each other often. Since that era the set had splintered, the scene changed, and Zak and he had rarely met up – and when they did, it was to their mutual incomprehension. It was a fact that he had never been able to square the early Zak with later Zak. In those early days at the start of the nineties, his friend had been a druggy and chaotic force of nature whose mushroom visions meant more to him than any daily routine. He had respected Zak then for being so detached from all the serious aspirations that even the most dedicated slacker took for granted – one day they would change tack, prove themselves. But for a couple of years at the start of the decade a bunch of them lived the same way, doing nothing at all as a kind of policy, nothing but laugh and talk and listen to music and now and then hook up. The important thing was not to win, since winning had been made to look so evil by a political culture that swept up any visible success in its graceless embrace. They were losers, but then they were trying to lose, in an era when only losers took the bus.

But Zak had not even bothered to take the bus – he had spurned any means of getting anywhere at all, and when others peeled off from that epic sleepover to take up their various professions he was left behind in his room, sucking on a spliff while the moon went through its quarters, the sun crawled along behind his curtains. Scott had gone off with the others to do his own thing, abandoning Zak without much thought, or thinking of it as any kind of betrayal. The last time they had really had a conversation was in the week when Scott got his job on the magazine, four years ago now, when Zak had mocked him for being sucked into that media world, with all the rest of the talentless peacocks. It was the breaking point of their friendship: whenever they bumped into each other after that, in Camden Market or up on the heath, Zak would stress the vast distance between their chosen paths, with Scott in thrall to some false god and Zak still following the footsteps of the Buddha – not, as far as Scott could see, the Buddha of the books he himself had read by Chögyam Trungpa but a very English kind of Buddha, a pale and skinny avatar who thought that everything beyond his front door was just samsara. This was late Zak, the embittered and righteous puritan – and this was where that Zak had ended up, lost in some dark corner, lowered into a hole in the ground.

A few of those who had partied together back in the day now picked their way from the graveside – but tentatively, he thought, as if they were unsure whether to stick around for a while and witness this death a little longer or run for the hills. Thirty was a hard age to be, ambivalent: either you became someone concrete and credible or you disappeared from the social sphere, though not usually as conclusively as Zak had. Their hesitant step between the stones of the already dead expressed this fear of disappearance; their relative security did not make them safe from some sudden overnight vanishing. Perhaps it was this generic fear that made all those people he must at one time have talked to at parties about music or books or sex, love or drugs, into a kind of inseparable mass. But when the crowd of mourners stopped outside the churchyard gate, brought up short by a stream of weekenders passing on their way to National Trust sites or down to the stony beach, he became aware of a movement at his elbow. He turned to find next to him the woman in black – but of course she was in black – who had caught his eye while the gritty rectangle was filled with Zak, or Zak's boxed body.

At the graveside she had been facing the sun, and her eyes had looked golden across that narrow gap, in the confusion of ambient light that bounced from the sea nearby and broke up around them in the air. Now that she stood beside him, he saw that they were a silvery grey, with a sheen like the sea's on the previous evening, when he had arrived in the hour before sunset. In that moment when she suddenly stood beside him on the pavement and smiled up at him boldly, he had one of those impromptu thoughts he would have liked to shut out – that he was not in her league. It was the kind of thinking he was used to from his brother, with his simplistic language of alphas and betas. He did not want to believe in such degrading hierarchies but, even so, some part of him subscribed. When she shook her head at him, still smiling, he recognised her as one of the gang from the height of the scene – she had cut her hair, that was all. He had talked to her sometimes at parties, although he had never got to know her that well.

'Nicola,' he said, with a note of triumph.

'Ah, yes. It took you a while to dredge that one up from the memory. I saw you eyeing me up across the coffin. What was she called again? Natalie, Natasha... begins with an N, I'm sure.'

They set off together through the village for the house where the funeral reception would be served. 'Ah yes, but you've changed your style,' he said.

'You, on the other hand, are every inch the Scott I used to know and love.'

He was taken aback that she recalled him so clearly, or that she said she did, that she used the word *love* and used it so lightly. Her once familiar playfulness came back to him – it all began to come back.

'It's good to see you,' he said.

'You too,' she said. 'God knows, there has to be some justification for this... awful thing.'

The house where Zak had grown up was at the end of a road that had taken them away from the sea, close to the back of the village – a big square house with many windows, all shuttered and the shutters all closed. Scott and Nicola joined the queue of mourners filing into the oppressive hallway and dimly lit lounge, where food was spread out on a long table and an oldish man with broken capillaries who might have been an uncle carried glasses of whisky and gin around on a tray. It was all perfectly decorous, everything organised down to the last detail.

Nicola sipped at her drink while he looked at her ringless fingers. Others of Zak's contemporaries stood about in groups of three or four, nodding across the room to one another but showing no real desire to mingle. He was glad of this; for all that the atmosphere was stiff and oddly false, as if everyone in the room was pretending that no one had died, or at least that he had not died the way he did, for all the awkwardness of muffled talk striving for a tone to fit the occasion, the pleasure of standing next to her outweighed other feelings. When she moved in close after a few minutes of silence, he recalled that trademark of her manner – her ability to ask a question lightly without making heavy demands or offering anything unwanted.

'Have you noticed how many of his friends are missing?'

'I suppose a few of them couldn't come,' he said, and looked around again because, in fact, he had not particularly noticed. 'Fred Acton is still in Beijing, and didn't Jake go and live somewhere in Eastern Europe? And then who was that guy who played the drums, you know the one who was supposed to be so wild – he became a lawyer in New York. And Dorothy is just so disorganised that she probably got the wrong day.'

'No, that's not it – they weren't invited. Zak specified in his note that they couldn't come. They'd let him down, he said.'

'I didn't hear that about the note. I knew there was one, of course.'

'His mother told me on the phone that he was very definite about who should be told about the day and who shouldn't. She followed his instructions to the letter, apparently.'

'Jesus,' he lowered his voice, 'what kind of guy issues invitations to his own funeral?'

Nicola sipped on her whisky with her eyes on the wallpaper, an old but well-preserved William Morris with a spread of leaves and birds – the only sign of life in the room. 'In other words, he wanted us to know who he blamed,' she said.

'Yes – his closest friends, in other words. I mean, compared to Fred or Jake or Dorothy we didn't really know him very well, did we? So it's a kind of revenge.'

'But it's also a sort of punishment to be here. It implies a contempt – that we didn't know him well enough to let him down.' Nicola laid aside her empty glass. 'I wouldn't have come if his mother hadn't rung me and been so nice. I feel nothing about this suicide except anger towards the person who committed it.'

She turned away, as if she would rather show her tears of rage to the rest of the room than to him. It was strange that he had failed to recognise her at first, now that she came back to him so vividly – and he saw that the Nicola he had known six years ago would not have said this, would have found a way around the feeling that lay behind her words. He saw the small physical changes he had missed in her when they met in the street, how her waist was a little thicker and the skin around her eyes a little tired. Some of the svelteness had gone, and with it perhaps the ability to leapfrog emotion – but that loss of agility had brought her closer to him, almost within reach.

Watching her profile as she scanned the airless room for the man with the tray of drinks, he wondered how come, in that brief era of mild promiscuity, they had never even kissed. But no – of course they had, he remembered: there was a night when they had tripped together under the apple tree in the garden of his rented flat and their lips had brushed. But that was all they had ever done; she had kept herself slightly apart without seeming aloof, at a time when there seemed to be more than enough intimacy to go around.

'You look a bit distracted,' he said, when she turned back to him with a fresh whisky. She nodded, her grey eyes catching the flickering candlelight from a massive candelabra that stood on a sideboard at their end of the room. Just then somebody, as if they had only just noticed the weird gloom and the general airlessness, suddenly pushed open the nearest shutters and flung open a window, making the orange flames gutter and sway and send up thin plumes of dark smoke.

'Let's say our goodbyes and go,' she said. 'I want to get out of these clothes. I feel so insincere in all this mourning.' She looked up with sudden warmth and smiled. 'Because you know it's going to sound strange,' she said, 'but I could fucking kill him!'

They took the first bus that came through the village. It was the wrong bus – it did not go along the coastline route straight into town but meandered endlessly through suburban housing projects, climbing and falling across the downs. These undulations were sickening after the muddled ceremony; the sight of all those hills covered in all the little grey houses, cut off from both town and coast, added to the nausea they had felt on abandoning the reception.

Their conversation also seemed to come and go in waves, like the bus following a route that at times appeared to take them further away from their destination. But they said enough to establish who they were now and what they were doing – that they had both had spells out of London and come back again, gone through relationships that did not last. Nicola had bought a flat in Manchester that she had never lived in, as an investment.

'Really it's a liability, and rather an ugly one at that. I wasn't sure what I was meant to do with my income, so I used it as a means to get into debt – the usual thing.'

'My brother is the financial success story in our family. He makes so much money that it doesn't really matter how he spends it. Of course, it helps that he has no ties or dependants. You remember Aidan.'

'I remember him being incredibly arrogant and rude,' she said. 'But then I only met him once or twice. You're very close, aren't you? Wasn't there some kind of romantic reunion when you were at university?'

'It wasn't a reunion, in that we'd never met before.' Scott was on the point of adding that it was the most meaningful event in his life, but he held back – his brother had no need to be painted into the picture any larger than he painted himself.

They had stopped at the lights, heading up a slope, where the road narrowed to a bottleneck. Nicola's eyes followed the cars as they wended their way past them down the hill; he watched her take in the movement around her. 'I must have started teaching soon after that last time we met – you remember, that night at Zak's when he made Tequila slammers and ran up and down the street like a maniac, clambering up on all the bus shelters.'

'It's funny to remember what a wag he could be, in his way.'

'God yes, Zak, what a wag he was.'

She put her hand on her belly as the bus lurched around another steep-angled corner, then turned and plunged again down an incline. The upper deck was shot from side to side and front to back with shafts of light; as they travelled through this dazzling crossfire, he noted a vulnerability in her that he did not remember from before – but perhaps she had only been hiding it.

'So you teach drama, you were saying, in Hackney.'

'Yes,' she laughed, 'I was saying that, it's true. You've been listening closely, Scott, I can tell. What about you?'

'I'm a staff writer on *Mojo* – you know, the music magazine. I review the new music, such as it is – mainly I review the old music, when it's rereleased. I interview the ones who are still alive. That's my life.'

She smiled wanly, her left cheek ablaze, left eye pierced by a white blade of sunlight. 'Yes, there was always music in your flat – it's one of my clearest memories of that period.'

'That was something that Zak and I had in common. He loved his bands for a while.' He could not help being drawn back to Zak; she also seemed to have a need to talk about him, no doubt because the funeral itself had not been much of a memorial. 'Someone told me that in the last year he didn't listen to music anymore. It's like he was denying himself the consolation of art.'

He wondered if this last statement strayed into pomposity, but Nicola picked up on it. 'And not just art, by all accounts. In his time he was quite the hedonist, wasn't he – but I heard that by the end he'd given up everything, all the stuff he used to do every day when we knew him, all the smoking and drinking and sex, the whole lot. It's like he was keeping himself pure – but I mean *why*? What for?'

'In a way I can understand his reaction. There's a mediocrity to our decadence, after all – it has no intellectual spine. We're like libertines without a philosophy.'

'I don't think that can have been Zak's objection, somehow. He was very anti-intellectual, really – or at least he'd always complain that I complicated things by overanalysing them.'

'Yes, it's true, he had a longing for the irrational in his life. It's like he wanted to surrender to some great engulfing belief, but he had too much education just to throw all his doubts to one side.'

Even as he said this, he realised that they were talking about Zak as if he were a type, not an individual. Neither of them had seen much of him in recent years; perhaps that was why it was so was easy to speak of him as if he were a concept rather than a person – or perhaps life, as it went on, became more conceptual and less personal. He tried to express some of this to Nicola, who raised her eyebrows then lifted her hand, shielding her face from the brutal light as the bus fell into town, juddering as it rounded the roundabouts.

'He was always a bit weird about women. I mean he was quite attractive at one point – at least early on, before all that frowning made him look like a little old man. Jenny said the first time she laid eyes on him she was smitten.' Nicola laughed. 'That's the kind of thing that happens to us girls, you know – we take one look at one of you mystery men and we're bowled over. But it was like Zak found the whole babe magnet thing too hot to handle, like it was beneath his dignity. She said he spent the whole afternoon basically talking himself out of a shag.'

Laughing, she fell against him at the next bend, and he wanted to keep her there somehow. 'Not surprising maybe that Jenny didn't make it onto the funeral list,' he said.

'Ah yes, Zak's list. I still can't get over the list.' She turned and shrugged, smiling into his smile. 'Let's face it, he was a head case but we loved him.'

'He was a head case but we loved him – an excellent epitaph.'

'He talked himself out of a shag is the one that should go on his stone.'

Scott had his arm around the back of the seat – he squeezed her shoulder. 'You're outrageous,' he said.

'Me?' she laughed. 'I'm just down for the weekend, trying to have a good time.'

The bus began its final descent to the shallow plain where the city lay, plummeting nose-down towards the coast road like a plane coming into land. Up front in the shaking cockpit, they watched themselves fall towards the sea's total whiteout, into a morning haze that had drifted inshore so that mist wound around the tops of the tall grey apartment blocks on the edge of town and drifted across the valley. Shrouded in a block of vapour, the Palace Pier looked as if it might go on forever, or at least as far as France.

The hotel terrace was deserted. An uneasy heat covered the seafront, filled with a greyish electricity, always on the point of sparking out or dying away – the kind of heat that made it feel natural to order a drink then go on drinking. They went to the bar, staffed by a different person from the bartender who had chased away the girl that morning. A small array of bottles, inverted in front of a frosted mirror, shed no glamour on the musty room: the livid green of Absinthe and primary colours of a golden Vermouth, blue Curaçao and magenta Campari only looked dusty in the south coast seediness of the New Europe Hotel.

They went back out onto the terrace with their lagers – but as soon as they sat down to drink the day fell apart, their focus dissolved, as if life was leaking from the frame into the landscape, so still and blanched and oppressive, losing colour by the minute. Whatever they knew about each other was not enough to make up for this energy drain, and their talk fell into a rough tangle of questions and lost threads of information, missing vital links.

Scott tried to dole out charm, as he knew he could – he knew that he was capable of giving people a sweeter sense of themselves, if only temporarily – but Nicola was looking for something else, it seemed. Even as she smiled at his snappy observations on culture and style, her face became masklike, her smile tight-lipped and almost grim. It struck him in a sudden flow of empathy that she did not expect much from him, or anything at all perhaps, but that he could make her happier right now, instantaneously. If there was a problem, it was not one of interpretation; he knew that she meant that they should go upstairs and have sex. This was something they had not discussed or even alluded to – they had not talked about her going back to London, or the fact that he and Aidan had the room for another night when she had just come down for the day with nothing more than a change of clothes. They had avoided the subject – strategically, it seemed to him now. So in the end it was easy enough to wave away subtlety and for him to suggest they go up and change out of their mourning gear.

She went with him up the two flights of stairs and hovered in the doorway. A pulsing light coming off the sea a few hundred yards away danced in the looking glass that hung slightly askew on the wall. Dropping his jacket on the bed, he waited for her to make a move he might reciprocate.

'What a beautiful room,' she said, breaking the silence, and her enthusiasm stirred and chilled him. He wondered whether a casual coming together of skin as a release from the afternoon's tension was all she had in mind, or whether her ambitions ran higher. In the end they simply moved towards each other, and he buried his head in her hair while she hid her head in his chest – and then they took off each other's funeral clothes, item by item, flinging them on the chair, laughing when the heap of black slid to the floor.

The short journey from clothed to naked and then the contrast between the sheets' coolness and their body heat made them delirious. The summer seemed to get to its point in those minutes when they moved together in a frenzy – and when the frenzy was over, he fell into a daze that was not like sleeping or waking but like the trance he once got from an Ericksonian therapist, in an office in Harley Street, at some expense. This trance was for free – but when she brought him out of it by pulling her arm away from his chest, he saw that what had passed between them was not therapy. It had not instilled him with calm purpose but filled him from head to toe with chaotic and flickering life. She rose and went to the bathroom, and he had perspective for the first time on her pale, dense body. He quickly turned his head away and looked at the ceiling. For once he wanted not to be the voyeur of his own experience, not to sing the burden of self-consciousness – but the cracks in the ceiling seemed to fuse with the lines of her limbs, and already he longed for a Nicola that he had not had, for someone else's Nicola or one that she kept to herself, one that perhaps did not exist.

When she came back into the room she too seemed altered, although only a minute or two had passed. 'It's strange,' she said without catching his eye, 'being in a hotel with you.'

'Really? What's so strange about it?'

She knelt on the bed then and looked down at him through her fringe; then she got up to wander restlessly around the room. She stopped at the dressing table and picked up her phone from where she had left it when he took off her clothes.

'This morning we meet for the first time in six years, at a *funeral* no less, and as soon as the body is in the ground we go to a hotel and fuck each other senseless.'

He gazed over at her, unable to hide his disbelief, but she leaned with her hip against the table, examining her phone, not returning his look. 'Yes, I know,' he said. 'I was there, remember.'

'We've kind of jumped the gun a bit, haven't we, don't you think?'

She sat down on the end of the bed and pressed the Talk button; in the sinking daylight he saw the green light spring on.

'How do you mean?'

'Foolish lovers,' she said carelessly, but in a tone so even that it was hard to think of it as false. It was as if she thought she was in a classroom giving dictation – she spelled it all out so precisely. 'Silly romantics that we are. What jerks we are to be so in love,' she went on, lightly, in the same cool way.

'It was sex,' he said, trying to emulate her lightness – and she glanced up at him, her eyes reflecting the phone's emerald glow; her nakedness was suddenly too much, intimidating.

'Yes, I know what it was,' she said, indifferently. She rang a number apparently at random, and he heard a distant dial tone before she snapped it off. 'I wish there was someone we could call,' she said, bending forward with her hands on her knees, as if in pain somewhere.

Her sudden coldness was unpleasantly erotic, her restlessness disturbingly familiar. He felt restless now himself and in need of some escape – but at the same time he wished she would come and lie down again and allow what was left of the afternoon to fall away of its own accord to its natural end. She seemed determined to pre-empt it, and her desire to control what they had just created and to call that creation a mistake recalled his first impression of her at the graveside. He was not in her league, not in anyone's language; she wanted something that he did not know how to give.

'You mean someone we could talk to together, someone from the past?'

She softened at the desolation she must have heard in his tone, switched off her phone and stretched out beside him in the fading afternoon light. 'But who do we know together anymore?' she asked gently. 'Where are they now, all those mutual friends?'

'It's sad, isn't it?' He picked up the theme gladly. 'It's like the network has just gone. We'll never have the same thing again, a gang like that, twenty people who see each other every weekend.'

'Oh well, it's not the end of the world,' she said, as if from an instinct to avoid any kind of backsliding, any kind of turning around. But then she brought herself up short, turned to him and stroked the shadow of his stubble. 'Why do you think that is?'

'Oh,' he said, determined to keep them on this thread, 'I don't know. It's like we've broken off into little groups – groups of one or two, depending on our state of mind. Some of us are too troubled, some of us are too happy. We don't meet well. There's too much tension between the haves and have nots.'

'So which category do you fall into?' She left him no time for an answer. 'Don't be one of the troubled ones,' she said, 'I've no room in my life for troubled people.'

'There's nothing for me to be troubled about,' he reassured her, 'or not anymore.'

'Why, have I just cured you of impotence?' She laughed. It was a brash thing to say, but the brashness suited her – or at least he could see that in another situation he would have liked it. 'But of course your trouble runs deeper than that.'

'Some of it may be sexual,' he conceded.

'Some of it always is.'

In the half hour since they had finished making love, the vivid sunscape of the room had darkened and the walls gone from golden grey to something quite luxurious, a Mediterranean blue. In this aquarium light he was overwhelmed by an adolescent loneliness, the trapped sensations of a boy who stood alone on a quayside, filled with an emotion he could not express. But perhaps this was his chance, perhaps with her he should try: an impulse came to pour it all out, tell her the substance of his dysfunction – that his ability to create women in his imagination was so developed that he could almost live through their imagined responses. When he saw a woman on the street, he would undress her to the point when he knew her inside and out, an illusion of intimacy that made real intimacy redundant.

Nicola lay propped up on her elbow, looking absently at him as if she were on a train and he was sitting across the aisle. He saw that she was ready and waiting, she had predicted this impulse to tell all – and for that very reason he did not give into it, since his fear of being predictable was as strong as Aidan's fear of boredom. 'Tedium,' Aidan would say, 'monotony, God I hate it.'

'What's making you smile?'

'I was thinking about my brother.'

'I don't remember him being especially amusing,' she said.

And then – but in the end of course it was all too predictable – Aidan flung open the door they had forgotten to lock and walked in on them.

The three of them sat outside in the hot sea breeze at twilight, hearing the Channel dragging on the stony shore. In the failing light, Scott saw that his brother had been drinking steadily all day; he bristled with artificial energy, his face set in a mask of alcohol and egotism. He would have been around town two or three times, finding people to latch onto in bars, short-lived companions to be discarded as his mood took him. Scott wondered sometimes about that brotherly connection, a gift they shared of making easy links with people – a gift that Aidan abused.

'Isn't it lovely out here?' said Nicola. 'So nice of Aidan to come up and persuade us to join him.'

'Yes, typically considerate.' Scott kept his eyes on the horizon, a milky line far out, not wanting to change anything in the ambience by paying any particular attention to it. He felt nervous for Nicola in his brother's company.

'So you had a good funeral, then,' Aidan remarked in a monotone that Scott understood held his brother's own brand of anger – an aggression that he would have stored up over the day. He had seen Aidan often in these moods, always provoked by a crisis over which he had little control, by any hint of an alteration in the balance between them.

'Well, we buried him,' he said, in an attempt to sound hard that only sounded fake in the deepening dusk – all aquamarine, a blue mixed by some cosmic painter, dotted here and there with points of light.

'And you gave him a swell obituary, I'll bet. Scott is so unpleasant about his friends when their backs are turned.' Aidan swung around to look straight at Nicola, studying her closely in the gathering gloom. 'And in

Zak's case I think we could say that his back is well and truly turned.'

'Who was it who called him an asshole only this morning?'

His brother raised an eyebrow, lifted his cigarette to his lips and spoke before taking a drag on it. 'Ah, but I didn't know him very well. He was never my friend.' Aidan turned to Nicola again. 'You wanted to say something?' In the broad shadow left by the hotel wall, cutting out the light from the setting sun, Scott saw a gleam of curiosity cross his brother's face.

'When we met before it was at Zak's place,' she said, 'in 1993 or so. You were already full of the joys of high finance, I recall. You had the women swooning all over you, didn't you? You and Scott and Zak had quite a competition going that evening.'

'It was Scott's place, not Zak's, in 1994,' said Aidan, who prided himself on his rat-trap memory. 'Your hair was longer – you were in a taffeta frock, burgundy. You told us you were going commando.'

'I was a good-time girl,' she shrugged. 'Still am, I guess, when it comes down to it.' She glanced over at Scott, who shrugged and picked up his glass.

'What I remember most,' said Aidan, his eyes fixed on her, 'is how at the end of the night you were running around, lighting our cigarettes, chucking us tins, trying to keep us all happy. That's a special talent, Nicola – you should try to hang on to it.'

'I'd like to think I have.' She reached behind her and pulled on the denim jacket she had brought down from the room. Scott saw her direct her gaze not at Aidan but slightly to one side of him, at the scattered street scene. At this time of night, there were only a few stragglers, stray couples down on the pavement. The scene was like an abandoned film set, as if the extras who only a minute before had been there in swarms had just left after working all the hours they were paid for; another set of extras was on its way for the nightshift. 'One of my friends still has a very romantic picture of you in her head,' Nicola went on. 'Do you remember Emily? You made a date and then you didn't show.'

'Emily, oh yes.' Aidan laughed, swinging back in his chair and running his hand through his black hair. 'I remember that I stood her up.'

'Yes, you did.'

'And you don't think that's the done thing, do you? But you have to recall the context, Nicola. A lot of kissing went on that night that never came to anything. Kissing without consequences was what we called it, me and Scotty.'

Scott nodded in agreement, without meaning to. But it was true – it had all been so innocent; their games had been so childish really.

Nicola leaned over to light her cigarette from a candle in a jar on the table. 'But then I suppose the consequences might have been pretty painful if you had in fact showed up for your date – for Emily, that is.'

'Well,' said Aidan, evenly. 'That's great feedback, Nicola, really, thanks for the information.' He stood, flexing. 'I'll get you both a drink.'

'I'm sorry about this,' Scott said, when his brother went inside. 'It's really so dull.'

'It is,' she said, 'such a waste.'

He watched her look away in the direction of the piers, the first spread with rings and streams of multi-coloured light, violets and oranges that smeared the air as they bobbed in the wind. The second pier, further off to the west, was a bright-burning shed of rust and weathered wood, its brokenness almost invisible against the fading sky. He was glad that she thought it was a waste – glad to know that she saw it as something dwindling that had once been alive.

'He's like the chairman of the board,' she said, 'in that pinstripe suit.'

Scott laughed. 'It's his armour you know, he needs it to survive.'

They sat quietly while bits of traffic crossed between them and the sea, and the wind rose for a moment and shook the halyards against the masts of little boats down on the stones, making that rhythmic knocking sound. Stars came out and were extinguished at once by the bartender, who threw a switch and flooded the terrace with a harsh electric glare.

'Here comes pinstripe himself,' said Nicola – but when Aidan stepped out onto the terrace they saw that he had been up to change. In black jeans and a pink silk shirt he looked less threatening – but more insidious, perhaps, as if he were wearing a disguise. He put a tray on the table and they took their glasses.

'Our room's a bit of a mess, Scotty. I can see you've been taking Nicola here on some kind of trip – and that's fine, of course, but you could have cleared up afterwards.'

'Shut up, Aidan,' Scott said. Already they were set into their groove of defence and attack. 'Can't you just sit down and be normal for five minutes?'

'Normal,' sneered Aidan. 'Jesus, who made you the normal police?'

'Why don't you tell us something about your day, Aidan,' Nicola interrupted.

'Aidan's day,' Scott took her up. 'What a tale of knights and chivalry that would be. Aidan nails the only willing virgin in town on her parents' bed. He chats up all the Australians in the pub until they realise he's just patronising them and he has to fight his way out. He breaks some petty regulation, doesn't pay for his bus ticket, just to prove what a rebel he is. Aidan's been having the same day for ten years, Nicola. He's the only one who isn't bored of it.'

A pinpoint of red shone fleetingly, far out on the horizon – a boat perhaps, or a lighted buoy. Scott saw his anger like that crimson dot, minute but sharp, hard to locate, isolated in space. Even when he fenced with his brother in this way, when he felt nothing for him but antipathy, he was lost in his need for that personality – stronger than his, less scrupulous – that he so resented.

'You know, Zak was braver than either of you,' Aidan retorted, jerking his head back and swinging in his chair, tugging at his hair in a brief repertoire of sudden movements. 'At least he didn't stick around to pick fault when he knew he wasn't up to it. Neither of you are any good at anything but chipping bits off people.'

'Don't compare me to that cripple,' Scott shouted. 'He didn't have it in him to live, so he decided to turn his failure into some Wagnerian fucking tragedy we'd all have to watch.'

'You call what you do living? You pussy around with your writing and women and music, as if there was anything faintly real or important about all that bullshit. You write about something you can't do yourself and fuck the ones who condescend to fuck you back. It means nothing, man, nothing.'

Nicola's voice came out of the blue, clear and startling – Scott had forgotten her for a moment. 'There was nothing brave about what Zak did. He had options and he refused to take them. He just ran himself down until he couldn't see the point anymore. What's brave about that, Aidan?'

'Simmer down, won't you?' Aidan retorted. 'I'm taking issue with my brother here, I'm calling out this lightweight on his so-called life.'

'And what about you?' Scott said, shaking with anger now. 'You keep up this image of yourself as some sort of anti-hero, battling against the bourgeoisie from the inside. At least I don't prop up my ego with some ridiculous self-deception.'

Aidan, laughing, turned his cheek theatrically. 'Slap me on the other one, brother.' He picked up his beer, drank and returned the glass to the table with a kind of taut control. 'I can't listen to you anymore, Scotty. Your words are empty. Your words actually disgust me.'

'Will you two stop it,' Nicola said – but with a stage weariness that Scott could see was not sincere. She was sitting forward in her chair and watching them with shining eyes, evidently fascinated by their conflict, wanting to see it to a conclusion. He and Aidan were not usually so eloquent in their attacks, he realised; she served them well as an audience.

'You aren't listening anyway, Aidan,' he said. 'You never hear a word that doesn't come from your own mouth. You're like a dictator – you're like a Nazi in a pink shirt.'

After a second or two of suspense, all three of them laughed, catching each other's eye – and then the mask of egotism fell from Aidan's face, and Scott felt a return of his love. He knew it would not last, it would not be long before his brother put his mask back on. But the atmosphere was transformed by their laughter; they would not argue again that night. Picking up his own glass, he watched Aidan drink, wipe his mouth with the back of his hand and glance up at the night sky in simple, involuntary gestures, grinning openly at Nicola. This was the Aidan he had first met in Glasgow, the one he loved to watch – the version of Aidan that only existed when he was not watching himself.

'Even you thought that was funny, Aidan,' said Nicola, still dabbing with her sleeve at the corners of her eyes.

'I'm laughing, aren't I?' he snapped back at her, as if she had pointed out a weakness. But then he relaxed in his chair and gestured with an open hand towards the sea, as if letting it go.

Nicola stood and crossed the pool of light between their table and the hotel door, closed now against a chill that had not yet arrived. The night was almost balmy, but with a brittle heat that threatened every moment to break and turn to something much cooler – and then the dark that now embraced them would send them inside. 'I'll get the drinks,' she said, and they watched through the tinted glass as she joined the one or two punters who stood around at the bar, waiting for the bartender to change barrels.

'Sweet in her way I guess,' said Aidan, after a pause, 'but essentially pointless.' He sat slumped back in his chair.

'What do you mean?'

'She's too precious for you, Scotty. You need a woman who can tip and run, someone who'll accept defeat. I mean that's generally been your rule. This one thinks too hard – she even thinks she understands us. And she probably has plans, if you know what I mean. Plans in general, of course, not a plan specifically for you.' Aidan gave him a look of humorous insinuation and sat back in his chair.

'As far as I know, Nicola isn't into weddings, if that's what you're trying to say.'

'She prefers funerals, I suppose – more erotic potential.' Staring into the bottom of his glass, his brother went on. 'But that wasn't what I meant, anyway. I mean she's the kind who thinks about the future – and that wouldn't fit in very well with *your* plans, Scotty.'

'Yes, okay, I get your gist. You think she's not right for me.'

'No, I just think that you're wrong for her.'

'Well that's great, thanks.'

'Then there's the complicating factor that she claims too much for herself, as women like her tend to. All ambition but not much flair. She's not the belle of the ball anymore, if she ever was.'

'She'll be back in a minute, Aidan.'

'Always the worry you'll be overheard.'

Scott looked around the terrace for somewhere to hide from his brother's judgments. He had not had time to consider what sort of future he and Nicola might have together, but his brother had already made up his mind. It was strange: he was the older of them, but it was Aidan who held sway, lectured him, criticised his decisions but more often despised him for his caution. But it was true, of course – he had always held back from committing to anything that failed perfectly to match his vision of himself. And what kind of return had he seen from all this waiting it out to get it right? As Zak had once said to him, to all of them, stoned and blissed out underneath an apple tree full of tripping light, *The rewards of hesitation are few*.

Nicola came out again then, carrying a magnum of champagne and three flutes on a tray. Aidan seemed to take her in anew as she took the bottle from the bucket and popped the cork so that it flew in a loop across the road separating them from the seafront. Then she filled their glasses, fell back in her chair and glanced between them.

'So have you guys made your peace?'

Without asking first, she leaned forward and took a cigarette from Aidan's packet. Scott watched the sway of her breasts in her top and saw Aidan watching her too, with that foxlike look on his face that women were supposed to find, as Scott understood it, menacing but seductive – the keen look of a single-minded man. To Scott, the contemptuous hunger it expressed was gross; but as Aidan's eyes rested on Nicola, he experienced a weird surge, an erotic flash, as if a camera had taken a picture of them, the cameraman unseen. It was gone quickly because he closed his eyes to it, but not before he sensed his own lust patched onto his brother's.

'We've smoked the pipe of peace, yeah,' Aidan was saying. 'But Scott and I will always argue because the man is just so annoying. I just can't stand watching him fuck up, Nicola.'

Scott shook his head. 'What can I say – we drive each other crazy.'

Nicola looked at them starrily with shining eyes, lit up by the champagne. 'When I see you two together, I wish I had a sibling. It feels sad that I never had a bond like that with anyone, that closeness you two have.' She laughed. 'The woes of being an only child.'

She held her glass up to the light, examining the bubbles with a look of childlike happiness, watched by Aidan, who was watched by Scott. She appeared so bright and separate as she sat there, lost for an instant in her love of the moment. The two of them could only throw shade on her, thought Scott, could only mar her bright separation with their twin shadow.

'Of course, we were only children too, until we met,' Scott said.

'Being an only child has its advantages, I can tell you,' said Aidan. 'Once I only had to look out for myself – now I have this man on my conscience.'

'Aidan hates to have anything on his conscience,' Scott explained automatically; his head was elsewhere, anticipating the next scene.

'It's a revelation to me that he has one,' Nicola laughed – but absently, still spellbound.

'People underestimate that side of me,' said Aidan.

'Aidan can afford to be underrated,' said Scott, picking up on his cue. 'No one will ever get him like he gets himself.'

Nicola looked over his shoulder at the horizon's dark line. 'That's a difficult thought for a Saturday night,' she said. Her tone had changed – Scott had the impression she was putting him down. 'How about this peace pipe?' she went on. 'Did anyone bring one?'

Aidan had something on him, of course. So it was settled – they would go upstairs and cut loose, as Aidan put it, once they had finished their drinks. For a while as the town grew quieter they talked on in their pool of light, as the traffic died to a trickle and couples ambled back along the front to their hotels. They were in the heart of clubland, where clubs pumped bass into the narrow stretch that went from their feet and out along the coast, the sound travelling with small clusters of white and red lights that were going east or west, crawling along so slowly that getting anywhere seemed nothing more than a game to kill time.

Nicola was chatting away easily now with Aidan – Scott saw her with her guard down, her weapons surrendered. His brother was only being accurate when he said she was not his style. She could walk into a room and furnish it with her personality; she was not like other women he had been with, who were hilarious or tearful on shuffle and repeat, who could only blurt out the things they felt in the moment. The women he had dated and lived with over the years had been shy and sad and marginal, with big hearts but little self-esteem. Things had drifted to a conclusion with them every time without him ever finding out what they really wanted. They must have wanted things, but whatever it was remained a secret that they kept to themselves.

He turned away from his history to the sea, which beyond a certain point seemed to enter infinite space but which closer to shore looked like part of the city. A shimmer came from the lit-up windows of buildings along Marine Parade and caught on the white horses – they ran in again and again on the black swell. What would happen, he wondered, to all those marginal women with their untold secrets? Something inside him seemed to ebb and flow, too fast for thought – and beyond the running crests he glimpsed their pale bodies, either swimming away into their element or spinning around in the waves, tangled in darkness, he could not tell. A wind blew up on the terrace then, still a summer breeze but with that taste of early autumn, a freshness that made the flesh ache for what had just gone, what was about to come. He had known the sensation before and recognised it now with a pang of sadness – because he had learned that, in his case at least, desire was only a regret for what must happen next.

They heard the bartender tell someone in the back she was leaving, and the lights went out on the terrace as they climbed the stairs with the bottle they had bought at the bar before it closed. Nicola entered the room first – Aidan had taken the bottle and handed her the keys – and she went to turn on the bedside lamp; but then she seemed to change her mind, leaving the room as it was, a dark glimmer with splashes of ochre and midnight blue.

They sat in a circle in the middle of the room and passed the pipe. It went around quickly to begin with; one of them opened the second bottle, and for a while they stared at it in silence, forgetting to drink. They stayed quiet, up in their own heads, while the pipe went around, watching one another get stoned. Scott could only see their faces clearly when cars passed along the road outside, when arbitrary splashes of headlight would come up through the windows. The day from certain angles seemed long and complex and from other angles drastically foreshortened; this was all he knew for a minute or two, and then he knew nothing again.

When they began to talk at last, their talk went on for a few seconds then petered out; they had conversations that were over in a matter of words. They peered into each other's faces, unable to see much at all, seeming to forget who was who – and then it all came back, and they remembered every syllable of what had just been said, believing it all over again. The cars passing on the road below threw their beams up onto the ceiling, and the light from the headlamps of the cars moved around the room like shooting stars on slow shutter speed, drunken compass points. It was as if he could see the world turning – uncertainly, not sure it was such a good idea to carry on, stopping and starting again.

At times lucidity seemed to return to all three of them at once, then the flow came back and it all made a kind of sense. In one of those clear spots, he heard himself talk on and on about Zak – the burial itself, Zak in a box. He already could not remember how his speech had begun, had no idea how long he had been talking, but he could not stop until Aidan broke in.

'Scotty loves funerals – he met me at one. In that case our footloose father was...'

'The beneficiary,' Scott finished for him.

'Old Maurice, the fisherman who caught more sea than fish.' When Nicola laughed, he added, 'Did you know our father was called Maurice Morris?'

'Scott doesn't tell me things like that,' said Nicola, with a hint of sadness.

'That's because it isn't true,' Scott said, powerfully aware of some control that had been wrested from him, as if his limbs were being manipulated from a distance, on remote.

'That's because Scott doesn't like telling lies,' Aidan said. 'He doesn't believe in it, doesn't think it's right. But I only lied about our father's name – and it made you laugh, Nicola, which is a small triumph for myself.'

She laughed again, then stopped abruptly as if she had heard her own echo. It was not the same room as in the afternoon; with the lights off and blinds open, it seemed aerial somehow, spinning in the sky between stars. Scott regained control of his legs and got to his feet; he went to the window, wanting to bring back a sense of where things were, but he found the sea as overwhelming as the sky. For a minute he had no bearings: everything seemed close to the point of suffocation, but also sickeningly far away. He swung round unsteadily, looking for Aidan and Nicola down on the rug, and he saw them in the shadows – but they seemed unreachable, even though they were almost at his fingertips.

'This isn't really that much fun,' he began to say.

Nicola got up and went to lie down on the bed. He heard her crying, lying on her side, her back to them both, looking so cut off, locked away in a private world. But she might not be inconsolable. Scott started to move towards her, but Aidan sprang up and got to her before he had taken more than a step.

'Oh, you are such a little pussy,' Aidan was saying to her, 'such a little cat.'

Aidan stroked her neck and kissed her hair, coming back again and again to his theme until it sounded like an incantation – or what it was, persuasion. Nicola rolled over onto her back, holding her arm across her eyes while Aidan rubbed her belly through her blouse. When he began to unbutton her jeans she twisted away, putting her hands down to stop him. He kissed her on the mouth – Scott saw her pull her mouth away then put it back – and in that moment she did look like a cat. She made the same shapes out of instinct, unknowingly, sleek and oblivious to anything outside her nature, as if she could walk a thin line without making mistakes. But it was not true, he thought, they had made a mistake – and he remembered it clearly, all at once. She had said something to him in the course of the day, on the bus, that was not true at all. She had said that they loved Zak, but they had not loved him, or even cared about him very much. This was what had been missing all day, which neither of them could find, which they might have found if they had been given longer to look – the heart, a heart. But she was right, they had made the wrong move, at the wrong time, and now they were living in the world that Zak had left behind, the world he had created by leaving it, which was all they cared about.

He wished she would stop what she was doing, sit up and turn to him and look him in the eye, so he could tell her what he had just seen. But she was lost in the moment now, in this time that all of them knew should

116

not be happening – and instead he lay down on the bed beside them to watch them fuck. He lay and watched them from a foot away, less than a foot, a few inches. He lay and watched his brother's hands move over her and knew how his brother felt; feeling Nicola through Aidan, he took her again, but in his brother's body. But he felt Aidan through Nicola as well, felt his weight on her and in her – the weight of his brother's body, his personality bearing down in all its recklessness and cruelty. But he had to watch, knowing that there would not be another chance, this intimacy was unrepeatable.

He watched as his brother touched her hurriedly and without passion, watched and stole their sensations and made them his own, shocked by their indifference to his presence, how bound up they were in each other. But he was caught up too in his own desire, which he saw as clearly as he saw his brother's watchface as it turned towards him and away again in rhythm, flashing the time over and over in luminous hands. Something was born out of the moment: together the three of them had made something, and it rose from the bed and floated to the centre of the room, a nastiness embedded in ecstasy, an amber ecstasy with a dead fly at the heart of it. Until now he had never admitted to wanting this thing, so horrible in fact, but now he reached out and took its smooth shape in his hands, touched by how small and hard it was, moved by its beauty. It would have been a crime against the moment not to take advantage of its beauty.

It went on like this for a while, a strange and dull eternity as the world kept on turning, while other things happened too – a low moan that drifted up from the street, a drawling voice saying something about the moon and a dog barking, down on the beach perhaps, a car door slamming. Then the street outside fell silent again; the traffic had stopped its flow, and the only light came from a streetlamp on the pavement close by their window, which shone up into the room and showed how the dark outlines of Aidan and Nicola were joined, how they clung to each other and came apart. He watched their silhouettes separate and come together again and again, gleaming wet from hairline to ankle with all the heat they were making, as they turned their faces his way without seeing him, their breath brushing his cheek. They went on like this until the pleasure was all used up – then Aidan sighed, slumped over Nicola for a second then rolled away, lay down between her and Scott and filled the room with the sound of his breathing.

Scott placed his palm on his brother's chest and felt the lungs empty and fill again, the heart thud against his hand. He became disembodied for an instant, falling into a dream perhaps, where he saw himself standing on a shoreline in sunlight, the sea at his feet and the tide coming in. He would have liked to stay there, standing on the shore and watching the sun go down forever in a perpetual sunset – but in the next instant he woke and returned to the room, this physical space that he could not simply abandon, to the bodies that lay breathing beside him. So he lay with his hand on his brother's heart and gazed at the window, where outside it was still dark, but a dark laced with streaks of silver, a silvery layer formed by streetlamps and constellations. If he stayed awake and watched for long enough, he would see it brighten. So he would lie like that until morning, with his eyes open, waiting for the morning light.

Carson's Trail

Shortly after his seventh birthday, Carson had flown over to England with his father for vacation, but now his father was sick. Soon after they arrived he had spent two days in hospital, but on the third day they sent him away with a bottle of medicine. Now he hardly had the strength to get out of bed and eat breakfast; he dozed in an armchair with his head nodding forward on his chest, or he watched TV – he did nothing now but sit and look out at Carson from behind a pane of glass.

Carson and his father were staying with Carson's grandmother in a bungalow in a village with a stream at one end, hills around two sides of it and a shop on the main street that sold everything, from Matchbox cars to envelopes to dog food. Beside the shop was a playground where Carson went to play whenever his grandmother could leave his father. She was over seventy and her small, lined face showed its feelings only in the rearrangement of its creases, but he could tell that it made her happy to see him swing himself or use the climbing frame or race about the edges of the playing field.

The older boys from the village were uninterested in playing with Carson, but they came almost every morning to his grandmother's garden. She gave them apples and biscuits and asked about their parents – and afterwards they fought or rolled each other about in the little wilderness at the back of the bungalow, or they played throw and catch with Carson's toys and teased him when he could not understand their accents. He would have preferred to stay indoors, away from them, but his grandmother told him that it was summer still and he ought to be outside. Carson only half-believed her. In the Nantucket summer he had just flown in from, even walking or lifting an arm made him break out in a sweat; here the wind seemed to tear through the trees from morning to night and clouds swept constantly across the sun, throwing huge cold shadows.

'And when the summer's over,' his grandmother said, 'the radio says we'll get an Indian summer.'

'What's that?' he said, although he knew – he liked to hear her explain things.

'It's a special kind of summer we get sometimes when the real one finishes,' she said. 'We don't always get it, but maybe this year we will.'

In the third week of his father's illness, the old lady helped Carson put up a tent in the garden. It was a windy day and while she wrestled with the ropes and the flysheet Carson watched her with love. He had not known before that he loved her – before it was nothing more than a word to him – but seeing her struggle against the gusts of wind, catching the edge of the canvas again each time it flew from her hands, made him know that he did. That week he spent a lot of time in the tent, sitting on the sheet of blue tarpaulin she had laid inside, while the light from outside changed shade as the sun moved across the sky. During part of every day he had to share the tent with the boys from the village, but in the evenings it was his until bedtime. On the day when it poured with rain from early right through and the boys did not come, Carson sat in the tent, in the greenish light thrown by the walls, and listened to the water drip from the trees. That was his favourite day.

One night towards the end of that third week, Carson was woken by a shout. His father slept in a bedroom overlooking the large, tangled garden at the back of the bungalow, while Carson slept on a mattress on the floor of his grandmother's room across the corridor. He heard his father call out several times in a loud, strained voice; after some time, the old lady woke and put on her dressing gown and went to him, but even then he continued to moan loudly and shout. Carson sat up and listened while his father shouted; he went on as if he could not help himself, saying things that Carson had never heard him say before.

'Oh my God,' he shouted, 'Oh Jesus, Jesus Christ.'

When his grandmother came back to their bedroom, Carson could see by the side of her face wet in the light from the corridor that she was crying. His father still called out, but for a while she only sat on the edge of her bed, scrabbling at the edge of her nightgown with her hands. To Carson it felt as if he was trapped in the semi-darkness of the room, in a cage made of sound: the bed in the next room creaked constantly while his father called out to his mother, who sat above Carson, rubbing her hands against the hem of her gown. Between the rustling of the gown and his father's shouts, if Carson listened hard enough he could hear himself breathing – short, hard breaths as if he was running away from something or standing outside the principal's office waiting for punishment.

In the end, the old lady went to the phone and rang the doctor. Carson heard her dialling in the hallway. She got no answer – she must have known that she would get no answer, but she called again anyway. The doctor would never answer the phone, however often she called; Carson somehow understood this, even at the age of seven. When his grandmother went to tell his father the news, his father groaned and began to sob. His sobbing was low and throaty and went on and on, like the sound of a wounded animal, like the horse with an arrow in his side that Carson had seen in a film about General Custer.

Carson did not like lying there in the darkness being able to hear but not see, and he got up and crossed the corridor to his father's room. His father's sheets were covered in raw-looking gobbets of blood, some of them already drying to a dirty brown. His father lay sideways in the bed, being sick into a bowl, his arms clasping his ribs while his mother bent over him, her head near his, holding the bowl steady. When she noticed Carson standing in the doorway, she let go of the bowl and rushed over, pushing him out of the room.

Later, when his father was quiet, she sat down on the edge of Carson's mattress and talked to him, told him stories about the village from when she was a girl, how she had played down by the stream with her brother and sisters, how they climbed over the wall into Miss Webb's orchard to steal the apples. She told him how once they had trespassed on Gale's farm and her brother got on the back of an old horse without a saddle and she got on behind him. She talked to him like this for a long time, for hours perhaps, but neither of them felt drowsy – and for the rest of that night he was allowed to sleep in the tent.

Carson woke with the dawn. He opened the flap of the tent and the sunlight poured in, as it had failed to for several days, with real brightness. Something had scraped the clouds from the sky, which stood above him blue and forthright, not brilliant but clear and giving off warmth. Perhaps the summer was over, and this was the Indian summer that his grandmother had almost promised him.

It was warm, but not warm enough just for dungarees, and he went into the bungalow to fetch a jacket. Inside it was quiet. Usually the old lady would be up making tea, but that morning he did not see her; he found his jacket hanging on the back of the chair in the hall and went out, closing the door gently behind him. He put his jacket on and ran across the lawn, jumping over the flowerbed onto the garden wall and down onto the gravel. At the gate he met the village boys; he was among them for a minute, while they pushed him between them like a pinball until he was dizzy. Then he fell over and cut his knee on the gravel and they left him and went into his grandmother's garden.

Carson got up without crying. He ran up the lane, the way he had often gone with his grandmother when they went out for a walk. The lane led up to the church and away from the playground with its one swing in the shape of a battered horse, which swung back and forth when he shifted his weight, squeaking because it was years since anyone had oiled it, away from the village shop with its popsicles and Feasts and model aeroplanes. Carson ran all the way to the top of the lane and then slowed as he jumped down the steps that went one side of the dip and up the steps again on the other side, where he entered the graveyard. This was where his grandfather was buried. He had been here several times since the beginning of his visit, and he knew where the grave was; he ran across to it now and read the name and straightened the jar of flowers that his grandmother had brought with them the last time they came.

Some of the flowers were dead, and Carson took the dead ones out and replaced them with fresh wild ones he found in the hedge. Then he ran out of the graveyard through the other gate and went down the lane that came out at the brook. It was a beautiful morning. Until then, he had not been sure what *beautiful* meant, but when he saw the light come back off the stream and shine in the dewy grass, he heard the word in his head. Taking off his shoes, he tied his laces, stuffed his socks inside, slung them around his neck and waded up the shallow brook until the banks became almost too steep to climb. He pulled himself up to the top of the bank, stinging his hands whenever he grasped the nettles by mistake, pricking his ankles on the thistles. He did not mind the nettles or thistles – somehow, they could sting him and prick him as much as they liked, and he would never mind.

At the top of the bank was an abandoned car, with only one door on the driver's side and the roof rusted through, the tyres long gone. He sat in the driver's seat and honked the horn, which made no sound except in his imagination. But in his imagination, the sound of the horn joined the other morning sounds – woodpigeons, starlings and robins, a dog barking somewhere, the engine of a tractor starting above him on the hillside. And so he went on up the road, towards the army ranges.

Carson knew that he must not trespass on the army ranges, so he turned off after the sign and walked on tiptoe down the gravel drive of someone's house. There were no cars in the driveway, but he clung to the wooded side in case anyone from the house called to him; he was ready to disappear into the trees. But no call came from the house, and Carson passed over the edge of the garden and through a broken fence, coming out as he knew he would at the watercress beds. He was proud of himself for finding a shortcut he had never taken; his grandmother had always led him the long way round to the watercress beds, by the road that everyone took. Feeling tired from all his running, he wended his way to the middle of the beds along the narrow dry path and crouched down. He splashed his hands in the water and washed his face, which he had forgotten to do when he woke up. But just as he closed his eyes and rubbed his wet hands over his cheeks, he heard a hissing sound, immediately to his right, right into his ear it seemed.

Carson stood quickly and confronted a black swan, which had approached him soundlessly out of nowhere on its webbed feet. Carson backed away and the swan stood its ground and extended its dark neck towards him, its red beak. He had heard that swans could break your arm or leg with one beat of their wings. He turned and ran up the narrow path, falling from it now and then and getting his feet caught in the watercress, until he got to the stile. Even with his grandmother he had never passed this point before, but the swan blocked the path behind him, and Carson climbed the stile and dropped over onto the other side, into the meadow. Looking back, he saw that the swan had not followed him but still stood on the path where he had found it.

Now he was in wild territory. Although he had not intended to come so far, he was glad. He would have something new to tell them when he got back home – something they might not have seen for themselves, or not for a long time. His father had grown up in the village, but he had never seen his father go through a meadow or climb a fence. At home his father would only walk from their front door to the door of the car; he would drive to the store and back, then sit back in his chair in his study. He could not remember seeing his father standing beside water, or under a tree, apart from the tree in the yard. When his father was a boy, he might have gone this way – but even if he had, he would have forgotten it by now. So Carson put his shoes back on and went on up the meadow.

There was no path through the meadow, which went in a steepish slope up one of the hills overlooking the village. The meadow was dotted with enormous rabbit holes, almost wide enough at the mouth for Carson to climb into, and huge bramble bushes. In places there was no other way onward, and he had to squeeze through the brambles with branches clutching at his jacket, pulling it off his shoulders, thorns sticking in his hair and scratching his face. But eventually he came out at the top of the meadow, where fields with crops began. He pushed up the middle wire of a barbed-wire fence and put one leg through, catching his trousers as he brought his second leg over so that he fell over in the grass, one barb snagging his calf. Carson lay in the grass, holding his leg and expecting to cry, but no tears came.

He felt a long way from home, but when he raised his head he could see past the meadow full of brambles to the village at the valley bottom, still where he had left it that morning, and he was reassured. He would have preferred to be back down there, in the village, in his grandmother's garden. At that moment he would have preferred to be there, even if the other boys were there too, pushing him around. But he could not go back the way he had come, through the barbed-wire fence and the brambles. So he went on, upwards, through the field – or rather he went around the edge of the field, not to tread down the stiff stalks of wheat. The sky was the same blue, enormous now that he was closer to it, and to protect himself against its vastness he let out a yell, his first word of the morning,

'Geronimo!'

The sky swallowed his word. The field was steeper than it looked, and the top of the hill seemed endlessly far away. Carson took off his jacket and slung it over his shoulder. He had come a long way with no breakfast, and as he climbed he looked around for something to eat, but he doubted whether he should eat any of the things he saw in the field. There was the wheat, but it was raw and hard and had bugs on it, and it belonged to the farmer. There was grass growing under the fence, but grass was what made cats sick. Now and then he came across a poppy, and he stopped and considered it, but he remembered a film in which poppies made a girl fall asleep, and he knew that he must not fall asleep. If he fell asleep now, he would never get to the top of the hill, he might never wake up, he might never get back home again.

But now even the word *sleep*, as it sprang to his mind and sounded on his lips, made him stagger in his climb. Carson went on, but he was blinded by the sky's blueness and by the sweat that ran from his eyebrows into his eyes. He kept his eye on the brow of the hill, blinking through the sweat, his feet dragging now, tugged at by the wet grass. The top seemed to come no closer and the sun became too hot for him; the sky seemed to be swallowing him up, as if he were climbing not a hill but a ladder, further and further up into the blue. He wanted to turn and look back at the village – someone from down there had told him once that from the top of the hill you could see his grandmother's house, as plain as day. But he knew that if he stopped climbing he would never start out again.

Even when he ran out of strength and could climb no further, even when he sank into the wheat and lay there panting and closed his eyes against the Indian summer sky, Carson did not look. He lay there with his eyes closed, not looking down – because what would he see if he looked? He knew what he would see; he saw it already in his mind's eye. The men arrived and carried his father's body through the garden on a stretcher, loaded him into a big black car and drove away. His grandmother knelt at the bottom of her wilderness; then she, too, was taken away. The boys from the village came and pulled out the tent pegs, the wind came and blew the tent away. The door was open but the sheets were stained with blood. The house was dark.

Accident on
Słowackiego Street

In the last July of the century, Carl met Karina in the
ticket queue in Victoria coach station. She stood next to
him in the queue and they got talking, watched by
London eyes in silent, gleaming London faces. When
she asked whether he had ever been to Rye – she was
going there for the weekend to stay with a friend – they
fell into conversation. For the first time, he heard her
say *day* for *they*, saw her eyes turn from grey to blue
with her changing moods, in the light that shifted
whenever a car passed the plate-glass window. She
stood turned towards him in the summer heat, her face
raised to his, and with his own eyes he saw in her a
quality that he had not seen before in anyone – a
connectedness, as if there was no gap between herself
and the world.

A month after that first meeting they moved in
together, renting a flat in Cricklewood, where they lay
for hours on the double bed and talked about where
they had been, what they had done. One morning, after
a week or so of lying together this way, she got out of
bed, took down the dusty curtains, washed them by
hand and put them up again. They lay together then in
a new light while she told him about the Poland of her

childhood, Solidarity and the shipyards where her father worked, standing in line for oranges and chocolate, the Sopot seafront in summer and the Zakopane mountains where she had skied in the winters.

'I grew up by the sea, but I love the mountains,' she told him. 'The sea is for lazy people.'

He was troubled by the gap in their ages, although its music was pleasing – her 23 years to his 32. But she told him it was good that he was older, he could lead the way. At times he was frightened to touch her, fearing that he might do something to change how she saw him or alter her view of the city where they lay, side by side on cloudy August afternoons, trading stories. Her past was so different to his own south London upbringing; whenever he talked about his childhood, mundane middleclass predicaments emerged in a whine and he cut himself off. If he tried to dramatise certain scenes where he had played the troubled soul or a rebel defeated by circumstance, she would only laugh and roll her eyes. She had her own understanding of him, which had nothing to do with the past. She was smart, a graduate in international relations from the LSE – her thinking was still fresh, not soured by years of disillusion. In the way she looked at things and spoke there was something eastern and exotic, as if she brought with her a mystique lost in time, left on the wayside in the exodus of ethnic Poles from Vilnius after the war – a clearness with something at the heart of it, like a piece of amber found on a Baltic beach.

He was bound to Karina by many things, but most of all by how differently she saw him from how others had seen him. Friends and girlfriends had sometimes been drawn to his impulsiveness; they would stand off and watch from a distance whenever he broke out of his reserve to do something reckless, like dangling from a fire escape or climbing to the top of a crane, drunk, in the middle of the night. They would stay on the ground and watch him climb, waiting to see if he would fall, avoiding his eye when he came down again, returned to earth. He had been with someone for a while who liked that side of him less, who persuaded him to see a therapist – and he had gone for one session, where he learned something about himself that he tried to forget. He could be reckless, but he could never set out with the intention of doing something brave; he could only allow himself in the moment to do something dangerous. That was just who he was; he had always been that way. But that first summer with Karina, he thought it was possible for him to be other things as well. Before Karina, no one had loved him for his gentleness or stillness – qualities that he had always despised in himself, in the belief that when he was sober he was simply timid and diffident. She loved his innerness and told him that she loved it; she loved his quiet passion, she said, apparently unaware that she was its only cause.

For a while, they forgot that there was anything beyond themselves; their love fell between them and the world like a curtain, leaving the world silent and dark. When she asked him to take her to his favourite places or introduce her to people he knew, he told her that it was all irrelevant now. None of the places he had passed through or the people who had taken up and discarded him, none of his previous missteps counted for anything anymore; together they had wiped it all away. They did not listen to the radio or watch TV: the history through which they lived went unnoticed, while the seasons grew huge and super-real, like giant dayglo images – summer a gold bar, shedding spurs of colour, autumn a rain-swept zenith, winter both endless and over in the blink of an eye. Then spring came, but Carl saw little of it apart from blossom in neighbouring gardens, a sky that moved through shades of blue and her grey eyes, reflecting it all back to him. Spring's bright, spear-like immediacy at times became too poignant; he spent a few minutes of every afternoon gazing into the sun, blinding himself to the flux.

Karina lived on the proceeds of black market labour, keeping up her student visa through sleight of hand, and Carl admired her fearlessness and head for detail – but he knew how stressful she found it to treat each day in England as if it were the first, as if she had only just arrived and had no footing. Polish people were used to playing the system, she told him, from decades of dealing with corrupt officials behind counters, but the system here was just as frightening in its implications. The English feared chaos, but then they brought it on themselves at every turn, too complacent or lethargic to impose any order. Even so, they might catch up with her at any moment, and then she would be deported – and if that happened, she and Carl would be forced to live apart, when it had taken them all this time to find each other. When she said such things, he would see again her love for him, feel his significance to her like a shadow overhead from which he had to run. But he did not run; he held himself still, froze until the feeling passed.

Summer turned to autumn again, and the rain set in. Karina often came home soaked through, walking from the station after waitressing in town. She would peel off her clothes and let them fall to the floor in a wet clump, get into bed beside him and shiver. One night she suggested that he buy a secondhand car – then he could pick her up from the station, and she would not catch all these colds. She was taken aback when he told her that he had never learned to drive, as if she had just discovered that he was lacking a limb. It was around this time that she began to pick fault with him for things about the flat, little features of their life that annoyed her, and he saw that their idyll could not last without some adjustments on his part. He had never intended to learn to drive, but perhaps it was a good idea. Living a hand-to-mouth existence, as he had for many years, he was used to looking for ways to add to his income; if he could drive, perhaps he could work as a removals man or make deliveries, maybe even run a cab.

So he borrowed money from his aunt for lessons, without telling Karina where the money came from. She tended to credit him with more assets than he had, no doubt finding it hard to believe that in over ten years of working in London he had failed to put anything by. When he tried to confess, when he told her that he really was penniless, she only said that he was too clever to stay that way forever; one day he would find his place in the world, and the money would come – not much, perhaps, but enough.

His aunt as she wrote him the cheque remarked that she was not a bottomless purse; he had paid for the loan with his dignity, but at first it seemed worth it. The mechanics of driving did not come naturally to him, but the struggle with something so purely practical came as a relief after a lifetime of wrestling with ideas he barely understood. Even so, he found that he could romanticise driving just as he romanticised other aspects of his daily life – his failure to make his mark, his inability to finish anything he started, even his poverty. While he fumbled the clutch on a steep incline, he would think of Neal Cassady behind the wheel of his

Cadillac, James Dean on the road to Paso Robles or the great Juan Manuel Fangio, whose daring was always rewarded, who was admired and respected even by his kidnappers. At the end of every lesson on a Saturday morning, he would come home and make her laugh with his tales of negotiating a roundabout with five exits, or overtaking a bus.

'You're so good at telling stories, Carl,' she said. 'You could make a living out of it.' And it was true that he had a gift, for which he had never found much use, for turning everyday events into something more than they were on the surface.

In the ambivalent light of that second summer, fraught with showers and ridiculous winds that came out of nowhere and tailed off at sunset, they walked hand in hand to the minimarket, where she bought apples and pears and a lottery ticket. They would go home, lie down together and lose themselves in each other for hours that seemed to last an instant – and afterwards, lying awake, he was often overcome with terror. Even as he lay beside her, emptied out in ecstasy, fear would grip him so hard that it stopped his breathing; she moved her lips across him, not seeing somehow that he lay petrified and breathless in the anticipation of loss. He had spent years steering clear of this scenario, fleeing at any hint that his need for the person he was with might turn so fierce, become so out of control. Would he have spoken to her at all, if he had known that twelve months down the line they would be so essential to one another?

He failed his first driving test, making countless small mistakes and one or two big ones. When he failed a second time, it came as a shock; he could not remember what he had done wrong. Karina assured him that it was not so important – he had tried his best, and now he could drop it – while he slapped the walls with the palms of his hands and shouted that he was too old to learn, he could not do what other men did, not even something as simple as driving a car. But he could not just give up on the idea; passing the test seemed necessary to their future in a way he could not have explained. So he took more cash from his aunt and bought more lessons – and at the start of summer, close to the anniversary of their first meeting, he tried again.

On the afternoon when he came home from his third failure, he found Karina lying on the bed in tears while their landlord sat in the kitchen, running through the inventory. Carl had never seen her so crestfallen; she had a resilience to catastrophe beyond his means, but their luck had changed so rapidly that even she was thrown. The week before she had fallen out with another waitress over something small and unimportant, and that morning her boss had phoned to say they were letting her go. A few minutes after the call, their landlord had dropped by to tell them he was selling the building, with a month's notice – and by that morning's post her passport had come back with no extension of her visa.

Under another star, none of these things would have happened, or they might have happened one at a time, in some way that was easier to manage. But they had all happened on the same day – and they seemed all the more cataclysmic to Carl because she had tried to warn him that they could not go on forever simply hoping for the best. He had not wanted to hear her warnings or to face all the complications that might come their way; now they were not fears anymore but facts, and he could only stare at them, willing them to disappear.

In their remaining weeks in Cricklewood, he went over in his mind again and again the events that had led up to where they were now, looking for the point when it had gone wrong, while Karina talked about packing her bags. And then she packed her bags. This was at the end of July, soon after his 33rd birthday; they had been together for just over a year. He had never been a decisive person; it was a problem with his driving that he never knew whether to hang back or overtake, slow as he approached a junction or try to make the light. He sat in their dismantled kitchen and watched her pack, then watched her call a taxi and helped carry her bags to the car. He went with her to Heathrow, hugged her at the gate and watched her fly away.

He saw her plane become a silver dot in the sky, then trailed back into town on the underground and sat in a cafe on Charing Cross Road, where he leafed through the *Evening Standard*. For the next fortnight his things were in storage, and he slept on friends' floors. It was hard to find a place to live in London that did not have some sad association with a previous age. Tooting was cheap, but he had grown up in the area, and the thought of going back to where he started with nothing to show for it was terrible – nor could he face a return to Brixton or Kentish Town or anywhere near the Westway, scenes of other disappointments, mediocre disasters that had not mattered as much. Finally, aware that it was an act of self-loathing, he hunted out a room in Cricklewood, a short step away from the flat he had shared with Karina. He had to punish himself for being the way he was, so easily intimidated by things that other men could deal with without even thinking – so he would make himself walk down the same streets and taste his defeat undiluted.

Summer drifted on; every week he got a letter from her with an eagle on the stamp, always about everyday stuff – conversations with her family, a dress she had made for herself or her new job in a small private school as an English teacher. He could not place these events, or bring himself to believe in her routine of shopping, planning for meals or visiting cousins. Gdańsk could only be the city of her childhood, the one she had told him about, with its sepia walls covered in bullet marks and portraits of unwanted leaders. Her new life seemed fantastical and unrelated to the one they had lived together; it was easier to think of her as someone who had gone to another world, who was no longer entirely alive.

On an oppressive morning in late August, travelling to work on the bus and skimming through her latest letter, he wondered if it would not be better for both of them to lose touch altogether. The upper deck was hot and airless, people around him were agitated and tense; no one wanted to be where they were at that moment, on a slow-moving double-decker in the stubborn heat. He did not want to be there, either; only the fact that he was born and bred in London had kept him there all those years after leaving college. Until he met Karina, he had disliked its sprawling anonymity, hated its extraordinary drabness, but with an intensity never quite strong enough to make him leave. Over the year they spent together, the city had appeared to him like a network of backstreets, secretive and sensuous, a haven where he felt safe and loved. He understood that this was a place he could never return to – but maybe, if they stopped writing to one another, he might adapt again to the city's stale afterlife, go back to living as if they had never met.

He watched as the weeks passed, believing that a sufficient number of days would allow his craving for Karina to diminish. He gazed at women on the street and fantasised about how they might replace her in his feelings, if he let them. But he did nothing about it, did nothing at all but come home from work and drink wine in his room, in the communal flat he shared with four others. As an experiment, he failed to answer one or two of her letters – but then he could not bear the distressed tone in her urgent notes, scribbled in breaks between classes, asking why she had not heard from him for so long. At the end of September, he spent a fortune on a phone call just to reassure her that his feelings for her were the same as ever. After that, he would sometimes ring her in the evenings, holding the phone from his ear to distance himself from her longing and despair, her anger. Her voice was often full of a rage he had never encountered when they were living together, a fury not with fate for coming between them but with Carl for allowing it. But more often in those late-night calls he heard an attachment to him that he found appalling and incredible. How could it be real, to feel so much for one person? How could they have let it happen?

On a night in the middle of October, as her voice swung through the now familiar arc from anger to love, he lay and eavesdropped on his housemates as they played Twister with their girlfriends in the cramped lounge – Twister or Risk, perhaps. They were strangers from another generation; they found him tragic and comic, as he knew from the incautious remarks they made when they thought he was out. He listened into their chat, holding onto the handset but drifting so far that it was a while before he realised she was repeating his name over and over, as if she sensed his remoteness. 'Karina, Karina,' he said in return. Over the phone that night he told her that he loved her, just as he used to tell her so face to face, every day, when that was their life. Now he said it to convince himself that what they had had together was still kept somewhere – buried and practically useless, perhaps, but intact and unspoiled even so. He promised her that he was only waiting for some windfall or inspiration to reunite them, as if the bad luck that had separated them might simply be reversed.

'But why wait?' she said, 'why not just *come*?' There was really nothing to stop him from joining her in Gdańsk; he could sleep on her parents' couch while they saved for an apartment of their own. She had found work easily enough as a teacher, within weeks of getting there – surely he would, too.

Of course she had said such things before, over the months of separation, and each time he had laughed as if she were just being fanciful – or, if pressed, he made a list of sensible objections: he could not speak the language, he had no relevant skills, he would know nobody in Gdańsk apart from her. He could not admit the real reason – that going after her again when he had already lost her once seemed absurdly hazardous, like climbing the Centre Point tower with toy magnets and rubber bands.

She appeared to accept his reasoning, that on some practical basis it was just too difficult – and each time she suggested that he should join her out there, she did so with a little less conviction. That night it sounded as if she was saying it almost by rote, and he longed for her former certainty. He craved her need for him and her attachment to him, even while it horrified him, even while he heard it diminish from call to call. Of course, there was a certain irony to the situation, because in his former life, when reckless acts came so easily to him, he might just have flung himself into the situation; it was Karina herself who had changed him, made him more careful and circumspect. She excused herself and hung up – for her, it was long after midnight – and he finished a second bottle of wine, tipping him into sleep. In the moments before he slept, he prayed to the dark, to the noxious autumn air that blew in through his bedroom window to bring it back, that old ability just to close his eyes and jump.

In the week that followed their conversation, he discovered a rationale for flying to see her at least: he would go over there, make love to her one last time and come home again; then they would be done. There was something ugly and sad about his intention, but the ugliness and sadness were as if in shadow, obscured. When he thought of his journey there and back, allowing the sequence of events to play out in his mind, his imagination was held at the border. He saw only darkness after the plane took off, time coming to a halt as soon as he left England. So he settled on a course of action – and then London itself behaved as if it was bent on his departure. The highways were just wind tunnels, cold winds sucked him down soulless boulevards full of faceless people, grey roads lined with reflective glass in which his own hunched figure appeared reflected, bent and indistinct, just another cipher in the street. It was as if the city was trying to show him that it was right for him to go; whatever happened, he must leave.

When they spoke again a week later and he told her that he had made up his mind to come over and take a look, she sounded delighted then doubtful, puzzled no doubt by his sudden change of heart, then delighted again. They fixed on a date in late November; she told him to buy a winter coat, that in Poland he could not depend on the anorak he wore all the year round, and a hat that covered his ears, and a pair of boots. He bought none of those things; he scraped together the price of a plane ticket, borrowing again from his aunt. It was the last time, she told him – and she wondered aloud why he had nothing in the bank for a rainy day. He could not give her a good answer to this question – but it was not as if he had not worked. For more than ten years since leaving university he had ploughed the rows in office after office, subsisting on his weekly salary, spending anything spare on alcohol, books, trips to the cinema. He understood now that there was something else he should have done – that it was wrong not to have any money. He had despised the material world because he could not grasp the mechanism that seemed to work for everyone else, because he himself seemed to have no substance. It had always felt to him that there was no place for him in that world – but he knew it was strange for that to be the case, when everybody else seemed to find one. What was true, he thought, on the evening when he set off to see her, as he counted his coins on the bar in Heathrow and eyed the upturned bottles of London Gin and Teachers, was that the year he had spent with Karina had been the only time in his life when he felt he belonged.

The sun had set by the time he landed in Gdańsk; his mind was dimmed by the Bloody Marys he had drunk on the plane. Heavy snow had fallen at his destination throughout the day and his flight had been delayed. Karina was there to meet him, wearing a black Russian fur hat, painfully altered in some way that he could not pin down, yet just as painfully the same woman he had talked to in the queue at the coach station on that hot day over a year before. She threw her arms around him, laughing and crying, her joy at seeing him again so extreme that it was almost repellent. He felt it too, but like a blade he wanted to thrust away from him as far as he could before it cut him again.

But then they stepped back from one another, and the difference in her became apparent again – or not in her alone but in them, in the way they stood side by side, the way they matched up. The match had once been perfect, and now there was a gap; he looked at her, wondering whether she felt it too and knowing that she must, it was unavoidable. But she smiled up at him from under the black fur of her hat, her smile tremulous and fragile, and he looked down at the snow.

Karina had come alone to pick him up in her father's Volkswagen. She had always been able to drive – she just could not drive in England, where officially she did not exist. England seemed suddenly far off, as if left behind in some other zone with its separate realities. Perhaps it was the drop in temperature to five below zero after London's dull mildness – perhaps the change in ambience was what made his country seem so distant, remote but hard-edged and heavy with facts compared to this cold white dream. The air was thinner than the air at home, and tinged with wood smoke. On reaching the car, as he leaned in to put his bag on the back seat and before he straightened up and she could see his face, he suggested that he should take the wheel. Then he turned and found her pressed against him and felt her warmth through all their layers, felt her beating heart and her intense animation, until at last she drew back and looked up at him with what he took for understanding. But of course she did understand him – she had always understood, always known him better than anyone else had. This was what he saw in that strange foreign light, the dreamlike and monochrome world where they stood together.

'So you passed the test in the end,' she said simply. 'I didn't know, Carl.' And she handed him the keys.

The airport was on the outskirts of Gdańsk, several miles inland from the sea. It was a while before they left behind the open fields, large blankets of snow turning blue in the dusk and dotted with new projects, signs of capitalist enterprise, fresh sides of concrete in a terrain that was otherwise timeless, undated. After ten minutes they hit the road into town. He had not driven a car since the day he failed his third test, the day when she heard that she had to leave England. He remembered the basics, of course, but it was a memory of something that he had never known how to do very well. He had always been a nervous driver, as his examiners had pointed out, overly hesitant, easily distracted by other drivers' manoeuvres. Karina said little, only telling him where to turn.

When they stopped at the first junction, confusing and snowbound and with the signs all iced over, signs that in any case he would not have been able to interpret, he glanced at her, and she returned his look. He saw that she knew he was lying; it was there in the calm set of her beautiful, open face – the knowledge that he was not safe to drive, and that the further he drove them the more danger they were in. He was convinced that she knew in that instant when their eyes met as the car stood at the lights, its engine thrumming through the handbrake, which he held in an unfamiliar hand. The lights changed, and he moved off again.

The darkness was weirdly underlit by expanses of fresh snow on either side of the road, a white space marked with isolated trees when they were still out among the fields and then, closer to town, broken up by building sites, wrapped in swathes of dirty plastic cladding that snapped about in the wind. The highway into town was covered in frozen patches and flanked here and there by houses built between the wars, large wooden cabins with smoking chimneys and rickety fences that kept in chickens, dogs tied up on long ropes, sometimes a goat or a pig. Looking out as they passed, he remembered a story she had once told him about her grandfather slaughtering a pig that had been fed all winter until it was ready; she had stood on the steps that led down to her parents' garden and watched it happen – and he saw the pig's blood scatter across the snow, red on white against grey plaster at the back of the house in the dying light. The land of her childhood was all around him, and for a moment he lived there; but he said nothing, only went on driving between the flat levels of whiteness, the almost buried hedges.

Karina put out a hand and stroked the side of his face, and he relaxed. The steering wheel slid icily in his grip as they coasted down the road that ran into the north side of town. The outskirts were left behind and the suburbs began, dun-coloured clumps of tower blocks with numbers written on their sides in tall blue figures, children running along icy pathways between them under the sallow glow from streetlamps. At intervals along the pavements were squat kiosks selling cigarettes and chocolate, newspapers and magazines, overhung by massive billboards, many of them featuring women's faces, some round and pale and open like Karina's, advertising items of furniture, ocean cruises, new apartments.

Between the mounds of blackened slush piled up in the gutters, the car seemed to move of its own accord, noiselessly over fresh snow. Now they were closer to the city and had left behind the dark glow of the fields, a dazzling array of illuminations came at them from the simple but gaudy storefronts – and then there were the lights in tower block windows high up in the sky, tail lights of other cars, red and green traffic lights. These lights and signs were all alien and incomprehensible to him, bewildering his senses; he saw before him a series of colours, brilliant but random, coming close and then abruptly vanishing, leaving him no time to think. As they approached a junction where the road crossed a tramway he began to slow, taking in the four-way street ahead, the pattern of tram tracks and pedestrian crossings, taking in the fact that he understood none of it – and he was aware of nothing more in that moment, other than her hand on his cheek and her face turned towards him, her look of acceptance and love.

The Sixth of November

Home again after five days away, he let himself into the flat, dropped his bags and flung open the garden door, letting in the cold November air. From a mile away he heard the faint roar of surf ripping at the shingle. At the start of autumn, gale-force winds had made the waves tear in, stripping stones from the beach and hurling them at the varicoloured huts that had been there for decades, smashing some of them to pieces. The storm was just coming to an end when he set off with Shannon and Dixie through a landscape of branches torn from trees and the trees themselves lying in ditches, on the long drive north to Scotland.

Now Shannon and Dixie were gone, the wind had died down and it was quiet again, with a lonely kind of silence. His body was stiff from driving – his arms felt cemented to his shoulders; he turned on a light and thought of destroying all that awful serenity with some loud music, anything with enough bass to shake the walls. Looking around his rented flat, he experienced the sharp disconnect that he sometimes felt between himself and this place where he had lived for several years, crammed full of his bits and pieces yet still not really him.

He was brought up short in his walk across the room to his old stereo by the pile of post that sat on the kitchen table, where his landlord had left it. Flicking through the subscription renewal reminders and offers of credit, he came to an envelope addressed by hand. The letter inside was also handwritten, and the writing was familiar, but he could not place it until he looked down at her name at the bottom of the page – and then he had to take a seat before he lost his balance, as if some invisible thing had come along and given him a hard push. His eye moved back to the top of the page, to the London address; he felt a presentiment, like a nudge from a messenger come too late – and he thought of that afternoon a few months ago, in August, when Shannon had so casually shown him on the screen of her laptop the cottage she had bought. He had the same feeling now of something taking place beyond his ken, a change that he had not foreseen and would not be able to avoid.

Dear Nick,

I will give this to you straight – I am dying. I have written a round robin email to most of the people I know, but I thought I should write to you personally. God, this is so strange, Nico. I feel like a character in one of those stupid epistolary novels we were meant to read in college. Clarissa, was it, or Pamela? I never even got halfway.

I only have a few months left. I know that we never became to each other what we thought we might become, but you are still my oldest friend, and I wanted you to have your own letter.

Much love,

Olivia

He flipped the page away from him so that it landed under the table. After an instant in which any thoughts were obliterated by his foreboding becoming suddenly so concrete, so visible, he dashed through the back door and down the steps into the garden. Struggling for breath, almost tripping over plant pots and crashing into the shaky fence at the end, he leaned his weight against the one stable strut. He breathed in cold night air and let his eyes respond to the partial darkness, his ears take in the silence broken only by the occasional car speeding up Viaduct Road or train pulling into the station half a mile away. This partial silence and near darkness was real and the letter just some bizarre fabrication by somebody pretending to be Olivia, using her name. And even if she had written it herself there was room for doubt, since she had always been such a hypochondriac, had always given shape to her days through imaginary sicknesses, exaggerations of minor conditions. Whenever they met, she would devote a good half hour of each encounter to talking about her migraines, the tendonitis in her knees from too much jogging, some ailment that caused her to run to the toilet every five minutes. Each time he saw her, the most recent complaint would be replaced by a new one.

He willed himself to doubt what he had read, but in the end the silence won out – it was too much. In the cold still air even the seagulls were quiet. The cracked ribs of the crumbling fence shone in the light of a quarter moon. A single dog barked from the garden two along – Dixie's friend, a chocolate Labrador called Brandon, stood in the middle of his lawn no doubt with his nose in the air, testing it for foxes. Otherwise the late evening had no interruptions; the sky was clear of planes or satellites or even stars, due to all the light pollution, and quite empty of the display that he remembered as a child, when the night after Bonfire Night was nearly as busy with leftover fireworks as the night itself had been, when the glorious failure of the Gunpowder Plot was commemorated in flashes and bangs.

He abruptly turned his back on the night's insistent hush and went inside – but his flat, full as it was of all his stuff, seemed so vacant for a crazy second that it felt as if not only Shannon and Dixie but he himself had moved out. On the spike of this transcendent loneliness, he knew that he had to see Olivia, to make sure of something, although it was Sunday and the hour was late. There would be one more train to London he could catch – he could not bear to get back in the car again, after all the driving hours of the past few days. Without bothering to turn out the lights, he grabbed his coat and house keys.

As soon as he closed the door behind him, he missed Dixie at the end of her leash. She was Shannon's dog, gone north with Shannon; there was never any question that she would stay with him. It made no difference that they had chosen her together, made an impulse buy together while on holiday, made no difference that it was he who had shelled out for her at the puppy farm in Kerry, 75 euros from his own wallet. It was irrelevant, in the end, that he had done nearly all the 'sit' and 'heel' stuff, doled out all the treats. Dixie had always been Shannon's dog. But only yesterday, as he drove away from that poky little cabin in the Highlands, Shannon's dog had chased him for half a mile down the lane – and when at last she fell behind, he had to park up by the lake and sit with his head on the steering wheel until he was calm enough to drive on.

If Dixie had been with him now, she would have taken his mind off the grainy details of the journey, all the dirt and decay on the last train up to London, bits of crap and beer spills; she would have distracted him from the seamy transition as the train crossed from Sussex into Surrey. As a child of the satellite towns, he had grown up on the estates that the line overlooked. It was only now, in middle age, that he had come to appreciate their extraordinary cultural sparsity, finding something soothing and ascetic in the faceless rows of identical dwellings. Whenever Shannon complained of their ugliness, he would tell her sincerely that he saw something magical in a landscape that had so little magic in it – and she would groan and roll her eyes and turn back to her book.

He wondered what Shannon was doing right now, at this moment, in her new home. He could imagine her putting books on shelves, hanging pictures, gazing out over the loch, but he had no real idea how any of it would make her feel. Over the time they had been together, he had gradually lost all contact with her inner life. It was as if she was a character in a long-running TV series, rewritten every season to keep the audience interested – the ardent lover of their early days crudely recast as the clinging, needy Shannon of the year that followed, then rewritten again as the bitter Shannon who saw broken promises everywhere, then for the final season as the Shannon who was hardly ever in, who busied herself at weekend workshops, where she learned to throw pots, weave rugs and tell stories.

And what was he to Shannon? It was difficult to tell, but he suspected that he had appeared just as generic to her as she had to him, as a *man* outlined so vaguely that almost any actor could have played him. Certainly, she had never understood that Dixie was not just a dog to him but a kind of canine Bodhisattva, who had led him through the hard straits into middle age. Surely she had no notion of his attachment on that summer afternoon when she came to find him in the bedroom, where he lay reading something she had left by the bedside – they had gone on sharing a bed for convenience's sake. She had perched on the edge of the same bed where in their time they had acted out all that passion, rage and indifference, and showed him on the screen of her laptop a photograph of a cottage in the west of Scotland. It was really no more than a shack, its eaves so close to the ground that the *For Sale* sign nudged the moss hanging from its roof.

'Look,' she said, 'there are actual *goats*. The goats are thrown in for free.'

He had got it at once – she was leaving him and taking her dog, she did not want him for a goatherd – and he had felt infinitely sorry for her as she sat beside him and clicked through the pix of her ideal home. If there was one thing he knew about her, it was that she was never one thing for more than half a year. For a while she would play the role of hermit, making her jewellery and spinning her yarns and walking her little bitch until some other real thing came along. She would blow around the world forever like a balloon, catching on branches and pylons and slowly deflating until she burst. But when she looked up from the screen, he saw a similar sorrow reflected back at him – her pity for him for being so stuck, so rooted to the spot.

None of this was ever spoken out loud, of course; they had got past the point of reciting their lines. Everything was communicated in gestures and glances that might have meant anything or nothing, most of the time, even to the notional viewer who had been closely following their story. Only at the last minute had she agreed to let him drive her up to Fort William, for the sake of closure as she put it. On the way they had argued, or at least for a few miles that spanned a junction or two he had kept up a one-sided harangue, spelling out why the dog was his, how much he had paid for her, how he had trained her for hours and walked her in all weathers. Shannon had raised her eyes from the map – she still used maps, she was old-fashioned that way – raised her eyebrows and shrugged; and that was all.

By the time the train left East Croydon and was making its final approach to Victoria, he was beginning to grasp the strangeness of his decision to come into London so late, to visit Olivia without any kind of notice. Was he really planning on ringing her bell after midnight? It made no sense – but turning back was unthinkable, and some strange imperative drove him on. He had been to see her in Lambeth on occasions over the years, in the house he was headed for now; always more decisive and realistic than him, she had bought when the time was right, embedding herself in the inner city when that was the thing to do. In the past decade their meetings had become more sporadic, and usually based around food. She had developed an oddly pedantic obsession with the art of cooking after leaving university, possibly in reaction to their mildly bohemian existence, living out of tins for three years in college. Their occasional encounters would leave him stuffed, wise to the joys of duck eggs, braised celeriac and capers but otherwise undernourished, hungry for the simple things they had savoured together in the beginning.

Getting off at Victoria and walking across the barren concourse onto Vauxhall Bridge Road, he felt a sharp pain in his temple, like a mental stitch. Thinking was important to him, or at any rate it was the only thing he would do until it tired him out; he thought and thought, but his thinking rarely led to any insight or awakening, rarely even to a thought about an awakening. He paused and hit his head with the flat of his hand, merely jolting the pain, then carried on across Vauxhall Bridge, which was deserted; there was nobody around to watch his struggle. It was cold, or coldish, and no one else was on foot – they were all on the buses that sailed past at that normal, reckless London speed. But he could not be bothered to fiddle about with timetables and stops; it was always easier to walk.

Leaving the bridge, he was met with the city's acrid stench, its early winter smokiness, so unlike the sea air he was used to. He started down Kennington Lane, then turned off to make his way through the Vauxhall Pleasure Gardens, so dark and empty, hoping to spook himself into the desired epiphany. Nothing came up to interrupt his thinking about this spontaneous and inexplicable pilgrimage – but after a while this very nothing took up all the space in his mind, until it was a black space streaked here and there with red and green, electric blue and magnesium white. As he approached his goal, the fireworks increased in number, but always at a distance, in colourful traces far away above tower blocks. There were not that many of them, but still it was happening: the tradition dying out in the provinces was still alive in the city where it had all started.

Keeping his eyes on the sky, he passed Pedlars Park and went almost the whole length of Lambeth Walk before turning into Olivia's street. Few people passed him on the way, and those he saw hung back in the shadows that proliferated wildly, thrown everywhere by the hard white light of the streetlamps. On Walnut Tree Walk itself, a toneless radiance shone from the redbrick fronts of terraced houses. He was alone, as far as he could tell; no one came or went, and he resisted the temptation to look at his watch – he knew that it was far too late to drop in on anyone. Olivia's windows were unlit and curtained, apart from one on the first floor, where perhaps her husband was awake.

Although he had seen her getting married only two years before, it was hard to remember that Olivia had a husband – hard to reconcile her married state with the bad fairy she had always been at other people's weddings, where she would make mocking remarks *sotto voce* about the ceremony, the institution itself, sometimes the groom and bride. When she went ahead and got married herself, he could only look on it as an extension of her old contempt into a strange kind of joke – strange, but all the same typical of the girl he had met in college when they were eighteen. Night after night they had stayed up, lying together in a single bed, fully dressed but with arms and legs entwined, reading satirical passages to one another from essays they would never dare hand over to their tutors, which they laughingly binned on the way to their tutorial.

After college, released into the fresh chaos that was London in the 1990s, there was a year or two when they spent all their weekends in each other's shared houses, before she bought the place in Lambeth. During that year or two, which he recalled as a series of frictionless highs and bottomless lows, their early innocence evolved into a growing diffidence. They became self-conscious with each other, looked away at key moments – a remoteness sprang up between them. She began to deride their simple connection, how they always greeted each other as if it was the first time they had met; she poked fun at their small kindnesses to each other, their present-giving. At the end of that year or two, they had parted company with an ironic agreement never to look back or rehearse any of it, never to speak of it again. And they had separated that way because, at the close of a long summer afternoon after a bottle of white wine or two, he had asked her whether it really made sense for them to live in separate houses. That had been enough to tip her out of diffidence into renunciation.

Now he stood outside her door, looking at his watch while the time passed. He had not waited like this, gazing up at dark windows and wondering whether to knock, since he was a student. Lost in thought and undecided, he failed to notice the boy sneaking up on him until he saw the Chinese banger dumped between his feet. In the instant before it went off – a moment weirdly stretched, seeming to take in other moments – he stared into the face of the rangy teenager who had put it there. The boy stared back at him, grinning. Then, when he lifted his foot to kick the thing away it exploded, he stumbled forwards into the boy's arms, and they both fell heavily into the gutter. The kid, lying underneath him, shook with helpless and triumphant laughter, as if they had practised this trick a thousand times without getting it right and tonight, at last, they had nailed it. He pushed himself off the tarmac and was still struggling to his feet and shouting down at the kid when Olivia's door opened, and Olivia herself peered down the tunnel of light that fell from her hallway. She turned and called behind her in a muffled voice – to her husband, he supposed – and then peered out again into the night.

'Sorry, man,' said the boy, who stood in the road and looked up at him through a fringe of dark hair. 'Just trying to wake you up – you seemed like you were dozing.' Then the kid took a step back and broke into a run, his footsteps drumming southwards through the quiet night towards Elephant.

'Nicky?' Olivia called from her doorway. 'Is that you?'

A tingling still rang in his body from the little explosion as he went up the steps to her Georgian doorway and embraced her clumsily, dazzled by the hallway light. She stood half a head shorter than him, in a white dressing gown and moccasins. A headscarf, wrapped around her head, isolated the livid, freckled moon of her face. He saw that she had not exaggerated her condition – the growth of every misgrown cell was written across her features, which were so altered that he would not have known her in passing.

'Same old Nico,' she said, as he let go. 'You leave me alone for years and then turn up at midnight with a bang.' She gestured behind her and along the well-lit passageway, where a man in navy pyjamas clutched the banister, blinking. 'Remember Clive?' she said, 'the poor dolt I married?'

His ears continued to buzz from the detonation, and in his aural confusion he thought that Olivia might be playing a trick on him; he even believed momentarily that this was not the same man he had seen her marry, that there had been another wedding since to which he had not been invited and this was her second husband. Picturing Clive in a morning suit instead of pyjamas, he recalled the noon wedding at Lambeth Town Hall, the sunlight dropping carelessly onto the pavement and the photographer, making room for a group portrait, who fell off the kerb and was almost hit by a bus speeding down Brixton Hill. Olivia, of course, had wept with laughter, giving her face in the wedding album a perfect mix of tears and smiles.

She sat down across the table from him in the tungsten glare of her kitchen spots while her husband, lingering by the sideboard, waved an opened bottle of red wine vaguely in his direction. Clive was some sort of NHS apparatchik, he recalled; in this setting he was oddly indistinct, his sandy head blending with a landscape of tasteful Swedish pine. Olivia vamped her amazement when he turned down the offer.

'Really? No wine for Nico?'

'I don't really drink anymore.'

'Well,' she said, looking at the table, 'I missed *that* change.'

'Yes,' said Nick, 'it's been a while since we spoke.'

Olivia smiled and looked almost beyond him, in touch with a mystery he could not even see as an outline, her round moon face full of a new knowledge. 'I'm touched that you came as soon as you heard, as if I might disappear in a puff of smoke.' She gave her husband a conspiratorial look as he stood leaning against the side. The shared experience of her dying had brought them closer, no doubt; their togetherness felt like something in the room, something vital and alive. 'You don't need to worry about how late it is,' she said. 'I don't sleep much at night. Do I, dear?' Clive's pale eyes focused on the side of her face, then drifted off around the kitchen. 'Clive stays up with me all night and goes to work in the morning. He's exhausted.'

She talked for an hour about hospitals and tests, about an operation with no positive outcome, the other cancer patients she had met along the way, funny things that doctors had said to her – and it was after all a little like the way she used to talk about her ailments in the past, except that now as she went on she began to wilt, turned paler, and her eyes stood out of her head. When she came to the end of her story, it was after one in the morning. Somewhere in the distance, bangers still went off, Roman candles shot into the cold, black sky. 'But

Nick,' she said, 'I haven't heard from you for so long. I have no idea what's going on in your life.' And she gave him a look that he realised, with a savage jolt, only she could give him, with all that had gone on between them, the history of their years.

He was seized with a great reluctance to tell her anything about the way he had spent the past twelve months, how his girlfriend had left him and how it had changed almost nothing – all this while Olivia had been traipsing in and out of hospital, while something was coming to an end for her, an end that she could see approaching. All he could see, when he opened his mouth, was a dog; so he told her about Dixie, about her obsession with rodents and her catlike propensity to sit in the lap of anyone who let her. He told her about the dog, but he did not say that she had gone, or where she had gone, made no attempt to unravel the tangled tale of Shannon and how she had left him for a field of goats. Now was not the time, in any case: Olivia's eyes were dimming – she was fading out. He allowed himself another quarter of an hour before standing to leave.

She came with him alone to the doorstep, leaving Clive to wash up, to wipe the sides, and followed him down the path to the gate. 'It was good of you to come all this way, Nick,' she said, putting a hand on his arm. He failed to respond – he looked away – and when he looked back she was smiling. 'So this is it. You're okay for the drive home?'

'Sure,' he said, knowing that if he told her the truth she would insist on him staying. Around them, the night seemed both huge and suffocating, a vast dome full of poisoned air. His question when it came rose up from an old part of him, a lost time. 'What did you mean, exactly, in your letter? That bit about becoming what we might have become?' He took a breath. 'I mean, were you just being nice?'

She looked down at her watch, hanging off her wrist like a broken twig from a silver birch, then looked up again into his face, putting both her hands on his chest; she shifted her weight from one foot to the other, but kept her eyes on his. 'You remember all the hours we spent back at uni, analysing one paragraph of a novel or one verse of a poem? You remember how in the end we always concluded that it could be interpreted in all kinds of ways?'

'Yes, of course I remember.'

'That was what I wanted you to do with my letter, Nick, take your own meaning from it. Not come to me for a gloss.'

He shrugged. 'I suppose I'm not too hot on meaning anymore.'

She sighed and let her head fall, looking down at his feet. 'I've got to be honest with you, Nick – you seem unlike yourself tonight. I'm wondering where he went, the guy I knew.'

'I think we just lost touch, Olivia.'

Shaking her head, still looking down, not meeting his eye she said, 'Maybe we did, Nick, maybe that's what happened.'

For a moment she went almost slack and rested her weight against him, and he could see only the top of her head. If he could have seen her face, he might have said something to dispel the effect of her words. As it was, they hung in the cold air with its heavy scent of toxins; and then she turned suddenly and went inside, closing the door without looking back.

He walked away quickly, zigzagging his way to the river then following the river along the embankment.

By the time he got to Victoria the station gates were closed, locked until four, and he joined a small group of people who sat slumped against the outer wall. A young couple, travelling from Brazil or somewhere like that, kissed as if they were alone together. Along the wall from them was a tiny waiflike girl, exquisite in a Dracula dress, untouched by her surroundings, and along from her a mouthy old soak in a flowerpot hat who crouched on his heels and yakked away at a woman with crazy eyebrows and a crumpled jaw. The eyebrow lady lay sprawled with her arms around a trolley on three wheels, which now and then teetered and spat out its load – cans of soup, ancient issues of *Vogue*, dog biscuits.

Traffic rumbled around the station, roared and farted, sending gusts of foul air across the discoloured facade. Despite the smell and noise, he could not keep his eyes open, and he slept and dreamed of a dog chasing a car that would not stop but went the length of the country in one long ride. Then the dog vanished off somewhere and he was down on the coast at last, driving along London Road and nearly home, crawling solo through a light that was neither dusk nor dawn. The road was empty apart from an old lady who walked towards him down the white line in the centre, laden with plastic bags. He slowed to a halt as she approached, but he could not for some reason get out of the car. He fumbled with the locks and threw himself against the car door – but then he saw rising from the beach a mile away a giant wave.

The wave shot high into the air and towered over the piers and Pavilion – a great wall of filthy water, dense with sand and stones, flecked with fish and seaweed and jetsam. This was his cue, it seemed: all at once the car door swung open and he got out and ran towards the old lady, who carried on walking towards him down the white line without quickening her step, apparently oblivious of the wave that now began its descent. But as he got closer, he saw that she was not an old woman but the young Olivia, dressed up as a bag lady, on her way to a costume party. She kept on coming down the road at the same unhurried pace, with the wave hanging in the air just above and behind her as if frozen, suspended in time. Their eyes met as she staggered theatrically, an old lady's wobble, grinning her satirical grin – and he broke into a run in the hope of reaching her before the wave could sweep her away. But even as she put down her bags, held out her arms in greeting and opened her mouth to call his name, the first white crest closed over her head.

Misfit Power

'How many houses have you lived in called the Rising Sun?'

'Yeah, but how many times have you seen answers blowing in the wind, man?'

'Yeah, well your old mum's a dustman, she wears a dustman's hat.'

'She wears cor blimey trousers, that's for sure.'

'Yeah, and boots.'

'Yeah, panties.'

So it goes on into the night, the gabbing and blathering, mild irony and occasional shows of spite, the dicking around, although each of us has to get up in the morning for his or her own reason. And I see the differences between the boy and girl reasons, more in the way they are expressed than in their substance – boy reasons all heavy and mischievous and monolithic, unaware of what is standing right behind them, girl reasons slightly too thought-out for their own good, balletic and greedy. I watch their tired faces gleam in the tiered candlelight that sheds so much heat in the unheated two-level dosshouse that is where we mainly live, see those candles lean too close and melt each other, so the wax drips in random places along the shelves, spattering bills and empty photo frames, bicycle clips, boxes of matches. No one is willing to call it quits, not Nutmeg with her beautiful hairy arms or

Paula with her endless supply of liquorice allsorts, Coover with his pissy jeans or Frazer with his face like post-adolescent death. And then there is me, Terry, who sees everything and nothing from every angle, not knowing which is which and not wanting to know, since I know in any case that knowing is never going to be much use to me in whatever layer of the universe they come up with next, in these real or unreal worlds.

The music keeps on pouring out of the speakers, cheap and battered old speakers that are not all they should be, just so much crumbling bass and waffling treble. But the music is really what it is all about. We could just stop fucking on about everything and listen to the tunes and it would be enough, for me at least. But when the talk turns serious, to weighty matters of head and spirit, there is no prising the voices away from their subject. The babble attains some gravity, Frazer and Nutmeg battling it out over gods and natures with metaphysical swords, Coover uncovering the worst excesses of his spiritual backlog, his sacred spendthrift ways, Paula stuffing the whole lot in her mouth and spitting it out again in rainbow blues and yellows. And then there is me just sitting, trying to block it all out and hear the sounds behind the noise, no matter how they prod me with their tongues and seek my opinion. They know quite well what I think, I have spelled it out to them enough times: opinions do not mean shit; they are of the moment and die in the moment, like some cheap and tawdry music. So in the end they give up stabbing at my ears and let me drift away.

Then it is Monday, another frigid February morning, and next door the cafe is already open – I can hear the ambient rattle of cutlery and chatter from where I lie on the couch. I am already supposed to be down there doing my shift, but I have slept through the others' morning routines undisturbed. I was sound asleep, in fact, until woken by my dream. Russell and I were standing on the landing of the old house, the one we lived in for the whole of 1989, with Gibson railing away at us through the banisters. I knew that within the parameters of the dream we and our father had come to some wordless agreement to keep those frail, silly struts of wood between us that would not protect a gnat from its own bite, because he had no trust in himself – he needed some symbolic barrier to prevent himself from hurting us, and in the dream the symbol worked. In the logic of the dream, we had agreed to stay behind those bars of shitty processed wood, knowing that if they were not between us he would come at us with his fists. Even within the dream I understood that the frail bars were his death and that our dad, dead so long, only needed to slip into my dreaming mind to come back to life. It was the total insecurity of the situation that made me spring awake and sit bolt upright on the lounge sofa, enraged for the millionth time with Gibson for calling himself a father just because in some dark moment he had spawned me, with myself for being so vulnerable in his eyes, so easy to hit, with my brother for being so out of reach now – for moving to another town, where he can dream his dream alone and not have to hear about mine.

I am still in the dress of the night before, I realise as I sit up on the couch, swing my feet to the floor and feel my head spin a little – but only a little this morning, at least by modern standards, the standards of the year 2000, this first year in a millennium that will never end.

'Only Terry would think it made sense to wear a dress in February,' Coover said last night – and then he grabbed the broom and played it like a guitar, the guitar

164

he cannot play, air strumming and singing along, 'Not sure if you're a boy or a girl.' And for a minute they all joined in on chair legs and tabletops and windowsills, knocking on wood with fingers and palms – because no one in this house plays an actual instrument.

'Some nights it's Saint Teresa,' Frazer announced solemnly, standing with his hands raised in the middle of the scabby carpet, a tin in one of them and a joint in the other, 'some nights it's Sir Terrence.'

'Come on, leave her alone, guys. She's not just some twink, you know,' said Paula – teacherly stern all of a sudden, like the teacher she used to be, unbelievably, until she was struck off or defrocked or whatever they do to teachers when they catch them doing lines in the girls' bogs.

'Are you making fun of me, Rizzo?' I asked her mock plaintively – and they all laughed, and I laughed, because I like it when they laugh at me, it feels good. It may sound a little contradictory, but when they mock me I feel accepted and embraced.

'You can laugh back at us, you know,' Paula pointed out to me once, 'why don't you?' But she is wrong, I really cannot laugh back at them; that kind of mockery is not in my repertoire. And anyway, I would not want to. She did not in the least understand my explanation – that to me my flatmates are like household gods, little demons that I keep in the fireplace, icons that I can rely on. 'You're so weird, Terry,' she said. And I was glad to hear it, because weird in her eyes is a solid positive, and because I need to keep those flimsy bars between myself and whoever – the barrier of weirdness, of unreachably kooky and strange.

But there is the other side to it, too. I am genuinely strange, strange for real, and that is how I like it. I am not just keeping the world at bay – I am keeping me at

165

the centre of myself, the weird mini-me I identify with the most, the freak who has squeezed through so many small spaces, who nobody can quite catch before I slip sylph-like between the fingers of the other dancers, slick from my own sweat and the sweat that drips and drips from the ceiling after hours out on the floor. I can take off almost all my things, get practically naked, and still they have no idea who I am.

I get up now – all these memories and thoughts have taken up, in real time, no more than ten seconds – and cross the floor to the bathroom, where Coover is actually jerking off. He makes no move to stop when I come in to brush my teeth; sitting on the edge of the bath, he beats away at himself in a parody of frenzy, rolling his eyes. It is so important for Coover to be gross and out there, this really great-looking guy who fucks everyone off with his grossness. He is so transparent, really – and although I would usually stick around and say nothing, because he is like a one-man sex show but somehow so unsexy, today I put my hand on his shoulder and he slows down and stops, looking up with a startled expression.

'What, Terry? What?'

'You don't have to do that with me.'

'Do what? Who's doing anything?' He whines and sounds all weaselly and desperate – but even that is put on, faked. He wants so hard to be the outsider, peak bizarro, pariah to the max. He has read all the books, seen the films and listened to the songs, and now he wants to live it, the lonely life of the one beyond the pale, the beautifully misunderstood, who even in his own circle is perceived as just a jerk, a yanker of chains. But that is difficult to be, not just because everyone is so reflex accepting of general weirdness around here but because they can all see the little boy blue beneath it all, cringing at his own cringiness. I guess that is why he laughs the hardest at my displays of kook; he envies how easily it comes to me, when for him it is such a strain to keep up the pretence.

'It's already over,' I say, taking the flannel and washing myself in front of him, turning him soft in his own hand in the space of a second, because I am really not his bag. As he put it once when we were out of earshot of the others, having a smoke, 'The whole point of a girl, Terry, is she doesn't have a dick.' This makes him sound kind of yeah, whatever – and he kind of is that, but he is also kind of okay.

'Gone, daddy, gone,' I laugh now, as he zips up, disconsolate, and hurries back to the room he shares with Frazer. When he leaves, I bring myself off thrice in quick succession. This morning turns me on, for whatever reason, whether I'm breathing the exhaust from some unremembered dream or spinning off Coover's simple reminder of our urges, it is one for the money, two for the show, three to get ready – and then I am ready to go.

There is so little going on down in the Black Rooster cafe that it hardly matters I am close to an hour late. Dashiell is douching the dishes while Phiz scats along to Beth Orton, lord help us. Daisy stalks the tables, looking glum and inspired, as if a new poem hovers in the back of her mind and she is just about to take out her notebook and scribble. Algren, the strange old man who runs the place, sits at the back of the kitchen beside the sink unit, avoiding my eye while I change into our uniform. We are an indie cafe, but we still wear set things, trousers fitting snugly around our hips and an apron with the white logo of a black rooster apparently crapping into a cappuccino. But that, as Dash always says, is the artist's fault, a design flaw. We were not involved in any of these high-level decisions, of course – Algren made them all on his own and a long time ago, a decade anyway. We are at least the second or third generation of staff; other waiters and baristas have come and gone to have babies, travel the world, start their own happy cafes.

'Greatly late but not lately great,' he says, as he often does, when I am dressed.

'Thanks, Algren,' I tell him, going out front where nothing is still happening, where I pour sugar into bowls and wipe sticky drips from vanilla syrup bottles and lounge against the counter with its metal top digging into my ribs. The pain keeps me awake whenever my eyes start to close.

'You turning up like this out of the blue has really made my day.'

I hear Dashiell's voice and open my eyes and yawn, loudly, in his face. Dear Christ but this man is beautiful, I think routinely, the kind of thought that everyone can hear but nobody minds because they are all thinking the same thing, more or less. Some people mistake Dash at first as slick or glib, but he is neither; he is as shaky and flaky as the rest of us, but still one of those rare people who surrounds himself in a kind of hush. I take a narrow peak at his olive skin and hazel eyes, that long defined nose and a smile cosmic enough to make the angels cry.

'I aim to please, Dashy boy,' I tell him, looking up as he looks down. 'I was thinking about you in the bathroom this morning – s'why I'm late.'

Dashiell bats his lashes and shakes his head and shrugs. 'Jesus, Terry, that's some corny stuff you've got going there.'

'What if it happens to be true?' I flick a bit of glinting cafe lint off his black sleeve. 'You coming out with us later?'

This is a stupid question. Dash is studying for some far-fetched degree in photography and never comes out on weekdays. For a man who spends so much time in a darkroom he has an amazing complexion. But I keep on asking these stupid questions just to let him know that he is the first on my list, and remind him of the one time we did get to dance – so spacily special, like an endless wank trance, like that place you go when you come so hard that your mind turns off and colours fly.

'Got to do some contact shit with my contact sheets,' he says, with an airy lack of meaning – and then he stands to attention at my side because the first wave is coming through, the midmorning caffeine junkies.

We all have our various relationships with these people, ageing cafe queens and recovering smackheads, freaks in the main from long-lost far-sides – or maybe only half of them are, but they are the ones who set the tone. There are also office workers from the jobcentre and American Express, retail navvies from the big concerns going into town and the littler concerns up where we are. There are the students who are flush enough to spend their money on a muffin or a caramel square, and the dogwalkers, because we allow dogs. Every now and then we get a yummy mummy with her gone parasol and mewling child, her Maclaren spokes and squishy vowels – sometimes even a yummy daddy – straying some way from their territory up in Queen's Park. I would sort of hiss at those people when I first worked here, muttering shit under my breath about dadoes and dildos, brushing crumbs into their laps and then apologising badly. Hell, we had dadoes when I was growing up – I know what I am talking about first hand, know how askew people's attitudes are up there in dado-land, with their bookshelves full of nothing but middlebrow schlock and their fucking direct debits, pretty little bank accounts all in a row, cars without a dent and perfect paintwork, their emotions without a hair out of place. I know the damage it does when people live in those bubbles and make a religion of normality, preach to the converted every weekend at the barbecue, knock around for a lifetime in their rinky-dink little marriage, their only rebellion some uptight but very much not out of sight extramarital fuck.

It was Dashiell who urged on me some largeness of mind – some tolerance, to use a classic dado term. 'It's not just unprofessional, Terry,' he said one evening last year, 'it's unfair. They all have their personality crises, identity shifts and identity thefts, they have their difficult lives as well. It's not like they're personally responsible for everything that's wrong with the world, is what I'm trying to say.'

'Nuts,' I told him. 'It is precisely their fault, all the rampant mediocrity,' I ranted back, 'the tediousness of the whole project, that UK plc thing they have going. They're complicit in it every minute of every day, totally tied up in the granular shittiness of it all.'

But later when I thought about it, I saw his point about their difficult lives and so on, and how my prime objection was just aesthetic, how it was all about how their lives looked to me – how I was being a snob. Who cares what they get up to, as long as they never expect me to join in? Dash made me see it in a word: none of it mattered to me personally, it was all just little England going about its business. They have their version of how it works and I have mine, and why should I give a crap about their lifestyles, investments or choices, or about how invisible I am to them most of the time – or how, on those occasions when they actually notice me, they actually wince? Why should I care? Dash keeps me honest sometimes.

'You dash me with your wisdom, Dashiell, you are my dashboard, my guiding light,' as I told him once.

'Well you know, Terry,' he said, 'what happened to you happened to you, but not because of them.'

'Yes, okay, I get that.' I remember this conversation quite vividly, because for once I dared to touch him, rather than wait for him to touch me. He was stood at the cafe kitchen sink with his back to me, and I went and leaned against him, resting my forehead against his spine for a moment until he stopped rinsing – and for a moment we stood like that until I knew, all of a sudden, that it was not a good idea for me to carry on standing. Then I could not stand anymore but had to crouch in the corner of the kitchen and groan while he came and put a hand on my head. It hits me sideways out of nowhere every time – or no, not quite out of nowhere; it is brought on by some signal emotion – and then I am undone, spun out, bent over my belly and aching like a bruised bollock.

No doctor has ever managed to put a name to this thing, but they tend not to look much further than their notes. At the start, before I knew better than to be too candid about my history, not yet seeing how ready they would be to fit me into their system of referrals, their one-size-fits-all cure for everything, I told the doc about how when I was nine my old man punched me in the stomach, bam, and down I went, spewing my guts out over his shoes while everything screamed in the air around me. Whenever the emotion flashes before me like a secret sign, it gets me in the same place, BAM.

It happens once a week on some dot or other, regular as clockwork, like a psychosomatic message from the past. And so at lunch today, this Monday, when everything is at its busiest, a car goes past, an old red car left over from the eighties – or maybe it is the face on a wild-haired man who orders a white Americano and cheesecake to go, or the dull clank of metal from behind me in the kitchen, or the stupid George Formby song playing on the PA. Whatever it is, I double up suddenly, fold in half and drop to my heels, and Phiz nearly trips over me and Daisy, beautiful pale Daisy with her slightly wilted face, stops what she is doing with trays and comes to my aid. Algren has gone on one of his wanders, as he tends to at the busiest periods, up through Kemptown to his mysterious old lady perhaps, in Bristol Gardens. We are stretched, but Dash helps me up and leads me out through the cafe to the street, and I lean against the wall in the alleyway that runs along and back from our building.

'Bad one, baby?'

'Bad,' I tell him, belching then vomiting in the space between us – lucky for him there is some space between us – from the sheer petrifaction of my guts, like my shit is turning to stone inside me and pushing everything up and out. Dash holds my hair away from my face; I keep it long to confuse everybody, even including myself, and for something to hold onto when I want to be held by my hair.

'You need to go back up to the flat and lie down,' he says.

'We're too busy.'

'No, we're not. We're fine.'

I straighten up slowly and look at his Adam's apple. It is bright and cold in the alleyway – wind-tunnel cold, freezing nipples cold. His apple looks raw. 'Wouldn't it just be so cool if Algren came and found us now?' I said. 'Like that other time.'

Dashiell laughs. 'That was crazy. That was perfect.'

This was an evening just before Christmas, impossibly hectic from all the frantic footfall and shopper flow, when I span out over something and ran out in the alleyway and Dash followed and asked me what it was. I had already told him the whole story. He did not even flinch when I said, 'I need to commit an act of violence,' just went back inside and got a couple of saucers and handed them to me. 'Go on,' he said, 'Algren won't miss them,' and I threw them at the wall with such force that they exploded in slivers and shards all down the brick lane. Of course, the instant that last fragment danced down the drain, who but Algren should appear at the top of the alley in silhouette – it was dark, the shortest day – saying, 'Algren won't miss what?' I thought that was both of us definitely fucked and sacked, but Dash took him aside; he must have explained my destructive act in a way that made some sort of sense, because all Algren did was come up to me at closing time, point his salt and pepper goatee at me and say, 'Kid, don't you ever break my crockery on purpose again.'

I put my hand on Dashiell's elbow now, feeling safe enough to touch his elbow. 'You're not even my best friend, Dash,' I say. 'I wish you were sometimes.'

He sighs, looking down at the top of my head. 'You know, Terry, you try too hard to be the It Girl or the It Boy or whatever – the It Person, anyway.'

'The It Thing.'

'Yeah, right. My point is that you try too hard when you are that thing already. Everyone loves you, even Algren in his weird and crabby way. You're like this prickly bear on dope and speed half the time and it's wearing you out.'

'There's some healing I haven't done yet,' I tell him, 'a cure I need to find for what I've got. I'm almost sure it exists. I don't know, some final intimacy, handing myself over to – to someone who knows me and uses me well.' I hesitate to say it, but what is the point, when he knows anyway? 'To you, is what I mean.'

Dash has heard this plea from me once or twice this past year. 'And then we wouldn't have this anymore,' he objects, meeting my eye and looking away. But I guess his real objection – I have pushed it this far and we have run up against it before – is that he actually has no wish to do any of the rough stuff with me, paddle or tool me, tug me down by my hair so my face is on the floor, spank the crap out of me, rake my back with his nails and pinch me. And I am still no nearer knowing whether it is me, because he would rather do all those things with his aunt than with some guy in a dress, or because he is just not that way tended. It would wake him up, I think; he is lovely, but he is asleep. But he cannot go near me, because he knows what I want is not to lie side by side in some cosy but coffinlike bed and to reach some deathly climax. Even with him, that would not be enough. I need to give myself over to him and know he will take me beyond my limits, and it will be done with so much love and connection that every ounce of pain yields a pound of pleasure.

'It's okay, Dash, I do understand.'

'No, you don't,' he says, looking pained. 'You can't. You don't hear me when I say you need a break, go travelling, work in a cafe on the other side of the world.'

'It's too prescriptive, sweets. What are you, my shrink?'

He sighs. 'Go home, Terry. Go home and listen to Dr Alex Paterson and chill out. Come back tomorrow when you're feeling better.'

He lets go of my cheek – his hand was there all the time, but somehow I failed to feel it – and turns on his heel.

I stumble up two flights of stairs to the flat and lie down on the couch, which is also my bed. It was kind of them to let me stay after Russ left town and our shared tenancy came to an end, but living in the central space of the apartment means that there is rarely a moment in the day I have to myself, unless I crawl home sick from work. We stay up all night, and I cannot escape – and they, of course, cannot escape from me. The boys share a room, the girls share a room, and they all invite me to sleep on their floor. Sometimes they say, 'Don't be silly, Terry, you can sleep in a bed.' But what they tend to mean is, 'Come and sleep in *my* bed, with *me*,' which could only ever make things worse.

Now I take off my Black Rooster uniform, dump it on the floor by the couch and lie with the late winter sun streaming through the open blinds. Down in St James's Street there is the regular carnival, a fucked-up jamboree, and for a while it is all I need to hear, all the ladytron aspirational gossip and boombox wanker talk drifting in through our cracked windows from down on the pavement. It takes me out of myself, so I wander my heady forest along a corridor of mental trees, to the soundtrack of that dumb word music, enter an internal wood whose branches do not reach out and grasp me, where the earth does not try to swallow me up. I relax my vigilance, knowing that this place has no predators, its shadows hide nothing too shady.

But it is impossible to sustain this state of trance; something throws me out into the void again, into that existential space where everything is brutal, forced and twisted. What triggers it is a dirty mystery with no clean solution – maybe just a word flung up from the street, just a tone of voice, or the changing angle of light as the sun descends; or maybe it was a door opening and closing somewhere close by or a car braking or a seagull landing on a chimney. I am aware, even with my eyes closed, of the dancing light of late afternoon, sunbeams struggling with zephyrs out to sea, and know I must have slept through much of the day. Perhaps it is the wind that alerts me as it blows through the girders of the West Pier a mile away, a pile of warped metal with its lacing of silvery wood, always creaking and shifting on its rusted stanchions, constantly threatening to collapse. I can feel those things sometimes in myself, little changes in the weather, small shifts in my environment, tiny and meaningless alterations. Ordinary flux does not matter so much – but the bigger flux, the big shift fucks me with its vicious reductions until I am this savage keening thing curled up on myself.

Some people masquerade as stalwart members of their small society when they are hateful and spiteful and everything they think is just smallness and meanness. That was what my father was like, even after our mother killed him. She threw him downstairs one night in that one split second when she had the advantage over him; and then we all stood over his body at the foot of the staircase, not knowing whether he was dead or just out cold, waiting to see whether he would twitch or shift or strike out again. After we had stood that way for ten minutes or so, still expecting to see signs of life, my brother Russell said, 'Well, that's him done.' We clung on to one another and laughed for hours, or so it felt, in a fuck the consequences way that was good while it lasted. Of course, at the subsequent inquest our father's mother said that her daughter-in-law was one of those wives who set out to kill their husbands from day one of the marriage. Old ma Gibson told the court that he was her sweet boy and could not have hurt a flea, that mum had constantly threatened him in her presence and that he would never have done all those things that mum said he did – hit us or steal her money or practice mental cruelty as if it was a sport.

I have to kill him all over again now and then, although to do so I have to bring him back to life. I have to kill him dead with a push again, until he lies again unmoving at the bottom of the stairs, stuck in his final position, in the last shape he threw; but for all that I must have killed him a thousand times, he will never be as dead as mum. She died in prison, after 18 months in which she failed to adjust to the rotas and details, the new routine. Russ used to pick up his guitar and sing that old country saw, *Mama Tried*, about the boy who spends his life in jail despite his mother's best efforts. In his gentle and bitter way he found it kind of funny, the role reversal – and because she was, of course, always threatening to kill our father, what granny said was true. During his occasional absences, she would plan to hide behind the front door and smack him in the head with the heavy porcelain cistern lid or poison him with mashed-up pills or just plain stab him with a kitchen knife. I am not saying that is good, just that he brought out the worst in all of us. Russ and I were always on at her, 'Don't do it, mum, you'll end up in prison, and then where will we be?' But despite her children's best efforts, jail was where she ended up and jail was where she died, leaving our paternal grandmother to bring us up in a state of foul complicity and lies, in dado-land.

That is what makes me angry, even now – that we ended up living out the rest of our childhoods on Respectable Street, among all those thankless people

177

who spent their days making castles out of sand in their soul desert, who made a show of despising the lowlifes half a block away, who flung the word *chav* at anyone who wore white socks, anyone at all blingy, just to make themselves feel better about their questionable place on the social ladder. That was our gran – but she was all we had, and we got along as best as we could. Even now I phone her when there is no one else around, nowhere else to turn, although she is the worst person to talk to at those times, since she has no belief in anything you cannot see. She cannot credit the notion that a child might be traumatised, or even upset, when there are plates on the table and napkins alongside them, when the beautiful ordered world as ordained by the BBC is broadcast from the sideboard. She does not see the wall-to-wall shame and hypocrisy in the midst of all those first-class dadoes. But still she is the person I ring sometimes, to get her usual short shrift – and then afterwards I have to break something, because I cannot go back and embody my dead mother or kill my dead father again. So I take it out on the crockery, go to Mind or Sue Ryder or Scope and buy a bunch of dishes and pulverise them in the alleyway, come rain or shine. Just to think of all those summer nights spent in the alley, smashing plates then sweeping up after myself, because to leave all those broken pieces of myself lying around would be antisocial after all, all those cold winter nights full of Channel rain and my frozen hands scraping up the shards and slivers. So many bags of charity shop china have gone down that road.

I can rationalise all I want, tell myself that she was right to kill him, it was the only part of their story that made any sense. But that is easy to say, in a way, now that they are both dead – and what does it change? Dashiell said to me once, during one of his pep talks,

'But it made you the person you are, Terry, in a good way.' Something has kinked me good, that is true, and it would certainly be a line to take – that some shitty little England tragedy, a careless crime with a crap victim who nobody mourns apart from his dirtbox mum, at least for me opened the doorway to a new world, the world I am living in, *this* world. Dashiell is right: it is impossible to regret it entirely. This world would not exist otherwise. How would any of us know what lay in the great beyond, if our mother had hesitated for a moment, held back one second from the fatal push? 'Tragedy is such a useless concept anyway,' Dash pointed out. 'It's all about finality, and nothing is ever final, is it?' Perhaps not – and it may well be that without those things happening I would never have met these people, my people. I might have gone on to be what I was brought up to be: an economic unit, plain cipher, sitting in a university library for a few years and filling my head with pointless knowledge, not afraid of Virginia Woolf but only because the life of the mind seemed so unreal, no wolves at all just words, then to trundle along between office and home and never know anything different, barely aware I was breathing, oblivious.

But that is still a rationalisation. Can we rationalise while we sleep? I must have slept for hours, fleeing consciousness at the first sign of danger. Now I open my eyes on the light falling dim all around me, that twilight world catching up with me again, feeling suddenly hyper and unable to let go of the smallest influence on my mind or body. It is as if our island has suddenly become one vast musician with a million tiny hands, playing for all it is worth. Inexplicable moments in sound crowd my mind's ear until I am scattered and lost in a mass of peals and knocks, rings and bangs,

179

scrapes and squeals, coming from all sides and all atonal, as if someone was hammering on a piano left out in the rain and dried out in the sun. In this midst of all this screaming influx, I hold onto my higher power, whatever it is – that thing I can cling to at least some of the time. Like the North Pole it has no substance; it is not a pole, is invisible and you cannot touch it, but when you are there you feel its presence, hold onto it with cosmic fingers. If I can just hold on I will not go crazy. But even just to stay as sane as I am right now, I need to burn all this awful energy into a kind of love, dance to the racket of this nightmare band as if it was somehow lovely, full of its own dark life – not my friend but not my enemy either, a mellifluous cacophony, a storm of shit and honey.

I am reaching that point when the tempest begins to die down, am almost ready to stand and go to the bathroom and splash my face, when the door opens down at street level and Nutmeg surfaces. Dumping her bag in the middle of the floor after turning on the light, she turns around and lets out a little 'Oh!' before coming over and kneeling by the couch. 'You okay, Terry? You had one of your days?'

'Yeah, heavy.' My lungs are like sacks of pain, as if I had been panting in the dark for an hour. 'You're home early.'

Sometimes when Nutmeg comes home early we lie down together and talk, or not talk so much as ramble. Nutmeg is the sweetheart of the tribe, Paula the great unmellow messer who gets things done but at a cost, Frazer the pale intellectual and Coover the addled pervert. Nutmeg is a dove, strangely young for all that she is ten years older than the rest of us, strong with a sensitive strength and as fair-minded as Anton Chekhov. Without her sweet nature and saintly overview, the flat would be uninhabitable – or more uninhabitable, at any rate.

'My cafe is not as popular as yours,' she smiles, and throws off her coat and her top layers until she is just thermals and socks and climbs in under the old army blanket so we lie shoulder to shoulder, squeezed. 'It makes me sad, the way they run it for themselves when it's supposed to be a co-op. They're all supposed to be so goddamn fluffy, but they're fluffy as fucking porcupines at the end of the day.'

'Yeah, well, it's not all paradise under Algren, you know.'

'I dunno – he lets you break his plates. He lets you guys run it the way you like and doesn't impose his vision.'

'I'm not sure he has visions,' I tell her. 'He's a hard one to work out, he doesn't even seem to care about the takings half the time.'

'And then you have Dashiell. You just need one person like that in any organisation and you're onto a winner. You okay now, hon?'

'You came in at the end of it,' I tell her. I am thinking how right she is about Dash, how he makes it all work out through the power of his presence, about which he is in denial, through the fact that he sees the micro and macro and talks it up with a flash of his teeth, so white and even, in that horny voice and with that smile, a grin of stellar proportions which unlike the rest of him seems extreme, too much somehow, when otherwise he is the voice of reason.

She is pressed up against me with her hair in my nose, so I smell her unwashed brown curls – self-cleaning, she insists – and the musk that is Nutmeg, with its hints of cinnamon and clove. Sometimes her closeness is comforting, and sometimes it makes me nervous; she is gentle and kind, but not in the end the heart of simplicity. She wants something from me, or at least it feels like she does. Last autumn, soon after I first moved in, there was an afternoon like this, with me clapped out on the sofa and her coming in early from work, when she lay down beside me and we hooked up, briefly. The whole thing lasted only about a minute or two – it was kind of horrifying how easily she was reduced to a puddle, as if I had melted her with my bare hands. From the way she skipped around for a while in the aftermath, I guess she found the experience positive and reaffirming, or whatever – more than just a relief, an actual connection. But for me there was something unwholesome about all that melting, the weird viscosity at my fingertips, the sudden shudder that passed through her muscles and bones and then all the softness and passivity. It felt close to repellent – but at least it enlightened me further on my own needs, how much I want someone to push back hard with equal strength, and not just push back but pin me down and mount me.

'Do you want to come out with us tonight to the Funky Fish? It's free fries night, remember, Mondays, it's cheaper than most other nights.'

'Yeah, maybe, Nuts. I thought you didn't like those big humping beats anymore. I thought you'd gone all Kate Bush on us, what with your clean-up time.'

'Well sometimes I do. It's different without pills, I grant you that. You should think about going straight yourself, Terry, with your condition.'

'What condition?'

'The condition you're in, that condition.' She turns her head, although it is hard for her to move without falling off the couch, and faces me at close range. 'You know, your PTSD. I look at you Terry and see someone in permanent shock from all the physical fallout from all the stuff that happened. I mean, you do have a condition.'

'Everyone has shit from their childhoods. I just have a low pain threshold, Meg.'

'Yes you do, and that's kind of my point, honey. That low pain threshold is not going to go away. It's part of you.' She leans up on an elbow so her kind, clear face hangs over me, haloed by the bald light from the bare lightbulb; her head throws shadow on my face and keeps the light from my eyes. 'All this running around and swallowing whatever you find on the floor has to end somewhere, Terry, that's all I'm saying.'

'The problem lies partly with the floor, know what I mean? I'd have to move out to drop all those bad habits.'

Nutmeg smiles. 'So move out. I'll come with you – we can set up together.' She has moved no closer than before, except in words, but still I have an urge to beat a retreat. But there is really nowhere for me to go; I am pressed up against the seat back as it is. It takes me back to that afternoon last year when we fucked and how, when the guys trooped in from their various McJobs, they picked up on the atmosphere straightaway. 'See how straight girls are falling for you, Terry?' Coover tackled me in the kitchen. 'Doesn't it make you think?' I flinch now at her closeness – she sees me cringe away, and a hurt look crosses her face. 'I don't necessarily mean as a couple, Terry. We could see how it went.'

'You know I can't do those things with you, Nutmeg.'

'I'm not asking you to do those things.' She sounds upset, but her face is cast in shadow and I cannot pick up on the look in her eyes, with the light behind, dirty halo ringing her head. 'I'm just saying it would be good for you to get away from here, and that I could go with you, and we could make something nice for ourselves somewhere quiet and healthy.'

'Okay, yes, okay. Good. Maybe.'

'Jesus, Terry, it's really not that tricky to say yes or no.'

She gets up then and leaves me on the couch, exposed to the glare from the bulb, harsh and artificial. I wait until she goes from bathroom to kitchen to the room she shares with Paula, then I get up and change into my leggings with the red and yellow roses and a silver blouse with frills, get my beanie and Tom Baker scarf out of the ottoman I use for a wardrobe, put on my tenth-hand trench coat and head out the door.

At the end of the Palace Pier, not the ruined one but the pier still intact, in the cold wind sweeping across from France, I take out my phone and ring Russell – my brother, my twin. We are far from identical. He likes country, bluegrass and Jim Beam while I need beats, no matter who from – Paul Oakenfold or Andy Weatherall, Jaki Liebezeit or John Bonham. Russ has chased his voodoo down his own road, his own way. Of course, we have kept track of each other since we were twelve, when our daddy fell down the stairs, since the spell in granny's house – but with some distance in between, besides a period of a year or so when we lived down here together, when we decided to pool our grieving for a while and see what happened. Nothing happened – or yes, there was something, but not what either of us needed, just a discovery of the limits to our twinship, maybe. But he is my brother, who was there when it all kicked off, the only other living witness.

'Happy birthday, bro,' he says picking up, recognising my number. 'Jeez, are you out celebrating it on some tundra somewhere, cos that's what it sounds like from here – the wind sounds like thunder.'

'Hmm, are you sure it's our birthday? Isn't that in March or something?'

'Such a polar bear,' he chunters on, ignoring me, evidently very stoned, 'up there in the Arctic on your weekend break. Or is it Antarctica you're at? Is that terrible racket in the background some poor penguin getting his flappers torn off by a killer whale? Too brutal, Terry, way too brutal.'

I know better than to engage with him on the level of free association – I try to keep it simple. 'How's south London anyway? How're things with the pranksters?'

'I'm not in south London, my boy, I'm in Whetstone, doing a gig. Or Totteridge maybe, not really too sure, but certainly it feels like a million miles away from snivilisation. You'd hate it up here, Terry, it really reminds me of wherever it was we grew up. God, I've literally forgotten the name of that place where we grew up. Isn't that crazy? I mean to say, isn't that great?'

'It *is* great, Russell – I wish I *could* forget. Or no, hang on a minute, maybe I don't. Maybe forgetting doesn't really help.'

'Well, I've forgotten anyway, whether it helps or not, bro. When are you coming up to see us? We're getting pretty good now you know, as in Flying Burrito Brothers good.' And he starts singing *Sin City*, as he so often does. It is his favourite song – and it has some nice writing in it, that I cannot deny, decadent and pretty, like granny's Home Sweet Home cross-stitch picking out a naked lady in a ten-gallon hat. None of that helps me get past the fact that the Flying Burritos lacked a regular drummer. I mean really what is the use of a band without a drummer? Same thing with The Doors – they had a drummer, a great drummer actually, but no actual bassist. And really and truly, what is the point of a band with no one on bass?

Russ is a pretty excellent guitarist – he can play the pedal steel as well. 'So you guys are still together then, the Boho Dancers?' He grunts in response to this; there is a thud, and I can easily picture him wedging his phone to his ear with his shoulder then losing traction and dropping it as he lights up. 'Are you getting paid for this one?'

'I'm flying solo tonight, Terry man,' he exhales, 'Otherwise I'd be doing it straight. I can't be going out there alone and looking them in the eye over my, uh, microphone, without something inside to keep me curly.' Russ has adopted these vaguely Nashville idioms, a twang he picked up since he started playing country so much, as if to put a few thousand miles between himself and where he started. But then he suddenly falls in sync with me, as he always does, even if just for a minute. 'You ring for any reason in particular, Terry? You sound a little, I dunno, blustery somehow.'

'Well yeah, I'm standing in a full force gale,' I laugh. 'I just wanted to hear your voice, really. I just miss you. I get why you left, don't get me wrong – I know we need to stay out of each other's range for a while and let it breathe and all that shit. I know, but I still miss you.'

'Yeah but Terry, my man,' he dives in, sounding anxious now. This is how he is – he burbles on for a while as if the world was just one big bourbon party, then all at once the anxiety grabs him. That is the way it is with me, too, only we are stuck in our own angst and make our different escapes – Russ to the melody, me to the rhythm. 'You don't sound too good, Terry, truth be told. I'd come back and live down there again, you know, at drop of a hat and all that malarkey, if you

186

needed me.' He begins to gasp between phrases, the way he always does when worry makes a grab for a piece of his mind.

'It's okay, Russ. It's better this way for the both of us.'

There is a pause as he unscrews the top from a bottle or puts the finishing touches to a joint. When he comes back he sounds distinctly relieved, depressurised, a little vapoured. 'Yeah, it is, you're right. Anyway, bro, thanks for the name again. Everyone really loves it.' It was me who suggested that he call his band the Boho Dancers. 'You know, we're thinking of giving up on being a band and becoming a group,' he laughs, 'like the Stones in '73.'

'Jesus, no, don't ever do that,' I tell him. 'What happened to the Stones was a tragedy, they've never got over it. If you can't be a band be an outfit, be a combo. Anything but a group, brother.'

Russ laughs again – and then he is gone, and I am alone again at the end of the Palace Pier, in the winter dark, with the breeze wrapping itself around my hips like some cold lover. Is it alone again, or just alone? It is never obvious with solitude where it stops and starts, when it began or if it ever ends, whether it is the worst thing or the best – the clearest and truest state. I regret those times when I have turned my back on everyone just to spend a while being miserable and lonely, because solitude deserves better than that – because, at its finest, it is a form of crystal-clear happiness. Now with the day's events behind me and the night's still ahead, still unlived, solitude stands with a hand on my shoulder like a friend, clarifying everything. The darkness beckons without menace, the cold has a stripped-down quality; suddenly, nothing is too close or too real – everything is cool.

So I go on standing in the dark at the end of the pier, looking down at the white horses in the water and out to the strange tower over there in Shoreham, stand there for close to an hour, despite the arctic weather. It is strange being who I am, even if life rarely sends me a spare moment to think about it – and stranger because who I am has been repeatedly in danger, for as long as I can remember. I never questioned it myself, even when our mother frowned as if I was being difficult just to add to her problems, my brother teased me over my clothes and haircuts, our father raised his hand. Kids at school and people on the street would come over just to laugh in my face – not all the time or even most of the time, but now and then they came over just to thrust their shiny little faces in my shady boatrace, my face forever in shadow. They scanned my features, curious as to how I dared to believe that being different was okay, not seeing apparently that they also had their differences, aligned as they were in their notion of sameness. It was like anyone who took off their uniform was immediately suspect; they wanted me to feel guilty that I was too little burdened by the problem of *me*, that I was cool with not looking or thinking or feeling like most of them.

After a while I came to realise that they only acted that way because they were so weighed down with guilt over who *they* were, caught as we all are in that old protestant mindwarp, a little world of blame and shame where there is always something wrong with you and it does not even matter who you are. On our tiny island of action and reaction where judgment abounds, it is not okay to be rich and not okay to be poor, not okay to lie in bed all day or go to work seven days a week, not okay to be meek or assert yourself, to get loaded or stay sober, to wear pinstripes or a shellsuit. These narrow shores are home to the guilt-trip capital of the world, where everyone always has a bad word to say for you, no matter what you say or do. You are always wrong, somehow, on this island, despite the fact that people cannot help who they are and have only themselves to work with their whole lives. All identities are mad, I realised early on, but in ourselves we have to accept our mad identity or die. So when people come up and peer at me from out of their shiny angry faces, it seems like a failure of imagination on their parts somehow, or an inability to look into their own deep dark truthful mirror.

Tonight, in the wind and cold, there are two truthful mirrors staring back at me, deep and dark, mirror of the sky and mirror of the sea. Just for a moment it is truly beautiful, and I am amazed all over again by those unnameable satellites, constellations I tried and failed to learn at school, big starry doodles above, then below in the water all the scattered shoreline lights, yellow and orange and white, broken up by the waves. But then I am no longer amazed – I soar into the mirror like a sea wolf, a flying fox or prehistoric gull, pulled out into space by my own spaciness, with no need for sidekicks or stimulants. Letting go into the darkness, with all that black light surrounding me, in a momentary panic I scurry to the edge as if looking for a ditch, like a wild animal instinctively seeking out the one place of safety, until it comes to me that I cannot hide but I have no need, wind and water are ditchless, endless places where everyone is equally free. And for an instant I live in that freedom entirely, not drifting or lost but *there*, in the heart of dark space, breathing and pulsing with every last inch of myself.

'A penny for your thoughts, Miss Fly,' comes a voice behind me, and I turn. It is Dash, thank the crazy gods, when it could have been one of those redneck types who turn up sometimes and pretend to throw you off the pier – although they never do, they are too chicken.

'Fuck, man, you made me jump.'

'I thought you *were* jumping, for a second.' Dashiell eyes me with all that ingenuous warmth he has, because he cannot help himself; it is just there, where he is, not a simple physical fact but a kind of hotspot in the universe. With my eyes I search his body for his camera; usually he has it hanging from a strap around his neck, goes out on image fishing expeditions, comes back with a sackful of pix. But tonight he is naked – that is, in his party gear, which in his case means some old blue jeans and a floral shirt that might have come from French Connection, and to keep him warm one of those Iggy Pop leather jackets, but too mint and undistressed to be the real thing.

'I was happy flying,' I tell him.

'Unaided?'

'Unaided, yes, believe it or not. Who needs drugs when I've got me?' I lean against the railing, facing out, as if to show him the sky. Wind whips through us like knives of ice, but I am sheltered by his hotspot, his mere presence. 'How are *you* here, anyhow?'

'I know your ways,' he says, 'better than you think.'

'It was a chance find,' I suggest, 'a felicitous guess. No one in their right mind would hang out at the end of the Palace Pier in February.'

'Yes, exactly, got it in one. Anyway, I wanted to talk to you.'

'Oh, right. Did Algren sack me at last?'

'No, but I think,' he begins – then he stops and looks around. 'Jesus, can we not go inside?'

'I don't think so, no. Inside means Horatio's, or am I wrong?'

Dashiell sighs and comes and leans against the rail beside me, shivering. We would have to be feeling tremendously drunk and patriotic to enter Horatio's, as well he knows. 'Okay, okay.' He has to get pretty close to make himself heard over the din of the wind. 'I really think you should think about doing something else, Terry. I'm maybe the last person to be telling you this, but it's not good for you – this whole sofa-surfing, living over the shop, 24-hour party thing. It's killing you alive.'

'So why are you the last person who should be telling me this?'

'Because I don't want anything to change – like, nada. So when I stand here telling you to change it all up, I'm also actually saying, Don't move, stay exactly the way you are, don't change a thing.'

'And why are you actually saying that, Dash?'

'Why do you think?'

This semi-rhetorical question is followed by a whole bunch of silence. 'We don't have to get farther apart, Dashiell,' I say in the end. 'We could get closer. I've more or less been telling you that's what I want for about a year.'

He tries not to look my way. Instead he bows his head into the stiff ocean breeze so that his considerable fringe flaps about, hitting him in his third eye a lot, breaking his concentration I guess. 'We've never had this conversation, have we?' he says, finally.

'Yes and no,' I say.

'I'm already confused, Terry, and you're not exactly helping me out here.' Now he turns to face me. 'I don't even know if I can be who you want me to be. I don't even know if I can be who you think I am.'

His uncertainty and vacillation for some reason take me back to a night at the end of last summer when I was

191

standing about where I am standing now, almost the exact same place, and an oldish guy came up and started snowing me. There were more people around that night because it was summer and still light, but even so I found him threatening – not so much because he posed a threat in any way but because I was having one of those days when loneliness seemed embedded in my side like an arrowhead. He came on so strong and gamed me, almost, to the point when I began to forget what he looked like – he was one of those blobby types who hang around on piers and so on, latching on to the frail and needy. He said stuff like, 'You know kid, some things are just supposed to happen.' He must have picked up on my struggle and recoil – I was painfully tempted to give in to this horrendous geek; at least he would suffocate my neediness, maybe even murder me – because he felt emboldened to go on with, 'What you need, kid, is to feel the pure fear. You're consumed by anxiety, kid. You need the fear undiluted, boy, the horror uncut.' For all that he sounded like some Poundland William Burroughs, for a devastating moment it felt as if he really understood me. I knew what he meant, and he was right – I was so bound up in all the minute and insoluble existential details, when all I really needed was the spike of terror that precedes death, the thrill of dread that obliterates the whole mental city like a four-minute warning. But when I saw that, I saw how easily he had played me, how transparent I must look, and I walked slowly away with him calling out at my back, 'Bitch, bitch, bitch.'

'I really think you're good for it,' I tell Dashiell now. 'But I'm not going to try to persuade you, you know. I mean, I'm not going to keep bugging you about it.'

'It would be a big step, Terry.' He shivers in his black leather jacket, his lips almost touching my ear. 'I mean, not just... not just crossing the line to be with you, in particular. I guess I've got to the point where I realise that I've never really given in to my feelings for anyone, however square the relationship, whatever the shape of it.'

'Believe me, I get that,' I shout back through the gale's loud wail. 'But it's the same for me. We could learn together, like we're learning together now. I like being with you.'

'Yeah,' he mumbles, suddenly covered in reticence – and I can just about hear him say, 'I like being with you too, Terry.'

Even just saying this freaks the man out so much that I have to laugh. 'Tell you what, let's pack up our troubles and heave the whole kitbag in the ocean and go and dance,' I suggest.

He moves his lips without saying anything, blushes into the night, shrugs into his embarrassment until I link arms with him and we march off the pier to the waterfront, steadying each other as we walk the slippery planks. But just as we step onto dry land, in that flash of tacky light below the arch that signals the boundary between pier and seafront, someone throws something at us – and I am not even sure what it is, but it feels like a bottle of piss, warm against our faces in the shabby downlight. The same person, I suppose it must be, yells some obscenity in our faces, vile and unpaid for, a little person's revenge on strangeness. For a moment there is a gang of them around us, chanting in a kind of magenta glow, a livid plastic hue cast down from the spotlit arch. Individual voices, individual words are lost in their loudness – but louder than any voice and nearer to me than their red-reflecting faces, I hear my dad say that I asked for this reaction, this is the response I provoke, this lynch mob are the carriers of justice in the common world. Because he was all for justice, my father – or for a levelling out, at any rate, the crush of the populus bearing down on wild cards and weirdos, in defence of the mass. That was what justice meant to him, a crushing as violent as it needed to be, taking care of the individual by flattening him out until he bled through his sides – the same justice as he chose for himself.

There are times when despair takes hold of me so firmly that I feel like a fish in an angler's grip, pulled off the end of the line, held by the tail and smashed headfirst into the stones of a bridge. I saw this once as a child and sometimes he comes back to me, the faceless fisherman – and when he comes, he takes me to a place beyond anxiety or fear or any nameable emotion, picks me up and breaks me into confusion, where I am aware of the hopelessness of my situation and nothing more.

It happens now, as we step off the end of the pier – everything goes black and oddly silent, and in the silence I think I mutter something to Dashiell about a fish, about an executioner's face – then I peel away from him and run down the beach towards the cold black water, darker down on the eastern side of the pier, where the city lights are further away. I keep on running until I have run into the sea up to my waist, into the icy water that is like a rock, not liquid but solid, and I am liquid inside the stone. It is a source of relief, the solidity of all that ice water holding me, to be captured within the great swell that stretches all the way to America and all the way around to the east and back home – to be held by the sea. The world has left me at the shoreline. I have solved my problem not by drowning but by becoming one with another element, all the air pushed out of me and water taking its place, water like a stone that embraces me until I have no air, and no words for feelings and no feelings, until I am neither alive nor dead.

Dashiell is with me in the water, shouting at the top of his voice, and I laugh as he shouts over and over, 'What the fuck, what the fuck.' I swim away from him through a sea as flat and cold as ice, unable to feel my feet or hands. Heading for a light on the horizon, some kind of ship perhaps, I find within the confusion a faith, or at any rate a simple block of unspoken knowledge, something apart from me that floats free. Dash swims after me, panicking a little perhaps, calling out, 'Terry, you fucker, we're both going to die,' while I keep heading for France – or for the end of the pier at least. The pier looks so stellar in the absence of moonlight, in its full dark splendour from below, with the towering stillness of its uplit but unridden rides, the mini-rollercoaster and the one that looks like Gemini spinning a mandala in the night when in spring it starts turning again, when the world starts up again, hurling all those lovers through space with all their innocence trailing off behind them like fire, safe in the belief that it will not just fling them into the Channel.

The vast weight of cold water below and cold air above is so fantastic, so purely novel to me – and terrifying, of course, because Dash is right it could so easily kill us. How long do we have, I wonder, in this degree of chill? Still, it is a great relief to feel those heavy expanses above and below and know for once where I am in the physical world, so simply elemental and nothing else. For a moment, in all that wildness of water and air, language seems to come apart, fly off and separate, as if words no longer cared about things and things were suddenly ignorant of the words that once described them. We have broken loose at last, escaped, us and all the words for the sealike sky and the skylike sea – and I want to tell him, 'I'm not trying to kill us, I'm trying to find the source of life.'

But there is too little air in my lungs and too much salt water for a statement of that length and complexity. Just in time perhaps, I stop swimming and turn towards him, to where he is right behind me, where he has chased me through this aquatic madness. I tread water and meet his eye while he bobs up and down in front of me, giving me a look so enflamed, treading water in a downshaft of pier light while someone far away and over our heads shouts, 'Man overboard!' All at once the cold water is impossibly painful, so overwhelming that I am aware of the danger of losing consciousness only as it happens. But even after I have lost all power of movement and thought, I feel his hand on my chin and sense our movement away from France and America, away from the fish and stars, back to our own narrow island.

When we get back to the flat, everyone is there. We are fortunate that it is just everyone, and not everyone else as well, all the hangers on, drop-ins and drop-outs. Tonight it is just the regular guys and dolls, who jump all over us with a manic and greedy concern, although their concern turns to other things when they discover what actually occurred. They assume at first that we must have been chased into the water by angry peasants bearing pitchforks, from the bare outline of the story. When they work it out – that I ran into the sea of my own free will, forcing Dashiell to follow me – they have other things to say.

'You're a fricking freakazoid, Terry girl,' says Frazer, shaking his head in woeful condemnation.

'That ain't no lady, that a dude,' Coover comes in on cue.

'No, but what a fucking, freaking, fricking freak. What were you doing, Tez? Do you think you learned them a lesson – like look how cold the sea is in winter, ain't that strange? You know, by taking to the waves voluntarily in that way you are sending out a very bad message,' Frazer goes on bombastically, pointing a finger. 'By letting them drive you into the Channel like that, you're basically letting the yahoos and galoots and whatnot know they've won.'

'Yeah, you need to make like Horatio and stand on the bridge,' said Coover, 'fight it out with the barbarian horde, *that* thing.'

Throughout all this blather, Paula and Nutmeg take off my wet clothes and sit me in front of the electric fire wrapped in a blanket. Dash is encouraged to fend for himself in the bathroom; the boys chuck him some of their more noxious items, incredibly smelly trousers from Coover and a hooded top from Frazer, stuff that Dash would never wear outside of an emergency. Normally, he comes across like one of those dressy hippies from 1968, all frills and fur – faux fur, of course, by now – and velvet pants. He was already dressing down for our night out, even before his leather jacket got totalled by the salt. This is the bit I feel bad about, helping to destroy an item of clothing worth a week of our wages. 'Was it worth it, Terry?' I can hear my mother ask, the way she always did whenever I acted up and there were consequences.

'What for is this lecture?' Paula asks the guys. 'I can just imagine if one of you was faced with an army of nasties you would really fucking battle it out.'

'They'd be standing shoulder to shoulder like the three amigos with one missing,' says Nutmeg, 'while everything around them turned to shit.'

'It wasn't really like that,' I say. 'They were being generally unpleasant and I just shot off, I just wanted to break loose.' I turn to Frazer, the more intelligent of the two guys. 'You know what it's like to want to break loose, don't you Frazer?'

'I suppose so, sweetheart.' He looks sheepish, feeling perhaps that I have singled him out, unhappy to stand in the spotlight. 'We're just jerking you around, Terry. We love you to fucking total distraction, baby. We just can't say it in so many words, most of the time. So we like, you know, express ourselves in other ways.'

'Wow, what a speech,' says Coover, who has gone over to the window. He gazes down into the street, his manhood challenged, as if looking out for the school of galoots, the eejit brigade – and if he finds them, he is thinking, oh then will he lay them to waste. I am deeply familiar with the way they think, my household gods, all their neat self-deceptions and world views, their ability to turn abruptly from assholes to angels and back again. When Coover turns around, his erection is uncomfortably emblazoned in the crotch of his grimy jogging bottoms, like a living badge. He is so grotesque and dysfunctional in his desire to depart from the norm, but grotesque in a way that makes him accessible to me – and he knows this. He relies at times on my understanding his need to be a total klutz. 'I say we hunt them down, round them up and throw them off the pier.'

'Ah but,' says Nutmeg, sitting with me now before the fire and warming her hands, 'that would be kind of like sinking to their level, don't you think?'

'The Nutster has a point,' says Frazer. 'We don't want us sinking to their level and we don't want them rising to ours. Tie a rock around them first, then throw them in. Otherwise the cunts will just float to the surface.'

'This is old-fashioned gallantry of the first order,' says Paula. 'You boys are like medieval knights, protecting the weaker sex.' She is on my other side, warming her stubby digits – the girls got cold, warming me up. But now the shivering has stopped; with all this life going on all around me, I feel a lot warmer than I have all day.

'Looking out for people of all sexes and none,' says Frazer. 'It's kind of in our culture, man. We were all medieval knights at some point in the past, back in the wastes of time. Or we were the dragons at least.'

'Can you toast me?' I ask Frazer. 'I mean with garlic and hash?'

Frazer heads for the kitchen, tugging on my hair as he goes. 'You want to go out now and dance your tits off, kid?'

'If at all possible, yeah.'

Dash comes back into the room. I figure he has been hiding out in the bathroom, avoiding all the stupid talk – now he stands in the doorway with everyone gazing at him. He looks fairly unrecognisable, almost like somebody else, in the hideous old hoodie and the stinky jeans. The flatmates all stare as one for a moment, as if wondering who he is and how he got in, until Frazer comes out of the kitchen. 'You want a piece of hash toast, Dash?'

'Uh, yeah. Whyever not?'

'Whyever not? Whyever not?' Coover repeats, slapping his thigh. 'What a fucking reply, man, what a cool response. I'm going to use that one next time, for sure. Whyever not?'

'Ignore him,' says Paula. 'He's like semi-imbecilic.'

'Nothing semi about him,' says Frazer, returning to his task.

'So come and sit down, Dashiell,' says Nutmeg, waving at the couch, drawn up close to the three-bar fire by which we crouch on the floor, the girls and I. Dash picks his way carefully between the bits of shit and debris that have collected in my living space until it has come to resemble an antique attic or a basement in a horror flick. Grossness abounds. 'Are you coming out with us tonight?'

He catches my eye. 'I suppose so.' He sounds gloomy, depressed, coming down from the adrenalin of being out in the ocean at dinnertime with a lunatic swimming for France. 'I don't really dance, as such.'

Nutmeg laughs indulgently. 'Ah yes, but then you don't need to, you beautiful bastard. Put all the rest of us wallflowers to shame.'

Dashiell looks a bit embarrassed by this gambit, so I intervene. 'Dash and I can maybe just sit at the bar and watch the dancers and talk about coffee beans and the correct use of the baguette.'

'He fucking dances or he's not fucking coming,' says Coover, who has strict views on almost every subject, nearly always made up on the fly.

'So that's settled,' says Paula. 'We all go down together. And now let us, in the hours that come between, get to the bottom of this here thing called life.' She laughs her laugh like a ritzy hyena, hilarity gurgling from the base of her throat.

Frazer fetches another round of toast, Paula drops a pill into everyone's palm. Coover, who has had the same temporary job for a year and a half, packing boxes in an industrial estate out near Lancing, who puts his money into invisible investments – but I think, on the whole, into porn in various formats – nips out in the midst of all this, having guzzled his toast and ingested his pill. He brings back a crate of light French beer in little bottles that open quick and slip down easy. Never at ease with being generous, he starts in on a big charade on the subject of bottle insertion, people doing themselves with random objects, while our eyes glaze over.

'Do you guys never eat dinner?' asks Dash.

'What do you think this is?' laughs Paula, waving a resin-dotted piece of toast.

'No, but I have cooked something,' says Nutmeg, starting to rise from her place with some difficulty. She would not normally partake – but tonight is special somehow, like the glitz at the end of the blitz, like one last party before the bombs are set to fall. 'No, but I have cooked something,' she repeats, and sits back down in the same place, beside me by the fire. She begins to weep, there are tears running down her cheeks to her chin, but no one notices apart from me – and I am stymied for a response, because to reach out and touch her at this moment might tip her over, or suggest we are back on when we were never on. But then of course I do it anyway, because I am stoned and impulsive, the way that Nutmeg does not like to see me; she has often observed that my impulses in these states are self-sabotaging, perverse and nonsensical.

For a month last summer I tried it the way she would approve, put a stop to my bad habits and grooved without stimulants. But it was no groove, just a slow collapse into an awful realisation that this, *this*, was why people got so mashed. The streets were not just grey, the people not just grey down on them, the constant activity not just cruelly pointless, the entire facade of the world turning its bland face to me not just bland, not just superficial – boy, in those weeks did I understand why people, including me, were always stoned. There was just no way to survive that deep engrained tedium without something to bend the mind. It is true that last August was especially bleak, I had nowhere in particular to live, was drifting from floor to floor, now and then kipping at the hostel, sleeping the odd night on the beach. One evening when I bumped into Meg on the Steine I told her all this, how my brother had left town, how I was trying to be abstinent, how I was practically homeless – and she was like, 'Terry, hon, you're just in a bad space right now, hey, you should come and crash at ours for a while, we can give you shelter. You'll see, everything will be alright under our roof.'

And she was correct, in that everything has been kind of okay since I moved in with these kindred bodies. I barely even knew them before I came to sleep on their couch – and now they are like the frenemies I never had at school, on nights like this my cosmic besties from the great beyond. They have given me shelter, and under their roof I have been more than alright, but I have never again experimented with druglessness, which equates in my mind only with wakelessness and sleeplessness and all the other lessnesses available to us in our short existence, a life made to feel longer but not richer by the lack of a vital ingredient. However much she takes me to task, I cannot or do not want to face it – I have no desire to head out into the world without my Midnight Cowboy shades on to look out on those streets of grey.

And it is not just space that is bad without chemicals to paint it – time is terrible too, creeping on in straight lines that never meet, on and on forever like a lost dimension trapped in an endless corridor. I told her this once, sharing too much as I always seem to do with her;

and of course she told me, 'Terry, that's just at the start. Give it a few weeks, or months or maybe a year and you'll begin to make up your own colour scheme, find your own rhythm. It doesn't stay so straight, it gets good and curly after a while.'

Now she is crying, and I reach out and take her hand. Her hands are small and ducklike somehow, like little ducks. In general, she is not a duck, more like some hippy emu with her long neck and legs and her gangly sincerity. But her hands are ducklike; they quack back at me as I hold them in mine.

'You told me it was all going to be alright, Nuts, and it is alright.' I feel my way with the reassurance, not knowing exactly why it is she is so upset. As luck would have it, everyone else is making a tremendous racket right at that moment; only Dashiell is perched on the arm of the sofa, holding a crappy cup of decaf coffee, awkwardly hanging over us. 'Is it about this afternoon? Is it about tonight?'

Even as I say the words, the music hugely impinges, coming down like a rain of hammer blows between my mouth and her ears, my mind and hers, me and myself. It has been on in the background ever since Dash and I came back, but now it seems to explode into a mad viral spiral of life, blasting out in all directions, concentrating on points where it can do most damage, those parts of the psyche where great pleasure and pain both hang out. The tune is one I must have heard about a thousand times, beyond famous and world renowned, a historic classic, but tonight I can name neither song nor singer. It is all just naked sound again, a black jagged scrawl in the air beneath the bare bulb, and not just sound in all its gritty matter but a shuffle through reality, as if the time signatures were shifting every second. I wonder .

whether Nutmeg is getting all this too, when she looks at me and mumbles as if repeating something,

'Go to him now, he calls you, you can't refuse.'

And I know then what we are listening to, and at the same time I have to translate the secret message she has passed on to me, impossibly deep but also quite possibly shallow, possibly important but also impossibly oblique, which may be based on a mistaken assumption or may be the truest word ever spoken. These possibilities shrink down to a dot, to the look on Nutmeg's face – and I look over her shoulder to where Dash still perches above us, evidently alarmed by the atmospheric traces of whatever is passing between us all, spoken and unspoken.

'Oh how does it *feel*?' he mouths automatically, I think, without volition, and to break the spell I swing round and say,

'Hey, Frazer, after this can we have something more, like, present day?'

Frazer takes charge of the playlists pretty much every night – he is one of those compulsive obsessive mixtape boys. And he is good, as no one would deny, a kind of wizard at fitting music to mood or, conversely, creating the mood he thinks we need, even if his tastes limit these adventures in mood music to the twenty years between, say, *Revolver* and *Steve McQueen*. Fraze will happily ignore anything that came before or after, aside from a bit of Billie Holiday, Chuck Berry and Patsy Cline. What saves this approach from itself is the wild variety to be found in that period, so rich and peculiar. Frazer loves Soft Machine the same way as he loves Linda Ronstadt, just because they lit up around the same musical moment, in 1971 or so. He is a kind of impure purist, fantastically pedantic but insanely open to all sorts of improv weirdness and MOR hell at the same time, loving the art for art's sake ethos, analogue studios and production values as much as anything else.

'Just for you, Terry, since you nearly drowned and everything.' And when Dylan is over he whips a CD blindly from the rack against the wall – it could be anything, he has no idea – slaps it on, and now we are listening to Meat Beat Manifesto singing *Circles* while Nutmeg says nothing but swings repeatedly from me to Dash mouthing soundless phrases, turns between us as if her neck is on a spring, in perpetual motion. We stay that way for a while, forever really, until she leaps up and leaves the room, and Dash is left sitting above me on the arm of the sofa, gazing down at me as I sit before the fire, while Frazer leans up against the wall and rocks backwards and forwards in time to the beat, Paula barks into the phone in the corridor outside and Coover bounces around the room like some whirling dervish boy.

We set out for the Funky Fish in the fullness of time. Nutmeg comes, brightened by the prospect of dancing, and I walk beside her while Dash hangs back with the boys. Paula has scheduled a meeting with someone on a corner further up in Kemptown, and because we cannot concentrate on our own objective we follow her, going the wrong way through those rings of fire, the fiery arches of the town's internal gates that separate one zone from another, invisible to the innocent eye, only perceptible by us, or so we say. These zones last no more than a block or two, but we see them clearly and ask permission of the spectral gatekeeper to travel through the hole-in-the-arm district to the scuzzy terrain of the falling-over drunk, through the bumboys' velvet goldmine to the dodgy fallout zone of the pills and thrills platoon, from the blues brothers' niche around the Ranelagh to the plush orbits of small hoteliers, with their Mercury mustachios and leopardskin wallpaper – and on beyond, into the region owned by rich denizens in their tall white townhouses, which stand half a mile from all the little shacks, thin-walled council flats, rickety beach huts and cupboards in which people crouch and pray that their walls do not close in.

We wait aimlessly on the corner of College Street, while Paula looks around for her connection. It is not far from midnight, somehow – I am not sure where all the time went. The time has gone somewhere, I want to announce, wrapped up now in my denim greatcoat with its furry lining, buried in its shapeless folds. Nutmeg is telling me again about her childhood, a subject that has infinite traction for her, a land within her being of almost infinite habitability. She tells me about it all the time, from a desire to communicate – not very subtly, it is true, but with good intentions – that the toys in the attic are not always broken, can be mended and brought down and used again. I am, as ever, in awe of her almost religious optimism on this as on most other subjects. The wind rips around and blows her hair in her face, the chill factor pretty considerable in this spot, on the junction by a bank and a grocers, where the road slopes up to the hospital; it blows her words out to sea, where they swell about with the waves for a moment before they are sucked below. She riffs on regardless, and I can hardly follow her, nor do I try very hard. 'We used to take off... prance about ... singing ... happy happy Eskimos ... and they would ask us to put on shows ... two Easters in a row, all the family ... sitting on the tassled settees, watching ... me and my sister

Cinnamon and the dog ... till Zebedee came and took us upstairs ... time for bed.'

I know she is telling the truth, in a way; this may be how it was, in a manner of speaking, from one angle – but I also know how the mountains of memories can overlook some deep shit in the valleys. I have a strong urge to attack, find fault and find holes in her account, lies she has told herself over the years to make the truth seem more attractive. Revulsion at her sentimental mythologising shakes through me like a shudder of cold, which is all she can think it is. I am Terry, after all, and often cold. So how can I tell her what a psychic chill it gives me to hear all this Home Sweet Home bullshit, her vision of a nest – not a sleeping bag on the street, not a sofa in somebody's living room but a real solid nest in a redbrick tree. I lived in that tree too, in the Quangle Wangle's Hat, and cuckoos would have been more welcome up there than us sparrows, fed by a hawk with a sharp beak and a beady eye looking out for rancid worms. If she scraped away at the veneer laid over her childhood by the years, she would surely rediscover all the many acts of petty jealousy, a crisis that went on for days now miraculously forgotten, carnivorous attentions from family elders, drastic turning points that she somehow missed at the time, when sweet picnics turned into endless bug-killing routines. These people you mention were not the happy Eskimos of your memory but your shadows and tormentors, chipping and cracking the broken spice jar that you are today, dear Meg.

Paula comes towards us, shrugging. 'He's moved,' she says – she has been talking on a payphone all this time, up on the hospital grounds.

Everyone is assembled on the shivery corner, waiting for guidance and inspiration. 'Who the fuck, what the fuck,' says Coover, teeth chattering.

'Steve. He's got the works, but we have to go and get it from up the hill. Marbles told me just now, over the phone. We just have to go up and find him and then we'll be, like, stocked up for eternity, or the end of next week. Whichever is the sooner.'

She is not making immediate sense because she is shivering so hard that her words fall from her mouth in haphazard shapes and patterns. None of us is dressed for this venture, apart from me – and me only because I got so iced over earlier and am still trying to get warm. No one else thought to dress up; we were meant to go straight to the club, not follow Paula on one of her wild drug chases through the night. She herself, for all her forewarned is forearmed, wears a yellow cotton dress over a bra top and leggings. Nutmeg is in a dress as well, spangled silver with black stockings, but at least she has on her battered parka. None of the others is even sporting a coat. Dash is caked in the clothes he was lent by the boys, Coover has on the same spunk-encrusted t-shirt he wore in the bathroom this morning, along with a pair of chewed-up Wranglers. Frazer has his white jeans on, just to be ironic, and pretty much a vest, really just a vest, to show off his biceps and quantities of chest hair. We are fucked, clothes and weatherwise, fucked to an absurd degree.

'We can't do this,' says Coover. 'This is stupid and insane.'

'And stupid,' says Frazer, slipping into their old Thomson and Thompson routine.

'Who knows, it might be the beginning of a great adventure,' says Nutmeg, who after all is wearing a coat.

'But also, in a very real sense, the end of one,' says Dash.

'Well, but,' says Frazer, who is reconsidering, 'the Bard said it best. Is it worse to freeze to death in a quest for an illegal high or actually not to have any way of getting high at all? Maybe we should all ponder that one for a while, get our little cells around it.'

'Yeah,' says Paula, 'it would make a lot of sense to freeze to death just thinking about whether we should freeze to death. Let's go.'

'Yeah, you go, we'll wait for you in the club,' says Coover.

'Oh no,' says Paula, who had turned on her heel, about to lead the troops into the windy night. 'Oh no, oh no, oh no. Not that way you don't, boy, not this time. Either you fucking come with me or I will personally stay up there in Steve Talbot's tent and take every last one of his pills myself, drop every last one of his tabs and smoke every last ounce of his gear.'

'Personally,' laughs Frazer, wiping his eyes, 'you would do that personally.'

'Wherefore the hyperbole, Polyfilla,' says Coover, 'and frankly why is the dude living in a tent?'

'He got kicked out of his house,' says Paula, 'and walk with me while we have this fascinating conversation.' So we follow her again; she is nothing if not persuasive. 'He was being antisocial, as were his clients, so his housemates kicked him out. His reputation precedes him, so he ended up on Whitehawk Hill in his dad's old army tent – been there since new year, more or less.'

'Fuck, that's awesome,' says Coover, genuinely impressed. 'We could all do that, save on rent, stop feeding the Man.'

'We couldn't all do that, Coover, because shanty towns within city limits tend to be taken down overnight,' says Nutmeg, 'ploughed into the ground by the municipal dozer, contents crushed.'

'Steve is apparently quite well hidden, I mean even in the daytime, behind a bunch of bushes and stuff,' Paula says glibly as we trail up the pavement. 'I mean, he's going to take some finding.'

'Aren't there other people up there, though?' said Frazer. 'I heard there was a kind of tent community living up on the hill, among the allotments. I met someone at a party who said they'd spent the night up there and it was, you know, jumping.'

'Jumping?'

'Yeah, like really happening.'

'Happening,' Coover snorts. 'You are so the new thing, Fraze. The kids are gonna be studying you in schools in the 22nd century, a one-day course in Frazerology.'

'At least I got a grip on the zeitgeist, man. You got a grip on jackshit aside from your penis.'

'Jesus fuck,' Nutmeg sighs, then she laughs as I raise my eyebrows at her.

'I know, right? Absolute barbarians.'

'This is where you get to show some male solidarity, Dashiell,' Frazer observes – and I hear in his tone how he finds Dash a threat, territorially and mentally, but also that he likes him in the way that boys like each other, a way I never really got. Even my brother is not a brother to me that way.

'I tend not to talk about my penis in public,' Dashiell begins.

'But for us you will make an exception,' Coover finishes for him.

'The level of debate is sinking low,' says Paula, 'and likely to get even lower unless we reach the top of this hill soon and sort it out with some kind of shutter upper.'

We are on Edward Street now, almost at the turning before the hospital that leads most directly onto the hill. 'It's interesting though,' Nutmeg says, 'isn't it, how differently men and women communicate.'

'Wow, someone has sobered up,' says Coover.

'For all that we try to be one of the lads,' says Paula, 'to fit in with all your baloney, it's true that there's a major split between boytalk and girltalk.'

'A definite schism,' agrees Frazer. 'I vote we go this way.'

'What, like, away from the hill?' asks Paula.

'I want to find the hidden village. It would have to be on this side – the other side is almost Whitehawk.'

'And what if there *is* no hidden village? What if, like so many things in these troubled times, it's just a rumour, a mirage, a barefaced lie?' says Paula. 'You're going to be wandering around for hours, boy, on your hands and knees in mud. In any case, how do you intend to get up there?'

'I had a friend once who lived on Rochester Street. He used to go to the end and get straight through onto this side of the hill. There's like a little gate, or a hole in a fence, something of that order.'

'And then you're what? Then you're lost, no?'

'This is like one of those interminable hippy debates that go on and on until somebody dies,' observes Coover. 'Come on, let's climb this motherfucker.'

'Well, I'm going the hidden village way,' says Frazer. 'I don't need you guys as back up – I'm going for a rumble in the jungle, no matter all the napalm death, agent orange and all the rest of it. I'm striking out alone, yeah, what a surprise.'

'That's okay,' says Dash, who has been conspicuously silent for a while. But no, that is not true – he is very often silent. Silence is his most frequent mode. Even at work when everyone is going all Rudyard Kipling around him, he manages with wordless direction to point us to our machines and utensils and stations, as if half a dozen invisible threads attach from him to us, pulling us gently into place. 'I believe in your hidden village, Frazer. I can almost see it when I close my eyes.'

'When I close my eyes,' Nutmeg murmurs dreamily beside me, 'I see almost everything.'

'Yeah, it's alright, Fraze,' I follow up, catching Dashiell's drift. 'We'll come with you. Just don't expect any fucking heroics, okay?'

So we peel off from the main crew of Paula, Meg and Coover, who head straight up the hill behind the hospital. In truth, their way will be so direct, almost instant, they will arrive at the radio mast on the crest in about eight minutes. Everybody understands at that moment the secret and not so secret agendas and covert motivations. There is a certain meeting of minds around this point – the knowledge that Paula just wants to sit down with Steve, loving the whole drug buddy aspect of things, Coover is too lazy to take anything but short cuts, Nutmeg is passively allowing herself to be jettisoned when she would rather be of our camp, Frazer gets bored easily and wants more stimulation than banter and highs can provide. And me and Dash – well, we cannot at this moment admit it to ourselves or each other, but we are on a search for the correct conjunction of time and space, a place to meet.

We watch the others go on their way up Whitehawk Hill Road, a motley trio of misfits who barely fit with each other, who would be lost in the real world with its hooks and splices, trapdoors and passwords, gatekeepers who know that the price of admittance can just go through the roof, pathways to information and modes of transport that only some can afford, minefields riddled with failure bombs, the riddles around success – who would be lost in that world if it really existed. But it is clear to all of us, in certain instants of contact between us, that such a reality is just the product of a general delirium magicked through propagandist hypnosis, on top of a collective will to be deceived. At least to me in this moment it seems obvious that the scary realm of hard-edged money machines and hard-eyed people is no realer than the flaws in the broken clouds, frayed edges of vapour shot through with reflected light in the inky sky tonight. There is nothing to be afraid of; reality does not know how to be cruel or kind, can only be itself, and then only for the split second before it changes into something else.

'This way, folks,' says Frazer, happily. He is not naturally gregarious – or he is, but only in short bursts. Unlike Coover, who depends on having people around to get some sense of himself in action, or Paula, who loves all aspects of mad camaraderie, or Nutmeg, who cares a little too much about others and what they think and longs to show her face but effaces herself, Frazer needs people only for as long as they continue to be interesting. He is satisfied by a brief exchange in which an idea has been given and received – then he is off again across the delta plain of his own intelligence, which he populates well enough without help from anyone else.

It feels like another night from the one when I went swimming in the sea. Only a ten-minute walk behind us, that vast chilly swell feels weirdly far flung as we trek up Sutherland Road, as if it exists but not in our dimension, mythical and powerful with symbols and stories of smugglers, invasions going both ways, not a real sea at all but one found in history books or odysseys spread by oral report, a chase across the waves that exists purely in mind or spirit, a hunt for something in the deep that has its own purpose and does not need the rest of reality to keep it alive. Only the sky is real now, black and full of stars, their stellar mass at first only a suggestion beyond the street lights; but then, when we get to the end of Rochester Street and climb over a wall onto the foot of the hill, unpolluted by all that unnatural light the sky is wildly sidereal, an emblazoned terrain of natural gifts.

'This is the way, huh?' says Dash, who has been walking at my side up to this point but now has to choose a single path and goes ahead of me.

'Far as I know,' says Frazer, who clearly knows nothing. But we all know that Whitehawk Hill, for all its significant connotations, the bridge effect – the barrier before and the way on to the vexed issue of Whitehawk itself – is a small hill in height and length. Because it is the first ridge going east out of town, it appears higher and longer, bulkier than it really is; and now of course, climbing it from an odd angle without a torch in the middle of the night, it assumes a certain massiveness, what with the intense brambles, the steepness, the lack of a clear way through.

The night sky takes over and covers us, even as the bush closes around us; a scuzzy urban underbrush opens up, scattered with discarded johnnies glowing in the dark, empty bottles of orangeade and fag packets –

things we cannot see but only sense, items of underwear and overwear and dead rats, poisoned by the residents of Rochester Street, human and animal shit, things that people have half-heartedly tried to bury but left sticking out of the earth, graveyards of hamsters and goldfish. Here and there, the undergrowth reeks; even in the dead of winter, something rotten prevails. My heart stands still for a moment when a shadow looms that turns out to be an elevated Frazer, perched on some sudden mound.

'Jesus, come on you guys, what's keeping you? We're going to lose each other like this.'

'Fuck it, Frazer, I'm struggling,' says Dash, wheezing emphatically, 'why aren't you struggling?'

'I *am* struggling,' says Frazer says, 'how would I *not* be struggling? I'm struggling better than you, that's all.' He stops about five yards away – not far off, but in this queasy jungle he feels remote – and sniffs the air. 'This is one fucked-up human paradise,' he says. 'Do you dig the epic nature of our quest, you know, on these shitted margins of the innercity, where men live like beasts and carry crossbows and drink cider out of cans?'

Dashiell laughs, but I can tell he is preoccupied, and it is hard to know at any rate how engaged he is with Frazer's most probably ephemeral vision of an urban jungle tribe, living out here on the edge. He knows and I know that Fraze will wake in the morning with half a page of mental notes, a sense of something quite unnecessary having been accomplished, a brief memory of a push through some dirty brush. He is like all of us, Frazer, taking his thing to a certain point then letting go of it before it becomes something he has to broadcast or patent. He does not want to succeed, as such, does not want to have dealings with any of the mechanisms that might popularise his peculiar vision.

Imagine that Jack Kerouac had never written *On the Road* but just kept it in his head, or he wrote it down but only showed it to five people, and you have a model for Frazer's pathological reticence in the face of the fully sanctioned realm of letters. And that is a shame, I sometimes think, because the guy sometimes has something to say – most particularly at those times when he is not lost in the crowd of two that is him and Coover.

'You're awful quiet, Terry,' Frazer continues, still not moving. 'Want to know what I believe? I believe you know that what you're looking for, in life I mean, is somewhere on this hillside, and you're just about to stumble across it, and you're in awe.'

'You may be right,' I mutter. Speaking out loud and clear on this rustling slope with its unseen presences would feel wrong. But as soon as he says it, it becomes true. Frazer is often the one with the word, who sets the tone. 'What are you waiting for?' I ask him a little louder.

We all hear – or is it only me, a strange reverb, an odd echo after my final word – reverb, the holding of a note, a long still extension of the same moment in time. In the instant of asking the question, it feels as if I have been dropped onto the hillside from the starry sky, dropped and only just landed, landed and only just got back on my feet, got back on my feet but only just opened my eyes to have my first thought. But it is not a thought, more like a pack of visions like a bunch of running dogs, racing down the slope towards me, flashing all over me with their instant grace, their instantly forgiven givens.

'Wow,' says Dash, did you feel that?'

'Huh?' Frazer is just about to set off again up the straggling slope of the muckheap, but now he stalls. 'Feel like what exactly? Georgia on my mind?'

'Yeah, something like that.' Dashiell and I are standing right next to each other – we have been all this time – and he suddenly reaches out and touches my chest, making real eye contact for the first time this evening. 'Georgia,' he says, 'do you mind?' His fingers begin to circle my left nipple through seven layers of cloth.

'Has someone down there taken a drug that I'm not privy to?' asks Frazer, who I guess can see none of this, or nothing clearly, but can hear the alteration in Dashiell.

'It's like a drug,' says Dash, 'but it isn't a drug. It does some of the same things, but it's more like a dream, one of those dreams you don't know if it's good or bad, it's just so powerful. It's like a story but you can't see the author – it just lives.'

'Fucking hell,' says Frazer. 'Dashiell, you have most definitely left me behind on this one. Where have you even *gone*, man?'

Dash says nothing this time. I have held his look, in a darkness where only the direction of the look is felt, the eyes are unseen, and we smile into each other as if we were both penetrating each other at the same time, but with smiles. While I hear what he says, I am not so sure that this extraordinarily sudden revelation, these abrupt accesses to intimacy, are not drug related. I have lived with Paula for long enough to know that what I do not expect to see, feel or hear, whatever is most improbable, is pretty much what to expect, at least half the time. She encourages these plastic breaks in logic, snapping the easily fragmented trajectory of the mind into space with her doses – and in truth we have rarely sought to discourage her from her habit of turning the flat into a big top, the street into a bazaar, the town into some kind of biblical outpost, divided between a rigid Roman rule and a domain of slaves' imaginations. But maybe Dashiell is right – maybe it is not a drug. Maybe something literally fell from heaven and converted us.

'You go on ahead, Fraze,' I say, 'we'll be right behind you.'

He grunts through chattering teeth, a pretty weird sound. All this standing around has chilled them to the bone, the guys, in their unseasonal gear; they rock on their heels in the breeze like icebergs on a mountain. Not me, though. If anything, I am a little overheated, climbing this hill in all these heavy rags. Frazer heads off again now without a word; he has found a rusty iron bar from somewhere and he beats back the bushes with it, threshing mightily. We hang back, allowing him to get ahead; a chill wind whips up just then and blows his threshing out of our ears. To all intents, we are alone.

'And then there were two,' says Dashiell, whose eyes have not left my face. I feel them, like two feelers, some moth-like antennae.

'Gimme shelter,' I say. 'I mean, that is, let's find some way of getting out of the wind.'

He does not seem remotely dubious about what I have proposed, although on the face of it the hillside has as much shelter as an old testament desert with a few barren shrubs – a few tall and handsome, but mostly trailing dewberries and those clinging weeds that grab at your ankles. He lets go of me with his eyes and allows me to go before him; and there it is, only twenty yards further on and hidden by an outcrop of lilac but otherwise unmissable, a little temple in the wastes, our own marquee, our personal pagoda. Unmissable, but Frazer must have missed it, this one-man tent that someone has put up and then abandoned – or at least they are not in right now; perhaps they have gone to a party. But perhaps Frazer spotted it and left it to us. He is capable of these subtleties, from time to time.

'What a find!' says Dash, from over my shoulder, as I unzip the flap.

We go in blind and torchless, scenting the indecent scents that waft from the tent floor, that busted banana split smell, odour of dried sweat and dark, rich smoke, blood even, spunk even and some stale meat-like thing, pepperoni left over from New Year's Eve perhaps, still permeating the tented space, so hidden in the midden that a little more vegetable matter does not matter. I feel around with my hands to check for slime, find none and lie down to one side, and Dash does the same.

'Ah well, not so much perhaps, but you have to start somewhere,' I tell him, sure of my ground for the first time in a while, as if I have struck out for the territory and found it. 'Feels like we've come a long way tonight.'

'Yes,' he replies, his breath on my face. 'It certainly does.'

'But you know where we've ended up? It feels like we're in Elysium, like we've actually passed over, we're in paradise like Frazer said but on the other side, some haven of contentment where everything's happened already, everything's contained.' He shakes his head in mute confusion – I can see that much, just about. 'You want another name for it? Let's call it the garden.'

He laughs. 'You're off your leash.'

'Yes, but that's it, Dash – I want you to put me on a leash, walk me on all fours around your floor and hit me with whatever cat o' nine tails you've got.'

He pants beside me from desire and fear in equal measure – and I feel it, his desire for oneness and strangeness, his fear of his desire for strangeness and oneness, his fear of who he is in this equation. I put out my hand and touch his cheek, which is surprisingly hot.

'She's off his leash, off her leash,' he mutters into my hand, sounding a little lost.

'You know,' I say, 'we should just enjoy the garden while we have it to ourselves. No one's going to find us here, no one knows where we are or even that there is such a place, that is aside from the original occupants – and I'm guessing it's party night and they're not coming back any time soon. No need for you to panic, Dash. I threw down a gauntlet, it's true, but that doesn't mean you have to pick it up. You can leave it lying there and breathe. So just breathe.'

Dash just breathes, we all just breathe: the scrubland around us breathes its smoky winter breath, cleaned by the lungs of the sea, while trailing vines scratch at the door, rats nibble at the guy ropes – but it is only flora and fauna and we do not flinch. The floor is firm and chill beneath us, but in time we get used to it; we lie side by side and listen to each other's breathing, while far away the winter air sends us back these echoes, strange traces of our parallel lives, us in different places, living under another name, doing the things we would be doing right now if we had never known each other.

'Your history scares me a bit, that's all,' he says after some time. 'It's just that it's so fucking *dark*.'

'But that's my history, not me.' In our tent there is a powerful addition to the strong aromas, hints of pre-cum and bee-sting, hints of honey.

'Can you see me, Terry?' His voice comes out of the vaporous indistinctness that is our universe, away from the wind and windy people and winding road shut out by the fragile mechanism of a zip.

'No, of course I can't see you, Dashiell. How would I be able to see you? Can you see me?'

220

'No, but we have different eyes and things, don't we? Your dark adaption might be greater than mine.'

'No one really adapts, I don't think – they just find ways to forget or pretend or they make it part of themselves, or they let it destroy them bit by bit. But that's not what I wanted to talk to you about, Dashiell, I wanted to talk about you – and if we can't manage that, let's talk about how it feels to be with you, next to you. Let's talk about how my astral body feels when I meet you in my dreams, yeah, how my physical body feels this very instant, lying beside you on the grand old slagheap that is Whitehawk Hill.'

He clears his throat. 'Shall I say how I feel first?'

'Sure, okay, shoot.' He has no notion how hard I am shaking with the effort not to say it all at once, loaded as I am on whatever love drug Paula plucked from her pharmacopeia. I feel like speaking just to avoid hearing what he has to say – but then I remember how none of this would ever have come about if we had not gone up the hill together and how context is all, how going up the hill together was his idea.

'I want to suck the living juice out of you, Terry, to be absolutely honest, suck and keep sucking.' He clears his throat again, to add his addendum, and I can hear that this is terribly difficult for him – he is not used to these disclosures. 'And you can rest assured I've never had that need before, and certainly not for anyone so...'

'Confusing?'

'Yeah, confusing. I have no notion what it would be like to be with you, Terry, and that really freaks me out – but also what would happen next and how it would look to us, let alone to all the rest, how it would be if we took each other home to meet our mothers.'

'Your mother.'

221

'Sorry, yes, my mother. She's fairly old fashioned, you know.'

'I know, you told me all about it once, you're from good country people. But I bet she blew through a few endorphins herself back in the day, Madame Poirier, don't you think, back when she was a mademoiselle? People are more open-minded than we give them credit for, as you constantly strive to remind me when I'm gunning the fuckers down. But that's all a bit of a side issue, you know. We don't need to plan a wedding, Dash – it doesn't even need to be a handfasting. It can just be the two of us, here in this tent.'

I am making it up as we go along by this point, so desperate just to hold his cock in my hand for a second and spiked by my own spiel, bewitched by words. The language itself is so sexy all of a sudden that every word we speak makes me feel more like fucking, until I am almost too horny to close my mouth – and all the time not knowing whether these words move him the way they move me, whether they draw him to me or push him away. But then in answer all of a sudden he is on me, getting through to me through all our many layers – he makes me come at once, as soon as he puts his hand between my legs, though through our many layers I try to hide it. I just kind of explode at the point of contact – but he got me to this point way back at the start of all this, six months ago, when we first met. With him, I have always been on the verge, the edge of coming. I think he does not notice or does not know what it was, the jissom is lost somewhere in the folds, although it is hard for him to miss the shudder that runs all the way from head to toe. But then his odd blend of innocence and experience, which makes him seem older and younger than me at the same time, has always been bewildering: I do not know what he does not know.

But then I feel his mouth on my mouth and I go blank, become a mental zero, as if the algebra of his mouth plus mine equals nought – and this lasts, this wonderful nothing, long enough for me to see the silence, feel the stillness until the rhythm of sex takes over, as it must, from the stillness that sex itself created. And then I work my way down, put my hand inside his borrowed jeans and shape my mouth around him just at the instant when he comes with a WANG, in my face. His taut frame seems to sob for a few seconds, then he relaxes, we relax and we are free, he lets go and we are for a moment at total liberty. We open our hands and fly away.

In the instant after we come, the night outside our tent seems to take on its own life, as if our climax turns me clairaudient. In a thicket beside us, a million insects try to make their minds up about the meaning of living; in the muddy self-seeded oaks that gods have sprayed up the hillside, sleeping songbirds dream of migration. Tonight the gods strike down benevolently, with gentle violence at the core until I feel our masks fall off, his and mine, in the dark where it hardly matters. They come after us when from instinct we turn and run and tear the masks from our faces, but in a kindly way, to reveal the mask that found our face and lived there long enough to become our face – the real mask, if you like, the translucent reality that we are *this*, we are all and nothing, we have only this thing that shifts continually, which we pretend is our true visage.

'Fuck,' he says, 'that was pretty magnificent.'

'Don't move,' I tell him – and I tell him about the masks as the little urban jungle wheels around us, the planet rocks from side to side. 'They come off when we dance and when we sleep,' I say. 'You know, don't tell the others this because it'll definitely creep them out, but I sometimes go and peer at their faces in the dark when they're sleeping, just to know what they really look like. That's the strange thing about you, Dash,' I tell him. 'You look asleep when you're awake. You're either all mask or all face – I haven't worked it out yet.'

'What you see is what you get,' he assures me. Then he clears his throat, a sure sign that he is about to say something difficult. 'Are we going to talk about what just happened?'

'I am talking about it, Dashiell.' Yes, but what I would give right now for us both to lose the power of speech – to let us be in the aftermath, let us go from aftermath to aftermath without submitting at every moment to the stubborn inquiry of our minds.

'Yeah, but I mean the logistics, ramifications, what might happen next. Those kinds of things.'

I pick up on his anxiety, I get it, these things would normally make me anxious too – but I cannot let him take us there. 'I thought maybe I'd move in with you and we could adopt some global babies, a litter of kittens, play house.'

He leans up on his elbow, a blacked-in shape against the backdrop of slightly luminous canvas. There is some spare light up on this hill, after all. 'That sounds really excellent,' he says after a pause – and I can tell he is barely breathing. His voice sounds new, deeper from the loss of an innocence he never knew he had, full of hunger, worry and the sudden shakes of responsibility. This is the voice of a different Dashiell – home-making, domesticated, pram-pushing.

'Oh well, I wasn't being entirely serious. Can you really see me living in a playhouse?' And I want to tell him, but these things are so hard to get across, that I know what I believe is not the alpha and omega. How can it be? I know that I am stuck in my point of view, at least for now, but I know it is not the only one. 'There is no long term, think of it like that, only this – this thing we both miraculously wanted at the same time which, unlike most things either of us have ever wanted, we've managed to lay our hands on.'

'But then I don't know what just happened,' he says, sounding bemused at what no doubt sounds to him like someone blowing hot and cold. 'I thought it was the start of something.'

'But it is – it can be the start of us doing the same great thing together, again and again until we die or it dies, or something puts an end to it, or one of us moves on or just moves house, or one of us falls in love with somebody else or just stops feeling these feelings, or one of us turns monastic, one of us becomes a monk and renounces everything and goes east, or west, or one of us wakes up one morning to find that what seemed to be the case is no longer the case. But until the changes come around we'll have this thing, Dash – this marvellous, temporary thing.'

'I don't know, Terry.' He lies on his back, talking to the tent roof while stuff bustles beyond its canvas walls. Black light surrounds us, broken here and there with dabs of other light, muffled starlight coming down on us from above – or is it from below? I feel turned around for an instant and it seems like the stars are somewhere beneath us, before I get my bearings. It makes me dizzy to hear him talk. 'I mean you sounded pretty interested in the future yourself, Terry, right up until we had sex. You were talking about it right up to the moment we came.' I shrug in the dark, and he feels it. 'I think it's more in you than you think, you know, the desire for whatever deal it is most people aim for, the thing that looks permanent and feels like it's going to last forever, even if we all know it can't – *that* thing.' He clears his throat again and turns to look at me; our noses almost touch. 'It's alright,' he says, 'I won't tell anyone else, but you don't have to deny it to me. You want something of your own you can keep, however fucked it is from the word go, however set to self-destruct. I can be the thing you get to keep for a while – that's the other way to look at it.'

Then we do it all over again, this time with gentle focus and sweet attention and not so many clothes on, this time with understanding and acceptance of who we are, where we are – and this time in accord, however fragile. Our understanding and acceptance that nothing lasts can itself only last for so long. I want to point this out to him, but he must know what is on my mind because he stops my mouth – and then he covers me in his juices, and I cover him in mine.

We climb the hill again, and this time it is charged, changed into something so neat and so right at first, easy to step on and up – but then it is hard going for a while, brambles interpose themselves between me and wherever we are supposed to be headed. I realise that I am singing songs in my head and the vast sky, with its icy spray of stars, wants to swallow me whole. Feelings wash through me as if released from their cage – an immense fear of loss, a fear of entrapment that is also perhaps a fear of loss, a fear of being loved which is also I suppose a fear of loss, an almost magical and mystical fear of loss, up on that hill. I stumble and stagger and cling to fronds of flora that are not even there, dark wisps of darkness. It is as if a great glowing angel is sitting on my chest, as if the best thing that ever happened to me is crushing the fuck out of my lungs and killing me.

Still I climb, and the system up here changes as if the stars have switched around on me in the time it took to blink. When I open my eyes again after that split second, the angel has gone and nothing is there – a no one is there who breathes on my face from up close, spelling out her absence. The cage is truly open now, and I am covered in the sensation of grief; it runs all over me until another switch occurs and grieving becomes me, until I *am* grieving and the grief is *me*. And still I go on climbing the hill, swallowed by darkness and blinded by my own being, by all these events in my psyche that have welled up and come between me and the world. They come and stand between me and the sky, until the black sky and the sightless eyes are one, to all appearances the same thing: a frieze of blackness hangs and everything else is destroyed, sucked away from behind it, until there is no longer a me who does not see. For a moment there is still the grief that fed the blindness, but then even that is gone, leaving only the darkness, leaving no feelings or substance.

I go on climbing, telling none of this to Dashiell – who fell from the sky, fell into my lap, is behind me somewhere. I know that I cannot communicate to him the overwhelming relief of no longer being, of creating something apparently out of my self then surrendering my self to it, dissolving in the power of my own loss, at the total disappearance of the loved one, the total vanishing. But of course a few steps on and she is back, my mother, if only so that I can see her go again, see her die of cancer, all those poisoned cells in her prison cell, waste away and shrink in on herself, pull back the edges of herself and retreat in space until she is a hand, a finger, a wedding ring, a band of gold on a speck of dust.

It is not lost on me that sex and drugs make these moments – they trick us into seeing what in the end we long to see, a kind of truth that seems so lasting, as if it has been waiting for us to discover it forever when it is just the product of our mind firing once and once only, creating retrospection and certainty as it goes. I know all this, but I hold on to the vision even so of my mother standing to face me, wearing her wedding ring and nothing else. She takes the ring from her finger then and drops it into the void, so it is just her left behind – naked in a way, alive in a way, at least vital enough to say goodbye or tell me her last wishes and hopes, her last vision.

'It's happened now, Terry,' is all she says, 'it's happened and we can't get back to the way it was. It's happened, and here you are and here I am, and I'm sorry that it happened but it happened.'

I stop walking and bend over, let the gasping do the talking. Dashiell comes up behind me, puts a hand in the small of my back and stays quiet – exactly when I need him not to say anything, he says nothing. Then the blackness around us has some sort of seizure, takes a fit for a minute in which it seems to convulse, darkness squirting more darkness from its edges, beating itself with its own wings. When it finally comes out of it there is a feeling of freedom, as if it has shaken itself free, thrown away a broken part of itself, stopped altogether a part that was malfunctioning or taken a hammer to a part that worked too well. And of course I am aware – more aware than ever – that the darkness is my mind; there is no space for any of this to take place except in there, my head and mental body, the body of my mind. The darkness quakes and everything shakes free, and the night is itself again, empty of hauntings, those spirits of love and loss. Free.

'Can you hear music?' Dashiell asks suddenly – and I have a hilarious mental image of his ears pricking up at some sound caught on the breeze.

'Absolutely,' I say. 'Unless it's just the wind in the trees.'

'I think we're almost there.'

'I think you might be right.'

The wind tears the notes of something, hither and thither, snatches of a song made unrecognisable by cold gusts ripping the melody into sweet random instants – or perhaps it is just the wind itself doing the singing. But even if it is just some Aeolian harp blown in the wind, this melody blown to shreds, I am reminded all at once how music fills an urgent need, one I had momentarily forgotten I had, a hunger that could kill by itself if left unsatisfied. It is our luck to live in a time when that need is so easily fulfilled, our hunger fed on all those moments in the history of song, like Iggy Pop on *Turn Blue* singing about all the things he takes that make him 'so damn ugly,' or Alison Goldfrapp swanning in on *Sad But True*, or Ry Cooder's steel guitar break on *Monkey Man*, or when we wait through sweet suspense on *Dark Side of the Moon* before all the alarms go off – or the rap on Galliano's take on *Long Time Gone*, when the band take it in turns to say, 'It might rain, and it might not.' Tonight I know that it will not, cannot rain.

'It's some sort of block rockin' beat,' he says, 'I think.'

'Yes, Dashiell, I think you're right.'

He catches my eye in the dark, even though our eyes are almost invisible – but we have grown used to all this blind communicating. We turn then and put our arms around each other, prop each other up for a while – and over his shoulder I see the town spread out below in all its glittering rows, bright rings of streets and the tilt of the seafront running in lights all the way to Shoreham, throbbing with life that would dazzle up close but looks so perfect from this far above. I feel him smiling in the dark – it already seems so historically significant, our time on this black mountainside.

'Thanks for doing this crazy thing with me, Terry.'

'I can't even feel the cold anymore, it's amazing,' I tell him. 'It's like you've warmed me through somehow, with all that free body heat of yours.'

'It's true,' he laughs, 'I'm not on a meter.'

And for a while we stand together looking down on the city – all lumière and no sound, as if its noise has been sucked into the black sky to leave that wild electric blaze on those streets thronged with denizens of some carnival abstraction, who from this distance are not only silent but out of sight, a wonderful illusion thrown together with the love of an amateur.

'It feels like we've sorted out the nowness for now,' I say.'

'Yes,' he says, 'you're right, Terry, the thenness of then is all that's left.'

This is lovers' talk, really, so kind to the world around it in a way that can only happen once and then never again – but we have to let it happen, I know that now.

'Look!' he says. 'Listen!'

The funny thing is we must have much marched straight past them in the minute before we stopped and talked. A crackling blaze shows their position, no more than twenty yards away, not townside but on the edge of the hill where it overlooks the Whitehawk estates, below the radio mast. We are actually above them on the hillside – they are across and down. Listening in, we can hear their voices calling, see sparks fly, before we hear the words or feel the heat. Paula's laughter, pealing distinctly, gloriously oblivious to the actual or potential unfunniness of anything at all, comes to us where we stand looking slightly down on them – it passes us by and flies over our shoulders, out into the sky over the sea. The rhythm of a faint but now I listen in familiar beat, sketched in and scrubbed out again by the wind, takes the same route.

We head for the camp, scooting between bushes, Dash just ahead of me and holding my hand. Before we reach the parting at the edge of the natural clearing – natural in that hippies and derelicts have hacked it out from the underbrush over the years – we linger for a moment on the actual summit, where the chill hits us squarely in the shoulderblades, taking each other in again, alone for one last time tonight. A moment later we go down and emerge from between the scrubby oaks, lilacs and buddleia, to stand before the fire. A massive pile of pallets burns in front of the dealer's handmade bivouac; waves of heated air come at us as we move into the open – giant flames are leaping, red and gold and full of black eyes. All the people spread around are tinged orange, basking in the glow. Frazer lies crashed out on the earthen floor by the tent mouth, laughing madly in some knocked-out bliss, while the dealer – Steve Talbot, I guess – sits with legs crossed and squinting into the inferno, like a wizened desperado with his face full of hair, all dreads and locks. But the others are all up on their feet, Paula and Coover and Nutmeg, dancing to the sounds from a surprisingly big beatbox, which blasts into the air the sacred sound of *Unfinished Sympathy* – a tribal address from the margins of the cultural nothingness that is now to the sky full of a black God that is also now, a sky filled with God and empty of everything else, from the now that is our sad pennilessness and smiling strangeness and our extreme identification with each other, a kinship that is rarely found in bloodlines. They dance around the fire now, the tribe, coming so close to tripping and burning then tripping and burning anyway, sheer heat melting their faces, to a sound that is now and which one day will be then and which has already come back to us from some primeval moment, a sound that has been here since the first Cretaceous ant climbed Whitehawk Hill.

And now Steve Talbot spots us on the edge of his encampment, where I see he spends his days and nights conjuring some sullied truth out of vanilla unmeaning, magicking the ground for all our benefits, drawing the circle and falling into it in a daze of raw ecstasy. His eyes are full of dark laughter and deep mischief, leonine and reckless, an Aslan look with a mane of dirty dreads – it is pretty fucking scary, to tell the truth, and for a moment I feel like a novice. His hand that holds out the spliff to us seems to signal a way beyond, in that way of merry pranksters.

'Try it,' he says, 'try it, you wayfaring strangers, you secret agents, try it and see if you can live with it.'

'Fuck, but this is *beautiful*,' Dash declares, in what was no doubt intended as an aside, more loudly than he meant – and the guys stop dancing now and turn to see us standing there, me in all my layers and Dash in his borrowed finery. And for a moment, all eyes are filled with the same understanding, because everyone sees what he means, because really it is – it is beautiful. Then Coover points to Dash, and says,

'Hey, look at the hoodie with the woody!'

And I blush and bury my nose in my boy's armpit, burrow into his chest and bury myself in his himness, and everyone laughs.

232

Afterword

Romance with a small *R* is a double-edged thing in our culture, despised but revered in the same moment by the same person. It's not just that someone who laughs at the idea of falling in love is called cynical – in ourselves we're divided between doubting that the dream kingdom has any worth at all and believing in it implicitly, as a tenet of our being. This is just the way it is, and has to be, because romance is essentially contradictory: it's a kind of freedom and a kind of trap, a kind of intense reality but also undeniably unreal, because what we call romance is a closed system. In other words, what happens there stays there and is only real there in the moment when it happens. As soon as the romantic is exposed to anything that lies outside it, it ceases to have any power or truth, it dies, which is why so much energy is expended in trying to stay in that place where it lives.

The place where romance lives is in the story. To tell the truth, I think I've always been just as fascinated by the closed system of the romance as by what happens in the romance itself – and the story, whether it's on the page or on the screen or in our heads, is where romance can survive untroubled by hostile elements. The art of capturing those golden moments and giving them their full effect has always had a great attraction for me. In those golden moments is what happens in the romance, the connection that we sometimes seem to feel between ourselves and another person or a place, a connection so time-limited that it could be said to barely exist – but its short-lived nature is what makes it so valuable.

What are the hostile unromantic elements that we want to keep away from us, keep out through our closed system? The hostile elements come to us in the form of a language that surrounds us every day, ordinary language that we hardly notice but which spells out our entrapment in various other systems, systems we can't escape, which are the air we breathe – our helpless attachment to the state, for example, or to our families, to the other circumstances we were born in. Romance is one way we can escape for a while the otherwise unavoidable realities of daily existence, but its power lies in entirely negating the importance of that existence, not just in denying it – by saying that those golden moments of connection are worth far more than anything else we'll ever experience.

These stories are various attempts to capture that state of connectedness while playing with all the forces that attack it – and in a story it's possible just to play with those forces, of course, without anyone actually dying in the process. Romance is ultimately a dream that we have to remain asleep to experience; people and things are always trying to wake us up, to kill the dream, and we ourselves will want to wake up as well. That's just the way it is. We can't stay there forever. So a romantic who tries to stay there for longer than is possible will feel as if they're living in both worlds, asleep and awake at the same time – lost, in other words. Other forms of lostness are always available, all the confusions that stand between our romantic selves and the objects of romance and want to wake us up: there is the confusion that comes from our egotistic attachment to the unromantic world, from certain views of ourselves as citizens of a state, although the state is itself just another fiction. There's the confusion of our history, personal and otherwise, which lies behind us and outside our influence, and the confusion brought about by our supposed identities – as *men*, for example. What even is a *man*? This is just one of the questions to which there can never be a satisfactory answer, which keep us from falling back to sleep.

But then the dream itself, which has its own rules, cruel and otherworldly, is also necessarily going to feel like lostness. It's inevitably going to feel like a fantasy, even at its peak intensity. These stories play with that feeling of a fantasy with an inescapable reality, a fantasy that has more authority than the ugly facts that threaten it, more even than the fact of death. This is not just because love is in some sense stronger than death – although that's also true, I think – but because death is co-opted by the system of romance as a necessary and fantastical endpoint, a final flourish that signs off on the truth of everything that has come before. You can't ask questions of romance, not least because at the very moment when you want to interrogate it and demand that it declares itself as deep or shallow, real or unreal, it finds some way to end itself – kill itself, no less, before it can be snuffed out by something that wants to prove that it was never alive in the first place.

There isn't much in the way of autobiography in these stories, written in a 20-year period between 1994 and 2014 – although I really did see a swan frozen into the ice from the train crossing the river at Malbork, and the incident of losing and finding the wedding ring also happened. The failed driving tests happened too, and the bit of dialogue about the Nazi in a pink shirt really took place. Otherwise, I've made it all up – apart from the locations, which are all real and known to me, from the village in Wiltshire where Carson climbs the hill to the suburb of Dublin where your man plies his trade, the street in Hove where Gumbo says goodbye to his old friend to the café where Terry and Dashiell work, which was where I came up with the story.

For a year or two at the start of the 2010s, I spent every weekend eating cake in the Redroaster at the bottom of St James's Street in Kemptown, Brighton – this was before the café was brutally gentrified and lost all its boho charm. After many visits, looking up from whatever I was reading to watch the waiters and waitresses at work, the flicker of an idea for a story came, but with that world fully formed. *Misfit Power* came out of that initial vision, but the vision derives from a variety of sources, the pop culture cliches that it embraces and the aesthetic of the iconic graphic fiction of the 1990s, particularly all the funny and heartfelt Maggie and Hopey stories that Jaime Hernandez wrote for *Love and Rockets*, Peter Bagge's Buddy and Lisa sequence in *Hate*, and the supremely weird Hugo Tate stuff that Nick Abadzis published in *Deadline* magazine. I'd always wanted to get away from the formula that seemed to cling to me in stories, with a singular guy or girl experiencing something overwhelming more or less alone – I wanted to have a whole gang piled on top of each other, talking shit, listening to music, taking drugs and falling in love. It was a side of the 1990s that I myself only glimpsed through doorways once or twice and rubbed shoulders with for an evening or two. I loved it, but I could never stay there and live in it, which I guess is why I wanted to write it down.

– John Ruskin Street, July 2023

Acknowledgments

Many people have contributed to this book, not least those who have given me space and time in which to write over the years. These stories were written or rewritten in Nottingham, Nanaimo, Dublin, Gdańsk and London – but mainly in Brighton, where for several years I lived in Martin's house on Stanley Road and did almost nothing but write and listen to music.

The music I've listened to has played a large part in what happened on the page, as much as anything I've read. Even when this book was still in embryo, my main ambition was that it should imitate in its feel the long-playing records we grew up with. When the Cocteau Twins' LP *Treasure* came out in 1984, I remember telling my friend James that I wanted to write stories that *felt* like their songs. I wanted this collection to read through the way we used to listen to a record album, one story segueing into the next. This book's original title in 1999, thought up by Hugh, was *The Vinyl Romances*, a name it lost because the play on vinyl/final lost its relevance – the endpoint of the last century now doesn't seem much like an endpoint at all – and because most of the stories about music that I wrote during the nineties have gone their merry way, as short stories so often do.

Writers whose influence hangs over these stories are too many to mention, but the most salient is probably Chekhov, the original creator of the *useless man*, for whom this book has so much time. For a long time no writer was more important to me than John Cheever, whose fixation on types of light at certain times of day became mine also and whose direct influence is evident in the *Housebreaker of Shady Hill* vibes of *My Animal*

Passion, the borrowing of an idea from *Angel of the Bridge* in *Sweetheart* and Carson's final vision in *Carson's Trail*, which is a nod to the ending of *The Swimmer*.

Many people have made decisive interventions on these stories over the years. Russell Honeyman read a first draft of *Passion* and pointed out that it needed a middle eight, which turned out to be the scene where Jerry gets stoned on the church steps. *Travelling South* was done as a writing exercise for a workshop run by Elizabeth Ingrams for Spread the Word in 2006. It was the first story I wrote about something outside myself, which in some mysterious way she showed me how to do – although it was a lesson I went on to forget again, many times. *Carson's Trail*, written a month or so later that same summer, came out of an observation by Paula McLeod, my therapist at the time, that while I believed I didn't remember my father dying – in real life I was two when it happened – in fact I did, it was always in me. I got up the next morning, went swimming in the sea, came home and wrote the story.

Carson's Trail appeared in an anthology for Stinging Fly, edited by Declan Meade, the first of my fiction I'd seen in print since I myself edited the school magazine. Many thanks to Declan, not least for convincing me that I wasn't entirely deluded and that this thing I'd been doing for so long wasn't just a byproduct of my dreamy and obsessive nature. Many thanks as well to Brendan Barrington, who included three of these stories in the *Dublin Review* and improved them with his editing, and to Anthony Caleshu, who published *My Breakfast with Gumbo*.

Instrumental to any progress I've made as a mental traveller is Lilith Wildwood, teacher and therapist. The courses I've done with Lilith have not just expanded the scope of my imagination but changed my ideas about what can be imagined, and the visionary parts of *Misfit Power* could not have existed without her helping me to travel through a world that would otherwise I would never have seen. The last scenes in that story may feel trippy, but the effect does not come from hallucinogens – not a single mushroom was eaten in the making of it – but from the awesome places we went in Lilith's guided meditations. Lilith can be found at her *Rebel Witch Magick* website.

The cover image, taken by me in January 2023 and rendered by Paul Arnot, shows the Tay statue in New Steine Gardens off St James's Street in Kemptown, Brighton. The sculpture was made by Romany Mark Bruce in memory of his friend Paul Tay, who died of AIDS in 1992. It was unveiled in 2009 to commemorate 'all those whose lives have been affected by HIV and AIDS'.

Thanks to Amina and Simon for the regular input and output in our writing support group, to Kerry for our literary road trips and to Russell as ever for the inspiration. Thanks to Imogen for keeping a roof over my head and maintaining me in a state of relative sanity, and to James for making everything feel alright. For all their help and encouragement over the years, thanks to Katy, David, Talulah, Kitty and mum. Thanks to Alva for all her support and for taking me to places I would otherwise never have gone. Thanks to Natalie for the proof-reading, and thanks to Paul for another beautiful cover. Thanks to my children for being lovely. And thanks as always to Richard, the best friend my writing has ever had.

... there is work to do before we say goodbye ...

If you enjoyed this book, you may also enjoy…

Anyone who catches my eye can have me

by the same author

London in the summer of 1999, reeling from a neo-Nazi bombing campaign, is the setting for this bizarre love triangle. Dean, temp and flâneur, has to choose between his stoner waitress Monika and Laura, a polyamorous bluestocking… or does he? A romantic satire in the tradition of *The Great Gatsby*, this novel shines a light on the metropolitan margins and captures a lost generation in its moment of truth.